OTHER BOOKS BY MICHAEL NOVAK

The Tiber Was Silver (a novel)
A New Generation
The Experience of Marriage (Editor)
The Open Church: Vatican II, Act II
Belief and Unbelief
A Time to Build
Vietnam: Crisis in Conscience (with R. M. Brown and A. Heschel)
American Philosophy and the Future (Editor)
The Experience of Nothingness

NAKED I LEAVE

naked i leave

A *novel by* MICHAEL NOVAK

THE MACMILLAN COMPANY

Library of Congress Catalog Card Number: 77-93284

First Printing

The Macmillan Company
866 Third Avenue, New York, N.Y. 10022
Collier-Macmillan Canada Ltd., Toronto, Ontario

Printed in the United States of America

TO K.

woman—risk—artist—critic

AND

lover-in-residence

NOTE

THE FOLLOWING DELIGHTFUL tale is fiction masked as autobiography; it is not—as enemies will suggest—autobiography masked as fiction. It has been generated out of passion, fantasy, and dream. Dark associations have been nourished. The thread and texture of the work are fictive, not historical. The resemblance of fictional composites to real persons is coincidental. What imagination joins, let no man pull asunder.

In our country it is not usual for philosophers to publish novels, at least under their own names. A novel renders a sensibility, not an argument. A sensibility cannot be said; it must be shown (co-created by the reader, lived through). No one, certainly, should mistake a Catholic for a Jewish or a Protestant sensibility. Or to speak more precisely: that of Svoboda for my own.

MICHAEL NOVAK

Oyster Bay, New York
The Feast of St. Patrick, 1969

CONTENTS

*"Naked came I into the world, naked shall
I leave it; nothing more do I desire than to
be naked in the sight of the Lord."*

—St. Jerome

MEDITERRANEAN I

◈◈

*"The gnostics believed that the angels
put to every dead person the same question:
'Where do you come from?' What will be found
here is what has survived."*

—ANDRÉ MALRAUX

1

THE ODYSSEY OF a Catholic in our society, if he decides to remain one, takes peculiar turns. Being a Catholic is not like being a Jew. A Jew is a Jew is a Jew; you can't resign from your race. But a Slovak can cease to be a Catholic if he wishes, and no one will notice. He can even cease to be a Slovak and melt into the American soup.

I am, I know, proud of the fact that I am part European. Hundreds of years of European soil, of the Carpathian mountains, of the river Charles, underlie my imagination. My four grandparents came separately to America before the turn of the century; destiny drew them, and they married compatriots in the valleys of Pennsylvania. One grandfather crossed the Danube by night, hiding from Austro-Hungarian soldiers as our ancestors have for a thousand years, to escape the draft. Our bones recall a centuries-

long struggle against Hungarian tyranny: a fierce pride of language
and roots and faith, a deep love of peace and farmland and
meditative virtues. (Under foreign occupation, what else could
we love?)

But now the future is open. America has burst our constrictions.
Where shall we go? What shall we become?

Unlike all those refugee writers who came to America during
the recent tyranny, I never learned to speak my native tongue.
My natural tongue is English, not my own. I do not have to
wrestle to gash sparks of one language by breaking it against
another: I simply speak. But what have I lost?

My tale begins in nakedness. Friends invited me to southern
France. After traveling all night by train from Rome, jammed
into a rocking compartment with a family of nine Gypsies from
Naples munching evil-smelling *panini*, I emerged into the glaring
streets of Toulon and bounced an hour by groaning bus until I
stood on a lonely corner of the village on the Côte d'Azur where
Jack and Marilou Prescott had a summer house. Dust covered
my shoes; I shielded my eyes. A telephone call, and before five
minutes had elapsed, a great, green Plymouth station wagon
crunched smoothly into the square.

"Eddie's here," the deeply tanned driver greeted me. "We were
just going to the island. Will you join us?" He had spoken jokingly
of this trip six weeks previously.

"Sure." I swung my two small suitcases into the back seat.

"How was Rome?"

"Fascinating."

Within an hour the four of us were running down the pier
toward the twice-daily ferry. Jack parked the Plymouth and bought
the tickets. Father Ed helped Marilou, a tiny, pretty girl of
twenty-seven, into the boat. I told the impatient agent in halting
French that the man running fifty yards behind us was bringing
our tickets. The launch strained against the tarred, dripping line.
Jack leaped aboard, and, with a scowl, the agent cast the rope
aboard.

"Good to see ya, buddy!" Ed punched my arm.

"Have you ever been out here before?" I shouted over the
engines to Marilou.

She smiled, her hair blowing in the wind. "Jack has."

"No!" Jack's lips formed clearly. "But I was on a yacht with a Frenchman on a cruise. He invited four girls aboard and served them tea. Naked women, teacups on their knees!"

Since I had been brought up in a pious family, and since, if the truth be told, I was almost if not quite a virgin (having learned a little casuistry), the image made me laugh; it also made me uneasy. I scanned the boatload of healthy people: only a few tourists like ourselves, most of them members of the island community. In white sport shirts, sun hats, and dark glasses, they appeared to be a normal sort. The spray of the Mediterranean kicked into the sun, and the French flag whipped loudly in the breeze. For an hour we cut through the placid, azure water, making ourselves ready for the break with the past.

Ed and I had studied for the priesthood together six years earlier. When I left the order, he was disappointed. For three years we had shared every enthusiasm, every new book, every adventure. Since then he had managed to be removed from two jobs; no matter how prudent he tried to be, he was too much a revolutionary for the Old Guard. There was never any definite reason, no breach on his part; he made people uncomfortable. His superiors had let him edit one magazine and then, after an end to that, launch another. It cost them 7,000 copies of one issue, which was banned after it was printed and had to be rerun minus an essay of his. He had already served in four different locations. "When someone preaches the gospel, move him." Rule One, United States Catholicism.

Emerald and brown, the island rose steeply out of the blue water. The boat's engines slipped into a lower, louder gear. Slowly we edged toward the wharf. A cluster of shops and a carnival of color and motion awaited us. Those on shore seemed to be dressed.

"Look!" Marilou tapped my shoulder.

I looked and laughed and tapped Ed's shoulder.

He, too, laughed.

The sign said in French: "Sunday Masses, 7, 9, 11."

I watched my footing as we climbed the small gangway. My heart was beating rapidly. I could count on one hand the number of women I had ever seen naked: one, and she only in the last year. "How can that be?" I asked myself. But it was true. Twenty-seven years old and absurdly innocent.

They don't wear pants
In the southern part of France
But they do wear strings
To cover up their things.

I learned the words in the basement of a Pennsylvania school. And it was true. It was difficult, at first, to figure out why some women covered their nipples, while others wore a patch of cloth, on a G-string, between their legs. A few of the men also wore a tiny cup.

"Marilou?" Jack invited teasingly.

We stood near a sign which prayed us, if we were to wander the island, to accept the conventions of the place.

"Let's start slowly." She giggled.

"Moderation!" Ed said. He was already pulling his yellow jersey over his head. He was tall and his chest was as white and smooth as a piece of ivory. A silver chain hung around his neck; from it a silver cross depended, gleaming in the sun.

We stripped to our swimming suits.

"I'd prefer to cover my top," Marilou was explaining. "It's funny, but I would. I suppose women differ."

We began climbing a rocky path along the western cliffs. Below us, a huge, prone, Nordic woman opened her heavy legs to the east and submissively allowed the sun to enter her precious harbor. In crevices, on flat places, lying upon their white towels or simply upon the stones, while the sea slapped delicate crystal spray against the sunlit rocks, dozens of worshipers were scattered. Burned maroon by the sun, no animals ever looked more beautiful.

The dusty, green branches caught at our legs, and we had to beware of turning our ankles on the rocks.

"Here's a good place," Jack suggested.

"Great place for a swim!" Ed agreed.

A formation of gray rock below jutted out into the sea. We eased our way toward it down the sliding, treacherous shale.

"Marilou's a little nervous," Jack had whispered to me. "She has a big scar on her tummy and it embarrasses her."

"I'll go with you, Ed," I called.

"Now's the time, boy!" he said in his deep voice. He began to peel off his trunks.

Almost without self-consciousness, I followed. We set our

watches in our shoes, and hid our rolled-up clothes under the stiff shrubs. Marilou was putting suntan oil on Jack's shoulders and offered us some. We accepted and she squeezed the white cream into our hands. We rubbed one another's backs.

"We'll see you later," Jack said. Ed had already dived into the pure blue water.

"Back here, in about a half hour," I called. I was never a good diver and wanted to avoid a belly-flop. Shifting all my weight, I accidently placed my right foot on a sharp pebble. I had to escape the pain. "Head down!" I thought and struggled to pull my abdomen into a straight line. Then the cold water crashed upon my ears, my nose filled with the smell and pressure of the sea, and my foot slapped hard behind me. The sea accepted me and pressed, bubbling, upon me. I reached out my arms.

When I surfaced, Jack and Marilou were laughing, but I waved and headed after Ed. He was a strong swimmer; I no longer saw him. I panicked. I had no idea how deep the water was, or what was living in it, or whether there would be anything to cling to. The rocks above plunged silently, sheerly, into the sea. Already my arms were tired. Don't be silly, I thought, and concentrated in the silence on slow and leisurely strokes. It occurred to me that no one who knew me knew where I was. Neither Ed nor Jack and Marilou were in sight—the latter two had gone in the opposite direction. Ed? He could be a half mile away by now. He had always been a loner.

The freedom of loneliness was delicious. The sun beat upon the water, an enormous skyful of sun, and I turned on my back to absorb it. The Mediterranean ran into my ears. I saw the silver, glinting spray shoot upward from my white, kicking feet and felt the water run off the oil on my brown arms. I felt a sharp, sweet taste—an astringent, penetrating taste of life. My heart surged with a mysterious joy, as if it would crush my lungs.

I turned over and began to take long, slow strokes, savoring the absolute clarity of the sea and sky. Around the next mass of rocks there was an inlet. I decided to swim for the inmost ledge. The sea was still, and my strokes set ripples running against the bleached rocks. I pulled myself like a primeval animal out of the water, taking care not to skin my knees. The stones were hot but not unbearable. As I climbed to the top, I heard voices.

Seven or eight French teen-agers were playing cards. One of the
girls was anointing her burned and flaking nipples with oil. Two
of the boys were arguing strenuously about the cards. Their
browned backs were black along the spine.

I sat awhile with my back to them, facing out toward the
cobalt sky and sea, running my hand through my dripping hair.
Already the sun was drawing my skin taut. For a long while I
sat meditatively. Down along the sheerest rocks the sea was
violet. Out aways the water was greenish, as though there were
a coral reef. Far out a white tanker rode motionless across a
spangling sea.

The voice of one of the girls was growing petulant, as she
accused the boys of cheating. But other voices broke through my
reverie more clearly: two heavy women swam into the inlet. They
climbed out almost at my feet, their great bosoms hanging slack.
I casually dropped my arm to hide myself and looked out to sea.
I counted to sixty and tried to imagine the taste of sour lemons,
but the sweetness was stronger, and I decided that after the
mammoth German women were safely past it would be time for
me to take to the water again.

I tried one further inlet, lay in the sun awhile, and tried to put
my life together. Then I plunged into the water for the final
time—the water first burned and then chilled me like ice—and
swam back toward our rendezvous. I hoped the spot would be
recognizable; my arms were aching. From the rock Jack, naked
now, saw me coming and pointed toward a series of rocks where I
could climb out.

We spent the rest of that lyrical afternoon on the island.
Families from France and Germany with rows of tiny children—
wealthy people, healthy people—were our constituency. At lunch
we sat at an outdoor café, where a French uncle bought a glace for
his niece, her breasts no larger than animated pears; she laughed
as they talked. We walked along paths of yellow dust as fine as
flour through the hills and ridges. Occasionally women, startled
by our appearance, clasped their arms in front of them; in our
bathing trunks, we were violating the conventions. When we
became aware of the disorder we were introducing, all of us but
Marilou stripped off our trunks. Our buttocks revealed that we

were newcomers, but at least we felt that we were being fair; we had the satisfaction of obeying the unwritten law.

I was surprised that it did not embarrass me to walk with Marilou. We laughed together at the sign we discovered announcing a dance that evening at 9 P.M.

"Imagine that!" Marilou said archly, blushing.

We stopped on a ridge overlooking the main beach and ate the fruit we had saved. Marilou passed out deep-purple plums and soft peaches; she handed Jack a thick bunch of large grapes. He tried to get his fingers around them to snap off smaller stems for each of us. We sat on the grass, dangling our feet over the ridge. I bit into a glossy, maroon peach and jerked forward to prevent the thick juice from falling on me.

"I haven't felt so good in years!" Eddie said quickly.

Jack began to lecture. He was writing a book on erotic literature in Roman culture. "Frankness solves part of the problem, but not all of it."

Eddie looked away.

Jack desisted. In his view, every celibate is inhibited. "I have never met an emotionally healthy priest," he once told me. "Not a single one. If you push them a little, out it comes into the open." His tone subtly reached out to include me. His researches into the psychology of sex gave him a power which he enjoyed exercising; I always felt he knew more about my unconscious than I. Since he was undergoing extensive psychoanalysis in connection with his book, and since he seemed to have read every book and article of erotic lore in six languages, I often found myself allowing him to take the role of magister.

Jack was a large man, six feet two, with broad shoulders. He had been born in Atlanta and still had faint traces of a southern drawl. His eyes, in his strong round face, were a surprising, innocent, limpid blue. He was quick, aggressive and easily provoked to hostility. His temperament was altogether Southern: soft, gentlemanly, considerate, but rapidly black and violent. There was a devil in him he could not slay, a devil he feared, a devil that humbled him to gentleness and lovely, placid conversation, while patiently plotting to strike in an unguarded moment.

He told me a story once about how after a publisher's party in New York an older man, a distinguished Catholic layman, had

offered to drive Marilou home. Hardly were they in the car than
the man made advances. Startled, she leaped out of the car at
the next stoplight. When she told Jack about it later, he took
his pistol (a Southerner always has firearms near at hand) and
went stalking the man through New York. Without a car and
at that time without funds to hire a taxi, he traveled by bus—
to the man's hotel, to the address of mutual friends, and even to
the publishing house the man had come to New York to visit.
Luckily, the man had already left the city and the long bus ride
tamed the devil. "I would have killed him," Jack said. "I was
mad enough to kill him. She was three months pregnant and he
knew it."

Below us on the beach were several hundred dark bodies drinking sun and air. They lay on their sides or sat cross-legged playing
cards, cribbage, chess, listening to transistor radios, or reading
magazines. Occasionally, two of them, or a whole group of four or
five, would arise, brush the sand from their gleaming bodies, and
run into the brilliant sea. Behind us we heard footsteps. A
middle-aged German couple were reprimanding their teen-age
daughter; there were tears of humiliated stubbornness in her eyes.
Her bulky, fleshy parents descended the white dusty path toward
the beach, and the girl listlessly sank to a seated position beneath
a tree next to us, crossed her lissome brown legs, and threw a
handful of pine needles at the ground. She didn't look at us at
all; her world was held tightly in her thoughts. She wore neither
G-string nor bra.

"What's the matter, Jon, a little much?" Jack asked slyly.

I blushed. "Let's go for a swim."

"That's what they taught in the seminary. An ice-cold bath,"
Jack taunted.

"I could use one," I said.

We rose and languidly began to descend the path. It was all
I could do not to look back. I hoped, somehow, that the girl
would be there when we came back. I was in love with a girl
named Vittoria in Rome, but it was an undifferentiated love.
To put it in a word: I needed a lover.

"I'll wait here for you," Marilou said.

"We won't be long. We have to catch the boat," Jack said.

We took our swim in the salty water. It felt much colder now.
We let the sun dry us, as we picked our way through the naked

beachcombers and climbed past the dusty bushes alongside the path to the ridge. We had to be careful of stepping on sharp rocks or on shale that would slide out from under us. At the top we gathered up our bundles of clothes and headed for the pier. The girl was gone.

The whole day had been so paradisaic that I have sometimes been tempted to think it was a dream. Seldom has the sky been so serene or the ocean so translucent. The world seemed open then, and lovely shadows haunted it.

On the way homeward in the dusk, we sat subdued and hardly spoke. We sat near the snapping French flag in the stern and sometimes felt the mist from the bow-cloven sea. The sun sank in the west like an orange translucent disc, behind a filter of air-meshed violet cloud. The Mediterranean sky played its twilight tricks: streaks of green and yellow light danced free and high above the pink and orange and mauve that dyed the horizon. The sea was rich red-violet in the distance, with lines of evening silver riding upon its undulating surface. The chug of the ferry's engines and its struggle against the tensile, resisting water violated the silent air.

It was a time for reverie. Nothing in my past had promised that I would find myself on such a ferry, at such a time. My life seemed discontinuous and odd.

2

My HOME CITY lies in a curving valley. Pressing upon it, wooded hills rise green and luxurious in the summer sun and flame scarlet in the autumn. Old houses, weather marked and sooty, are stacked in dreary rows through every valley. Thin clouds of reddish smoke rise from the open hearths of the mills of Nazareth Steel. The mills, which once employed eighteen thousand men and now employ seven, wind for twelve miles along the shores of the brown Rolling Rock River. At the Point, where the Ponawatomac meets the shallower, coffee-colored Rolling Rock and their mutual waters gurgle against rusty orange rocks, there is a double-tiered baseball stadium where in 1929 Babe Ruth, before 14,000 persons, poked an exhibition blast that was still rising when it cleared the red-brick right-field wall at 415 feet. Nearby, there is an incline plane which ascends the hill (townspeople boast) at the steepest angle of any incline in the world. From above, on a balmy summer night you can look down upon the stadium's illuminated infield and brown, worn outfield. You can look down upon the arc of soft light over the stadium, the sluggish rivers, the twisting blue gas flames of the mill's tall stacks, and, beyond the bridges, the streets of the heart of the city. The Fort Bedford Hotel, the fourteen-storied Pennsylvania Bank building, Grey Hospital, and a set of shiny new downtown motels dominate the streets. Great stone churches preside over the edges of the circle.

You look down, and you imagine the entire valley under fourteen feet of water in 1889 and again in 1936—imagine the waters swirling against the concrete bridge at the Point, dammed up and become a whirlpool into which houses and boats are sucked, and you see the whirlpool explode into a spiral of flame as the oil upon it ignites. You think of two thousand human beings drowned and burned alive. Vividly you see the profiteers who pillaged the wreckage and, in their haste to remove rings and watches, cut off the fingers of the dead. You recognize that some of the city's ten millionaires received the first large funds of their investments from the immense surplus which the staggering generosity of the peoples of the world contributed to the stricken city.

Conemaugh is a beautiful and a forgotten city. One hundred twenty thousand strong in its metropolitan area, it is becoming a city of the aged; there is no work, no future, for the young. Its humiliation saddens me. Here fortunes were made, inventions which helped to revolutionize the world were conceived, a gateway to the west—long since superseded by Pittsburgh, Louisville, St. Louis, San Francisco—was thrown up in a silent forest. The township of Scalp Hill attests to the last episodes of the Indian

era. The river Ponawatomac and "Ponawatomac Big Town," as
the Indians called their few paltry huts at the Point, appear on
every map. To the south, at Bedford, the main road of the early
British expeditionary forces was cut from forests so thick they
awoke awe in young English soldiers. "We do not see the skye,"
a lieutenant wrote home to Liverpool. "Savages lurke a yarde
away, utterly invisible." Strong men were snatched as hostages
from army columns. To the east, a sixteen-year-old girl was kid-
napped and hurried overland to the Ohio. Years later, an old
woman, she returned to write an account of her marriage and
her life in the tribe; she had fared no worse than some of her
schoolmates, married normally. To the west, at Bushy Creek, a
bitter struggle set the stage for the white man's final triumph
over the Indians of Pennsylvania: a triumph full of murder,
plunder, and mass imprisonment. Too many historians have lived
in Boston for Pennsylvania's stories to be familiar; they lie in
the memory like gray, powdery embers, awaiting flame.

My home, in short, was built by bloodshed. Every automobile
now whining down the Pennsylvania turnpike, skirting the highest
and most tortuous of the inland hills, skirts past the violence
which is our truth.

My grandfather came to Conemaugh in 1887. The clapboard
opera house, the mud streets, the ugly telegraph lines shine from
old daguerreotypes with a somber poverty. Yet, by the standards
of the world, Conemaugh was rich. My grandfather, Stephen
Svoboda (our name means "freedom," my father has always
pointed out), came to the city on a tip from his brother John
in Connecticut. "Lots of work. Many Slovaks needed." My grandfather, who was twenty, was determined not to work in the mills.
He had a little money; his parents in Slovakia were shopkeepers.
He wandered over the hillsides, out the trails and deeply rutted
roads. Near what was later to become Mohawk highway, not far
from where my father now lives in a suburban development,
my grandfather purchased seventeen acres of land, at present
part of the estate of one of the wealthiest men in town. The
purchase made, my grandfather returned to Slovakia, to the hills—
so like the hills of Conemaugh, only steeper and sheerer—of his
native Spiš. There he was reunited with Anna, his fiancée.

We do not know how many brothers and sisters my grandfather

had. It is a struggle to unearth the smallest details about his
family. Were he and Anna married in Spiš? Almost certainly.
When they returned to Conemaugh—how long was the boat trip?
was it arduous? were they ever afraid?—the flood had already
wrought its worst. Stephen began to construct his house. For a
while, his efforts at farming proved successful. In 1892 little Anna
was born; in 1895, after a frightful delivery, Stephen junior; in
1897, George. Then in March of 1902 my grandfather's first wife
contracted pneumonia. He was driving her down the muddy,
deeply rutted roads to the hospital when an axle of his wagon
broke and Anna was flung against a rock. The rain fell in solid
sheets. The horse reared and the broken wagon pitched on top of
her. Stephen frantically heaved against the load. Anna's hip was
fractured jaggedly. Her face was rain soaked and ashen. She
never spoke again. Well before he reached the nearest farm, she
was dead.

Stephen sold the land, which he now detested, and went to
work in the mill. He didn't turn to drink; he worked. He moved
his three children to the Bottomlands, the Slovak section near
one of the central mills. In 1903 he married a sixteen-year-old
girl, blond-headed, high-cheeked Margaret Pravo, who took his
children as her own. She bore Stephen two more sons, John and
Alex. Alex was only eighteen months old when Stephen caught
his arm in a conveyor belt and was pulled in and crushed to
death before his shouts were heard in the immense din of the
mill.

Margaret Svoboda drew one thousand dollars insurance from
the mill in exchange for the life of her husband. She turned to
doing housework. My father John and his brother Alex quit
school when they were eleven and went to work.

In 1919 my father, aged fourteen, walked into the employment
office of the mill and asked for a job. They put him with three
other men handling the two halves of a sand-filled template, each
of which weighed three hundred pounds. Inside the template were
openings in the sand for four brake shoes. At the top of the
template was a hole through which molten steel was poured from
a huge metal bucket. My father was responsible for carrying and
pouring his own molten steel, and he was expected to pour

twenty-four acceptable shoes a day. During his first week of work he was sent by the older men to fetch a left-handed monkey wrench twenty inches long, then a bucket of whitewashed coal, and then a box of fresh steam; his face stung with each successive burst of mocking laughter which greeted his docility.

He was glad when the great strike of 1919 threw him out of work. He left the plant whistling, with an eye fixed on the mounted officers of the state constabulary who were all too eager to use their long, lean clubs on the skulls of workingmen. (It is resentment, not fascism, that runs deep in America; the outcome is the same.) Two days later he was applying at Hansen's Dairy. Did he have any experience? No, so they put him to work in the packing room. He disliked the cold and the dampness; he used his first week's pay to buy a pair of sneakers which would take the wet floor better. Rushed one day by an order of three hundred Santa Clauses for a party of Rotarians, Mrs. Hansen called him to cut the ice cream. My father chose the red ice cream he liked most—strawberry. He packed the ice cream in the mold, plunged the mold in hot water, slid the perfect forms on a tray and swiftly put them in the freezer. Mrs. Hansen arrived as the trays were being taken to the trucks.

"Lovely, lovely," she was nodding—until she noticed that they were not made with raspberry.

"The order slip didn't say nothin' about raspberry." My father showed her the paper.

"God*damn* it!" Mrs. Hansen threw a fit. "Hurry, you! Do them all again. Do them all. Hurry now!"

"Mrs. Hansen," he said, confident in the knowledge that the mills were reopening, "you can hurry. I'm quittin'."

When he returned to the mill, my father caught the attention of one of the bosses. He was picked to be millwright on one of the mills: when something went wrong, he was responsible for stopping and starting the mills. The company recorder logged every minute the mills were stopped. Every minute a repair required beyond what was specified in the company book had to be explained. As long as the mills rolled, my father could sit in his little glass shack and read. When a warning whistle rang or someone came running, his responsibilities began. The sound of

the whistle often meant a death or serious maiming. Faced with
a breakdown, his job was to invent the speediest possible technical
solution. The machines came first.

My parents went on Sunday picnics with Emil and Mary
Budik, who lived two houses down. Emil was twenty-nine, a strong,
handsome, black-haired man, and at the mill he directed a team
of men at the brick pits where the steel was heated. One day
Emil was giving orders at the edge of a huge pit. The bricks
were white hot, and faint traces of steam crackled from below.
In the noise it was impossible to shout; Emil was directing the
men on the cranes with his hands and extended arms. There was
no guard rail. He swept an arm, stepped backward, lost his
balance, struggled desperately, and fell into the pit. Instantly one
of his men grabbed a hose and others leaped to help. They played
hoses on Emil for fifteen minutes, blindly, into mounting clouds
of steam, until his body could be recovered. My father could never
after that endure the sight or smell of boiled meat.

My father in those days was anticlerical, irreverent, and even
somewhat antireligious; my mother was a deeply religious, cheerful,
believing Catholic. She loved ceremonies, ritual, prayer, not for the
spectacle, but for the feeling she gained of unity with God. Her
own father was an extraordinarily meditative, prayerful man—I
remember seeing him often "saying his prayers" on his knees
with a rosary wrapped around his fingers and a sweat-worn prayer-
book in his hands. He kept his prayer aids in a round black wicker
basket from Czechoslovakia; he spoke little, but then gently and
to the point. As a child, I could never woo him with artifices as
I could my grandmother and my uncles and aunts. He was severe
and paternal toward me.

The pictures of my mother as a girl of nineteen show a strikingly
girlish face, with lustrous eyes and delicate nose and chin, altogether the kind of face the Roaring Twenties gloried in. Her
parents owned considerable property in the prosperous next
borough beyond the Bottomlands; her uncle was a highly successful
undertaker. Her side of the family was the distinguished one. Her
values were shaped by the responsibilities of station and commitment to duty which are important to families of modest wealth
and position. The Catholic religion was a perfect support to these
Protestant values. To be good is to do what will never bring

shame. To see life quite clearly is to be aware of one's responsibilities and duties. The most basic value of all is fidelity to family.

For the family was the matrix of religion and culture. "The family that prays together stays together"—long before the slogan was printed in black letters on billboards from Hollywood to Pittsburgh, the ideal had been imprinted in my mother's responses to life. "Always stick together, boys. Blood is deeper than any other tie. Believe me, one day you'll come to see how important family is." They named us David and Jonathan because of the friendship of the two biblical heroes—and because my father had such a deep sympathy with Jews that we often wondered whether his family had Jewish blood in it.

My mother saw to it that David, who was four years my senior, and I made our first communion, went to confession at least twice a month, and to mass every Sunday. Her faith was so lively that ours was, too. Our fidelity was even heightened by the fact that the two of us went to the public school. We were both altar boys and choir boys; we were excused from early classes on special feast days like December 8, the Feast of the Immaculate Conception, in order to take part at mass. In my own grade, I was the official Catholic. When Miss Abernathy, the fifth grade history teacher, stumbled on the name of the reigning pope, I supplied in a firm, knowing voice: "Pope Pius XII." Once I corrected her when she was too severe on the Renaissance popes by asking her whether she knew how many of the 262 popes were saints—the batting average, my voice implied, was rather high. I was a fiercely proud Catholic, not least because national pride was at stake. Where we went to school, most of the children had American names and were Protestant. Wrinkling their noses at "Svoboda," ten-year-olds used to ask me what nationality that was—Polish? "American!" my father had taught me to say. Flustered, they would ask, "But where did your—er—ancestors come from?" "Slovakia," I would say, recognizing that precision didn't help matters much. "Part of Czechoslovakia," I clarified. "The eastern part." Poise worked so well that one Irish American in high school paid me his ultimate compliment: "Are you Irish, on your mother's side or something?"

My father was one of the millwrights who agreed to stay inside the mill during the strike of 1937; it was a critical moment in his life. Kitchens and dormitories were opened up inside the mill gates; big-fisted pickets made strikebreaking inadvisable. On the first day of the strike my father was at home on his day off. A black car loaded with five brawny men drove slowly by the front porch; the driver tooted the horn and shouted, "You won't go to work tomorrow if you know what's good for you." My father stayed home the following day. But he went to work the next. He had watched the union organizer from Detroit get railroaded out of town by the city police, at the mayor's orders, and judged that the union offered him too little security. He was confronted by his superintendent about the missed day's work: "Johnny, you're either on our side or theirs." He opted for management; he became, in time, a foreman.

My father favored the unions, but he personally didn't want to get involved. He hated to see the men come into work drunk, especially the Monday after pay day; he sent home anyone unfit for work. "So you'll lose your pay!" he told one angry Slovak. "You'll keep your life." On another occasion a drunk he told to go home picked up a two-inch iron rod and rushed at him as if to crush his skull; my father thought his time had come but stood his ground. "Go ahead," he said. The man lifted the rod, then stopped. My father hated the conditions at the mill, and he hated irresponsibility. As the unions gained power, washrooms and laundries were built; no longer did the men have to go home covered with grease, or stow their greasy clothes in rudimentary hiding places; no longer did wives wrestle with grease on tin washing boards; no longer did a man's grease-stiff clothes suddenly burst into flame from the heat of the furnaces and burn his entire body. Wages rose; insurance and pension plans were established; elementary safety laws were enforced. After the Second World War, however, the Conemaugh mills became too expensive to operate. New plants with new processes sprang up in other cities. Nazareth Steel gave Conemaugh the fragmentary business unprofitable to take elsewhere.

But my father had a decent salary. My parents were the first Slovak family in our city to move "up on the hill" into the suburb where the city's mill owners, doctors, and lawyers lived. David and I went to one of the best public schools in our part of the state. Mother was nervous in her new bridge clubs and women's groups; she never quite felt accepted, and she couldn't compete with the sophisticated, ironic gossip in which middle-class women expend the substance of their lives. Bridge club ladies have terrified me ever since we moved (when I was seven and David eleven) to the large house on the rolling lawn.

My mother was a kind woman; she seldom spoke ill of anyone, and when by chance she did, the failure provoked instant apologies and two or three days of praise for the offended party. My mother was innocent to a degree that hardly seems possible in a society afflicted with advertisers, merchants, propagandists, liars, and hustlers of every sort. Her moral horizons never extended beyond the confines of family experience. She didn't believe in malice. She reinterpreted everything so that "the good side" came upper-most. She could be cool under pressure. When in the early days eight feet of taut five-inch chain snapped in the mill and coiled like a whip around my father's head, knocking him unconscious and raising swellings as big as grapefruit, she never panicked. She sat with him in the company hospital for the two weeks he was unconscious and nourished him on soups afterwards until—without compensation—he was able to go back to work. Had he died, she would have been twenty-nine years old, with two children to support through the Depression and one thousand dollars insurance from Nazareth Steel to pay for the funeral.

My relationship with David is difficult to state. Perhaps the simplest statement is that we never achieved the friendship of our biblical namesakes, except possibly when we were children and built tree houses in the back yard and played guns in the wide fields and orchards near our home. Whatever we played, David always had to win. It was forbidden us to say we hated each other; blood brothers above all should love. But there was certainly hostility between us. What are the prospects for the human race, if two brothers who come from the same home cannot speak to each other? David never understood me, or perhaps I never understood him. He was my mother's favorite: seemingly gentle, kind, hardworking. He was very intelligent; he always got better marks than I did in school. When on graduation from St. Margaret's Catholic School (my mother's scruples caught up to her by the time we were old enough for high school, and we

transferred from the splendid public school to a much less sophisticated, lower-class Catholic school) I won, as David had
four years earlier, the Outstanding Senior Award, it was widely
recognized that his trailing glory had more or less singled me
out in advance. I was a better athlete than he, but not by much,
and I had none of his crisp brilliance and—the ingredient so
indispensable in high school—personality. When he went to a
Jesuit college in the Midwest, I resolved never to attend a Catholic
college and to head east. It was an immense surprise to everyone,
myself included, when I decided, after graduation from college,
to enter the seminary.

Ironically, David had by that time left the church. Somehow
he became fed up with the Jesuits, and came to think the whole
Catholic Church was a fraud. There were some painful scenes
at home when he announced these views; my mother wept. "See
what I mean!" he said desperately and bitterly. "Sheer sentiment!
That's how they get so deep a hold on you. The Jesuits at least
pretended to be logical. So long as no one really raises doubts."

David was a hero, later, in Korea; at least, he came back with
a Purple Heart and gold battle stars. My poor eyesight and a
football injury kept me from emulating his wartime prowess;
secretly I had always known that he would someday come back
in uniform, with medals, and be the center of attention. The
event fitted our relationship perfectly.

Just after I left the seminary, I went to New York "to do some
writing." My mother was certain I would end up in Greenwich
Village and return one day with a stringy blond in sandals, with
dirty feet. "Why don't you get a job?" she asked. "You could
make a thousand dollars by September and help your father
pay for graduate school."

"Mother," I tried to explain. "You're only young once. I haven't
been anywhere. I haven't seen anything. This may be my last
chance. Besides, how can I work and write?"

"You could write in the evenings."

I suppose I wore a look of contempt, or exasperation, or both.
"Mother . . ."

"Why do you have to be a writer? Who wants to marry a
writer? You'll need a regular, paying job."

"Who knows if I'm going to be a writer?"

"Well, if you don't know, why don't you get experience with a good firm. Look at David . . ."

"Mother, Uncle Frank hired him and, besides, he likes banking. I don't want to be a fat, middle-class banker all my life."

"Don't you speak of him that way! Would you were a little like him. At least he knows what he wants to do and has some stability."

I almost threw my book to the floor. To fill the silence I started to say "Mother . . ." and took refuge in the easiest strategy I knew. I got up and left the room with purposive silence, the only slap I seemed allowed to deliver.

3

FOR TWO DAYS Ed and I sat on the porch of the Prescott house on a hill on the French coast. Below, the brilliant blue water curled in a white line on the sweeping beach. A French cook prepared our meals and minded the Prescott children. We sipped Pernod and talked of love, freedom, the meaning of woman, and other rare themes. Ed fancied himself a philosopher—he and Jack were, in fact, professional philosophers. And as an English major, I was even more professionally a philosopher than they, and for more people. Common sense, the instincts and emotions, the concrete word: these are the lifeblood both of literature and good philosophy; they are my credentials for profound discourse, but that was in another land and, besides, a long time ago.

We watched the sun set late in the evenings and, on the

night we returned from the island, talked by starlight until the sun rose again in the chill damp dawn. During the day we slept.

Eddie was in the throes of a decision to quit the priesthood, and we were living through the struggle with him. No one spoke directly to the issue, but almost everything we said bore upon it. A Catholic priest is ordained "a priest forever." The priesthood is thought of as a character, a mark never to be dissociated from the personality. The priest by his ordination becomes sacred in his very person, dedicated to God and linked mysteriously to the person of Jesus Christ. The conception is awesome and magical. To break from it requires an inner agony that is searing and intense, particularly if one retains one's faith and one's attitude on almost all other matters. It is easy to become an atheist and to reject "magic" in one fell swoop. To go as Eddie was going— to reject the priesthood because it was making him a bureaucrat despite himself, to reject, as it were, the priesthood in the name of Christianity itself—was shattering, particularly in 1962 before the path had been worn so smooth. Moreover, it was not the sacredness Eddie was protesting; it was the destruction of that sacredness by managerial values like obedience and prudence which he detested. He was far from being a pragmatist; he had reverence and a sense of mystery; he was, if anything, an active and effective idealist. Eddie was reshaping his whole attitude toward women and toward his own identity; in the process, the sacredness he had hitherto attached to celibacy and chastity and restraint was under painful questioning. The trip to the island was of high emotional importance to him, although his efforts to explain why were faltering and he was checked by a long-standing reticence.

"Say, would you like to drive to Cannes for dinner?" Jack invited us Sunday afternoon. It was four, and we were having an after-breakfast drink.

"Sounds great!" Ed slapped his knee.

"Well, better get ready; it will take us at least two hours to get there."

At precarious speeds, Jack whipped the green Plymouth around curves. The wheels screeched as we veered to avoid an oncoming sports car that was, as we were, straddling the painted center line. The narrow highway was flanked by whitewashed trees— trees like those Albert Camus had crushed against two years earlier. Begonia-scented air whipped loudly through the windows; it was impossible to converse. You only live once, I thought, deciding to relax. Impossible for Jack not to live dangerously; his demon demanded danger.

Near Cannes, Jack wheeled the car up a narrow, winding road toward a castle where he and Marilou had discovered a restaurant. On top of the hill we came to a tiny ancient village, whose streets the station wagon could scarcely navigate. At last, Jack gunned the car into a lantern-lit outdoor garden. Three tables had been placed together, and a dozen young playboys and pretty girls looked up in surprise and then disdain. Jack braked the car, turned sharply, and wheeled it swiftly down a narrow alleyway behind the dark stone building. Three gaunt chickens scurried from our path. Wheeling rapidly, Jack spun the car around a corner, backed up, and came to a quick stop. "Well, here we are. Ed, bring the wine." He pointed behind the back seat.

We walked jubilantly down the dark cobblestones, past refuse drums and a gray stringy mop. Under the lanterns a waiter greeted us with a bow and showed us to a table. We ordered slowly, smoked, and began sipping the first of our three bottles of Pommard. The Frenchmen at the table opposite were making jokes about us, but we tried not to notice.

Jack was in rare form. For our amusement he dredged up scores of fascinating details of erotic lore. "There were women in ancient Rome," he said, "whose vaginal performance was so good they could shoot carrots across a room. Honest."

"Some more Pommard?" Marilou asked me. Such conversation displeased her. You could see a silent rage gathering within her.

"Thanks," I said.

The cuisine was excellent, but no better than the mellow, fragrant Pommard. We were rather heady with the wine near the end of our dinner, when the first grape bounced across our table, hitting no one. We looked up and the French youths laughed. A tall young Frenchman in an open blue shirt waved.

"There is no Frog who is not a bastard," Jack said, with the bitterness of two years' living in France.

"Just overlook it, dear," Marilou counseled nervously.

Jack tried to resume our conversation. A second grape sailed just past his head.

"Goddamn it!" Jack threw back his chair and walked across to the far table.

I crumpled my napkin and set it on the table. I had not been in a fight since grammar school. Jack had been in at least two brawls in Paris, for one of which he had spent a night in jail. We watched as he spoke angrily to the blue-shirted man. There were five men and seven girls at the other table.

"If anything happens," I whispered to Ed, "take Marilou and get into the car."

Jack's voice was getting louder. Two of the Frenchmen were rising to their feet. Jack's fist suddenly flashed and smashed into the face of the blue-shirt. Chairs began to spill. Girls screamed.

"Take her to the car," I said, and with cold heart crossed the eating area. One of the Frenchmen was trying to get hold of Jack from behind; Jack had thrown a chair in the path of the red-shirted one. I swung with what I thought was a karate punch at the neck of the man on Jack's back. A flash of pain went through my knuckles, and I grabbed him by the shoulders, slid my forearm around his neck, and threw him to the ground. Blows were falling all around. One of the girls picked up a wine bottle, and I grabbed a glass of water and dashed it in her face, shoving another girl against her. Jack laid into two of the men with his fists while I grappled with a third. The man I had thrown to the floor got up and came at me. I was afraid for a moment, but threw a punch as hard as I could. It hit his nose with a soft, crunching sound. Just then something hit me heavily on the back. Then someone was grabbing my arms. The pressure was released and I saw that Eddie was beside us. The three of us held off the others until the lights of the Plymouth bore down on us. At the same moment Jack and Ed got the idea of grabbing the tables, and overturned two of them in the path of the opposition. While Ed and I jumped into the car, Jack called several more imprecations down upon Charles de Gaulle and all living Frenchmen, and in a roar of dust the Plymouth leaped through the last flimsy table in our path and down the roadway.

We were uncertain of our escape until free from the narrow streets. Marilou drove aggressively, rocking the Plymouth around the last two corners.

"W-w-we didn't have dessert," Ed said jubilantly.

Released by sight of the open road, we began to laugh.

"One thing I don't stand is a pompous Frog!" Jack said, throwing back his hair.

We were all breathing heavily. Marilou was quiet but obviously disturbed. The violence disgusted her.

"My hand is really aching," I laughed.

Jack turned in the seat and said appreciatively, "Let's see it. I didn't think you had it in you, Jon."

There was nothing to show except bruised knuckles. But the hand felt twice its normal size.

"When you pick 'em, you like to pick 'em big, don't you?" Ed cracked.

"At least you won't spend tonight in jail or tomorrow in the hospital," Marilou said drily. She pulled the car over to the side of the road. "Here, you drive. I'm too nervous."

We looked back anxiously through the rear window. Jack got out and crossed in front of the headlights. His shirt was torn and there were smudges of blood on his face.

"You're such a mess!" Marilou said as he entered the car. Ed reached for a sweater from the rear and offered it to her.

"It wasn't serious, honey. You can't let a bastard like that insult you."

"He was just being smart in front of his girlfriends."

"Well, he has to take the consequences then. He can't treat us like fools just because we're Americans."

"Oh, you're so defensive and so combative. Everybody's always picking on you."

Ed and I sat back in silence. The car speeded up and the white trees flew past.

"We never did pay for dinner," Ed said quietly to me.

"Or for damages," I added.

The excess of adrenaline began to subside. My hand still throbbed. I wondered what my mother would imagine (surely not the truth) if I told her that we had dined at a castle on a hill near Cannes. And that high culture ends inevitably in acts of international aggression.

4

WHEN I LEFT the Prescott's late one afternoon, I traveled by hot,
bouncing bus to Cannes, past the road to the castle restaurant,
past the restless cobalt sea. In Nice that night, I stayed in the
cheapest hotel I could find. On the train the next day I lived
on a sandwich and an *aranciata*.

The train was crowded, as usual. I was lucky enough to find a
seat, facing two wool-suited workingmen and a girl in a black
dress. I sat beside a huge woman and a sleeping boy of eleven.
The train rocked from side to side and the hot sun beat upon my
arm. The clicking of the rails lulled me into a kind of mindlessness.
I studied my fellow passengers, as they studied me. No words were
exchanged. We were on exhibit, our lives intersecting for a few
rocking hours. The girl was a teacher, perhaps. Wisps of dark
hair escaped from under her arms. I noted the contours of her
lips, her bosom, her waist; without an effort I mentally undressed her.

My thoughts, insofar as I would allow them to focus, moved
dully but irresistibly toward what I knew would happen in Rome.
Everything had, without design, been set in motion. The grip of
Sarah Douglas on my imagination was at last being broken. She
seemed, especially after the last three days, far away. I had not
thought of her at all, even once. She had not wished our relationship to be serious. And though I had once thought that I might
one day marry her, I found it difficult to bring her image vividly
before me. I could see her, slim and untamed and immature, and
feel almost unmoved. A wave of regret, of contrition perhaps,
followed. All the more eagerly my thoughts focused upon Vittoria

—*la mia* Vittoria *di* Roma—her accent fell distinctly upon my
inner ear. I heard her laugh. I felt the solid, firm warmth of her
presence at my side. I saw the narrow turn of her ankle. My
fingers closed upon her full breast.

A soldier slid open the door of our compartment, looked in,
and then slammed it. The old woman muttered an imprecation
and slid it open several inches to preserve a draught. Outside,
the countryside lay whitened by the sun, dusty, blinding hot. No
breeze blew and the dirty air stirred by the train beat upon us
without cooling us. After a while the workingmen unpacked huge,
moist, smelly sandwiches. They offered one to the girl. Politely
but resolutely, she refused. They were about to offer one to me,
but I averted my eyes.

Am I, at twenty-seven, I wondered, beginning to taste freedom?
As the train rocketed along, I had a feeling of great power and
yet also of powerlessness, of a kind that often afflicts me, as if
despite surprises and novelty everything has already been decided,
as if I have lived through all this before. Often I see a face or
catch sight of a building—like the buildings around the Pantheon
in Rome—and think, I knew that man many years ago, or, I
have lived here before, when it is certain, by objective criteria,
that no previous acquaintance was possible. I seem to myself a
Jekyll and Hyde: sometimes detached, sometimes passionate,
observer and doer. Sometimes I feel that I decide nothing, that
my life speeds along on predetermined tracks. Sometimes I feel
that I have absolute freedom to decide who I am: each moment
I start from zero, each second of life is staccato and fresh, now,
and I can begin everything anew.

A complete and thorough world view was presented me with
my first breaths. The hairy fingers of the priest rubbed soiled salt
onto my infant lips and roughly loosened my shirt to violate the
hidden nape of my neck. Thus today alternatives take root in
me only slowly, like the grass that gradually loosens the walls of
ancient cities. The Catholicism of my parents was gentle, sober,
reasoned. By the pragmatic tests of their lives, it worked: through
suffering, through joys, through routine, at each moment the
myths and rituals and sacraments of the church spoke aloud and
spoke sense. In the delicate, exquisite sexual symbolism of the
eucharist they weekly bit with a love-bite into the flesh of God,

eating him, becoming God. On the other hand, their Catholicism was uncritical. Like a chameleon, the official Catholicism they knew changed colors; it went wherever the needs of family, law, and order went. It never erred. It never learned. It taught all things true, good, beautiful: whatever is discovered to be true, good, beautiful, it says it has always taught. Never surprised, never dismayed, it ingests the imaginations of the ages. It announced no novelties; everything good it found to be a return to tradition. My parents' Catholicism never experienced revolution; the most it allowed was renaissance. Catholicism taught its children to look backward.

But what, then, of the individual, pitting himself against mother church, pitting himself against history, demanding an undetermined future? What if one does not wish to have been programmed in advance? What if one desires most of all to find out for oneself?

I was taught that in order to commit a serious sin one must give sufficient reflection and full consent of the will, and I was instructed, in the seminary, that my vows would depend for their validity upon the freedom in which they were made. In a sense, those were lessons in liberty. And yet so many forms of behavior had been already classified, and in the seminary I had poor experiential knowledge of what I so willingly denied myself. I had long practiced making "free" decisions: when I was thirsty, I used to count to fifty before allowing myself to sip from a water fountain, and sometimes when the count reached fifty, I would turn away without drinking at all. While I counted, I did not let myself think about what I would do. At fifty, spontaneously and firmly I would decide.

Or is freedom the exhilaration I felt the night of the brawl? Not merely the burst of danger and novelty, but the release provided by violence? Sarah had once cried out in exasperation: "You're the most *reasonable* person I've ever met." I didn't think I was as inflexible as she made out, and I have certainly struggled all my life with instincts and impulses. But possibly she was right and I must let go. How will I ever find out who I am if I do not run some risks? Apollo and Dionysus—one must flirt with both.

The excitement of a clear chain of ethical thought drove me onward. Why had it taken me so long to begin to be free? My life seemed much shorter now than it ever had; youth had almost slipped from my grasp. My three years in a seminary were like a dream, a set of brackets around a period of my life which had disappeared: I had lost three central years of my youth. Supposing that there is no God, supposing that there is no immortality—I felt my passion for life rise with every pitch and beat of the clicking, rushing wheels. I had been cheated. I had been cheated. It was rushing away, and perhaps I had not ever lived. Perhaps I had lost years of my life. Each grain in the hourglass—don't wait for the next!

Several times the train rushed through dark tunnels. Hurriedly we raised the window against the hot, cindery, black air and, when we burst into daylight, hurried to slide it open. My thoughts began to lose their sharp edge and reverie replaced concentration, though the glow of liberty remained. I thought of Sarah in California. Her image remained remote, and I somehow could not bring myself to the emotions I wished: of affection, of love, of commitment. After all, she had not wanted, yet, to "become serious." She wanted to finish her degree. I had once loved her, there was no question of that. Or perhaps I should say that I knew that she had awakened love in me. The love slumbered now, and it seemed idle to prod it. I would have to wait. Wait while the time flew, faster than the posts outside the train: day by day, year by year, as youth disappeared, wait. I pictured her short blond hair and slender figure; pictured her in tennis skirt on the courts at Barnard, and heard the *bonk, bonk, bonk* of the ball as she easily defeated me on the hot gray surface; pictured her in summery white cocktail dress as we drove in the cool of the evening along the Hudson; pictured the sunlight falling on her impassive face—always slightly impenetrable to me—as we drank Bacardis on a terrace, in the noon sun, overlooking the hills of Connecticut. Yes, we would meet again, in due course; her almost total selfishness, her imperviousness, her bright, cynical mind attracted me. She was a creature of a different sort from any I had ever known; she toughened me and was good for me.

Meanwhile, the center of my affections, revealed by the weight of gravity in my thoughts, revealed by the anticipation and the joy, pointed to Vittoria: Vittoria the brown-skinned, the raven-eyed, the black-haired, the lissome, the free. A fresh creature,

placid and demure on the surface, but unspoiled. Awed by everything, romantic, acutely self-aware.

Is it common, I wondered, to love two women at once? I did,
equally. Or rather, unequally. These were two different kinds of
love. I loved Vittoria for now, and it was a love sweet and sad
because the time was short. I was a little afraid of Sarah, afraid
of her indifference and her fickleness. Yet it does her injustice to
suggest that her love was weak because her realism and her
determination were strong.

"What you have to understand, Jon, is that I can't afford to tie
myself down. I intend to remain single until I'm thirty, and if I
can hold out longer, I will. There's nothing you can't get without
marriage that you can get with it if you have the guts. And I
have the guts."

"Why do you waste time with me?"

"Because I want to. As long as I'm enjoying it, here I am.
When I get tired of it, phwwt!"

"Maybe I should pop you into bed. Maybe I should try to make
out . . ."

"Don't you think it's a relief not to have hot little fingers
climbing all over you? When that's what I want I can get it.
Besides I don't quite understand you. I'm intrigued. And there are
things I rather like about you."

We held hands, embraced, kissed—my hands explored a little.
I liked to cup her malleable breasts, through her sweater, in the
palm of my hand and to slide my fingers on the cool flesh of her
thighs. In those days I would go no further. How could that be?
I was twenty-five. It is difficult to explain how powerful and
strong the ideal of chastity remained for me. When I met her,
I was still in the trailing brightness of my seminary days. I never
had the view that sex was dirty or evil (though I had been taught
a hearty disgust for masturbation, which made it all the more
attractive). But I had accepted the idea that sex is holy, sacred,
precious, rare. *Do not squander your seed* was, I suppose, the
commandment as it came through to me: *Save it for the only one.*
Fellows and girls together with me in graduate school would have
found this attitude, had we spoken of it, odd. I resented missing
the fun I thought they were having. But I also felt that sex for
me still had mystery and magic attached to it, and the taboo

I accepted made my sexual appetites explosive, not to say cosmic
in their implications. No mere eating and drinking, or scratching
of an itch, in my consciousness. By the time I was going seriously
with Sarah, however, I wasn't sure I could hold out much longer.
The idea of saving for one sole investment was becoming a drag.
Half of me had always wanted to experiment—even in the seminary
I had told Eddie on more than one electric-aired, juicy, spring day
that it was all I could do not to jump on the first broad I saw.
Now three-quarters of me could wait no longer.

It must be hard for those who did not grow up Catholic to
understand—even to believe—that countless young Catholics are
chaste far beyond the normal complement of years, and for a
long time do not seriously miss the sexual experience they lack.
In a way, they love their chastity; it has its own peace, liberty
of spirit, and joy. Yet, at a certain time, the fruit ripens and the
juices must flow. If the young man or woman has been chaste
not through duress but through choice, a new choice is made fairly
peaceably: the move from purity to achievement requires but a
single proud step. Afterwards, I have heard of persons pinning
medals on themselves to advertise their, shall we say, bar mitzvah
to the world.

In any case, Sarah never asked for more. She was content. My
dedication to chastity was new to her and strange. In her circles,
innocence was a matter of age and accident; no one *willingly* was
chaste longer than external circumstances warranted. It was surely
assumed that a male by seventeen and a girl by twenty had had
their appropriate come-uppance. With me, Sarah was curious
and respectful. We spent many hours in each other's arms. Our
lips lay pressed together quietly for many moments; our passion
was, most often, serene. The fact will defy credence, but we even
slept beneath the same sheets one night, unclad, affectionately but
without making love. I wonder, now, what it cost her.

Now, again, with Vittoria, marriage was out of the question. It
was a good relationship. Vittoria had lived for two years in
England; her English was pleasing, though not faultless. But,
for all that, she knew as I did that she was born for Italy and I
for America. The very first night we were together she had said,
under the immense dark pines of the Terme di Caracalla, "Do
you know why I said I would come?"

I walked along the path with her, matching her steps, silently. "Why?"

"Because you said you were leaving Friday. It would be more beautiful." She looked up shyly. "Do you understand? Am I being silly?"

"I think I understand."

She extended her hand, almost losing her white shawl. "And look at the stars. Look at the moon. It is beautiful, *vero?*"

The night was warm and fresh. We couldn't concentrate on *William Tell.* While the singers vibrated with emotion and sound, and the chorus filled the air with counterpoint, we sought seats in the last row, twelve or thirteen rows behind anyone else, so that we could talk. I had been trying to get Vittoria to come to the opera with me for more than two weeks. She worked in a jewelry store on the Via Condotti—she knew I had bought a pin for Sarah.

When I met Vittoria that first night at her home, she left the building without asking me up to meet her mother. When the bell rang, she knew it must be me and descended. After we had greeted each other and began walking toward the opera, she pulled my arm and stopped me in the street.

"First tell me," she said. "Excuse me. Are you—a Catholic?" I laughed. "Yes."

"Good!" she said, resuming her walk.

"What does that mean?"

"I don't know, but I am glad." Perhaps she had told her mother so, to disarm some of her fears. But wasn't everyone in Italy Catholic? And what did that prove?

"May I put my arm around you?" I asked during the second act. She hesitated and her dark eyes were troubled. "Where?" I laughed. "On your shoulder."

Her heart beat faster as I clasped her arm. After a while the stiffness left her back and she allowed her weight to rest against me. Through her shawl I could feel her flesh; electricity was passing between us, beneath the moon, as we sat in the gaunt red ruins and tried to listen to an aria here, a chorus there.

Afterwards, we walked in the park and down the wide boulevard. She had promised her mother—who had been horrified that she was going out with a stranger and, worse, an American—that she would come home early; she declined a trip into the city. We stopped at a café and had a cappuccino. The young men and older, unshaven workers eyed us with hostility; we tried not to notice.

As we walked toward the park, where the pines already glistened in the night, we tried to piece together patches of our lives, to present ourselves to each other quickly, filling in our identities. Every point of similarity, every mutual interest, however tenuous, exhilarated us. Love is staked heavily against fate, and each point lowered the odds against us. Dreams were taking flesh; each step seemed too reassuring to be true.

Memories, memories. As the train rolled from side to side, fruitful glands warmed; a delicious erection pushed hard against my zipper. I longed for Vittoria. We had had three beautiful days. She was alarmed, and yet excited, to know that I would return to Rome for two more weeks after my trip to France. I longed for her. I wanted to make love to her. We were ready, I knew. If the delights of the opera, the beach, the Borghese gardens, could be so keen, what lay ahead of us?

On the beach at Fiumicino, she had let me kiss her breasts. The sun was scorching hot. No sane person comes to the Italian beach during the noontime hours; the beach was empty. We lay upon her towel on the salt-and-pepper sand, having drunk heady red chianti and eaten ham sandwiches and juice-laden red-violet plums. Her figure was chunky and full. When I slowly pulled her bra away from the whiteness and rubbed my teeth against their center, she pulled back, wrestled, suppressed a long, low cry. Her head moved violently from side to side and finally she pushed my head away. "Gianni! Gianni!" She was very quiet and troubled, and slowly replaced her straps. For a long time we listened to the waves. We were both glad when clouds began to form in the west and a cool wet breeze arose. There was nothing to do, nothing to say. We had crossed a boundary, and only the oppressive knowledge of the shortness of the hour prevented our pitching camp and occupying unknown land. That night, unsettled, restless, discontent, I boarded the train for Toulon, and Vittoria waved a sad good-bye. We had arrived upon a ledge from which there seemed to be neither descent nor ascent. We said a farewell meant to be anticipation.

5

ROME WAS BATHED in the quiet cool light of early morning. The train wound slowly through the hump-backed hills. We rolled past dark cypresses, a silver water tank, sleepy green and pink and buff apartments. When I stepped from the train, the still air radiated the coming heat; dust and engine fumes soured it. Sweat gathered on my back as I shifted the weight of my bags; there were a thousand yards or so to walk. I had napped only fitfully during the night; heat, desire, and longing had prevented sleep.

The unmistakable scents of Rome lay upon the air: the dampness of ancient walls, the calcium of a thousand years' decay. I asked for the number of the bus to Piazza di Spagna. A wizened man in a thick-threaded coat pointed to a sign three lanes away. I walked cautiously through the rows of waiting busses, holding my breath against their acrid exhausts. Workers crowded the aisles. The fountains of the Piazza della Repubblica gleamed in the morning sun, and already the flags of Rome and Italy flanked them—maroon and orange; green, white, and red. The bus rambled swiftly over the rough streets, swung wide around a corner, and sped swiftly through the dry, gaseous air of an illuminated tunnel. At the Piazza di Spagna, I dismounted and walked two blocks to the Nazione.

Paolo had not forgotten to reserve a room for me, but it wouldn't be free until noon; when I told him I hadn't slept, he said, "*Momento*," and went to speak to the *padrona*. He returned and gave me the key to a room I could use temporarily. Paolo owed me several favors; I had translated letters, signed with lipsticked kisses, that he received from an American girl who had fallen deliriously in love with him after two dates, and I had helped him conduct the phone conversation when she called from Milan. She had cabled her parents in America that she wasn't coming home as planned but was returning to Rome. They had telephoned instantly from Long Island. She was telephoning Paolo to assure herself that he meant to marry her. Paolo stood beside me, dismayed.

I set my bags in my temporary room. I would call Vittoria as soon as she arrived at work, and we would go to lunch together. Perhaps she could get the afternoon off. Today we would make love; I would take the proud step. The hotel room did not seem so dreary as before, but I walked up and down, unable to sit or lie on the bed; the air was stale and confining.

I decided that I would go out for some breakfast, and then I would telephone. Or else walk over five blocks and surprise her in person? The prospect cast new brilliance upon the day. I shaved quickly, whistled fitfully, put on a fresh shirt and lighter trousers, and pulled the door happily behind me. I slowed my steps on the stairs and casually left my key with Paolo with an apology about needing breakfast first. Out in the streets again, I no longer felt tired. I bought *Il Messaggero, Il Tempo,* and a left-over copy of *Paese Sera.* For kicks, I also bought an *Osservatore Romano.* I looked at my watch and figured the papers would keep me busy for an hour. I sat in the shade, ordered *caffè latte* and a roll, watched the people in the street, and then began to read.

Nothing held my interest. When I turned the last page, barely forty minutes had passed. I tried to sit still and watch people pass. I paid for my breakfast with a neat stack of lightweight coins and began to walk slowly toward Via Condotti. I tried to loiter. When I got to the jewelry shop, however, no one but the proprietress seemed to be inside. I ambled past, to look at hats, bikinis, and cameras; I went into a shop to price a lace tablecloth. Then I turned back up the street. Still she wasn't in sight, so another stroll. Perhaps she was in the back room. Perhaps she wasn't working at all. I forced myself to look at goblets and crystal, silver and cutlery, comparing prices and appraising styles. Then I could tolerate it no longer and marched directly to the jewelry store.

I was about to ask Signora Mimosa if Vittoria was in. But as I entered, Vittoria stepped from the back room with two black trays in her hands.

"Gianni!" she called.

"*Ciao!*"

The electricity which one day scientists will identify leaped between us. Vittoria flushed. Our minds seemed transparent to each other. Consent was exchanged. Signora Mimosa discreetly walked through the curtains into the back room.

"I didn't expect you."

"I've been waiting for an hour to see you."

"Waiting?" Her eyes sought out where I might have been waiting. "I have been here since eight and a half."

"I've been walking up and down for a half-hour, trying to see you."

"You should have come in."

"I didn't want Signora Mimosa . . ."

"She likes you, Gianni."

"Well, if she likes me, will she give you the afternoon off? Can you come to lunch with me?"

Vittoria frowned. The dimple on her chin grew deeper. "I have promised to meet Mamma at lunch. And this afternoon— the Signora has decided to take inventory. I couldn't ask her today. I am so sorry."

I glumly rearranged my dreams. "What about dinner? I would like to take you to the Hilton."

"The Hil-ton?" She seemed to blush lightly.

"You've never been there? We'll have an evening *all'americano.* V*a bene?* It has been six days since I've seen you!"

"Six days!" She groaned. "Okay, Gianni. The Hil-ton. I will have to come like this."

"You look lovely." I looked past her shoulder, then leaned forward and kissed her on the cheek. She turned her face quickly and met my cheek with a kiss, too. Each second we held seemed to seal our covenant. When I left the shop, the policeman on the corner looked at me, was amused, and bowed to me as he waved me across.

If stimulation alone counted, it would have taken me hours to fall asleep. But the bouncing and the long, tortuous reflections of the night before had exhausted me. When I awoke, hot and sweaty in the afternoon heat, it was six o'clock. Vittoria would be free just before seven. "Vittoria!" my heart sang.

As we got into the taxi, I wondered what would happen if I had misread her intentions. Would she be shocked when I took a room? Would she hate me? I was also unsure whether I could sign in calmly: should I use a fictitious name? Sign "Mr. and Mrs."? No, they would have to check my passport. There were a thousand ways the evening could go badly.

The air was hesitant; the sultry breath of the evening sirocco had settled on the city. The gray stone buildings and the domed churches had lost the bright glare of the afternoon and were, in the evening light, resting in a subdued, richer orange and gray.

Vittoria had somehow managed to change into a black evening dress. I had never seen her so precisely, so delicately made up. Her eyes were brilliant. She smiled bravely and happily.

"Gianni," she said. "It is a beautiful idea. I am so excited to have you here again."

Her feet rested on the raised center shaft; her finely nyloned kness turned toward me and at a corner swept against mine and remained there. I put my arm around her. Our eyes caught. We kissed. Finally, our hearts pounding, she broke away, looking right and left.

"Gianni, everyone will see us!"

I caressed her small hand in mine. She had long slender nails, and I ran the pads of my fingers along them. We felt trapped in the taxi. It seemed that everywhere in the city there were windows and eyes: all through our relationship we had felt we were living behind glass. Absently I made little circles with my index finger in the palm of Vittoria's hand, round and round on the firm, lined flesh. The taxi climbed away from the city. We did not speak.

When I had paid the cab, Vittoria took my arm. The doorman opened the way before us. In the lobby I looked for directions to the cocktail lounge. Both Vittoria and I were uneasy. Women in mink shawls and golden shoes, gentlemen in crisp dark suits walked back and forth or sat, bored, waiting in brightly colored chairs. Our eyes accustomed to the evening dusk, we were awed by the sudden blaze of furbished bronze, soft rugs, gleaming chandeliers, and brilliant splashes of green, violet, and yellow. After seating Vittoria in the cocktail lounge, I sat only for a moment. We clasped hands across the table.

"Vittoria, I want to take a room."

Her eyes were full of affection, but a question crossed them as she nodded.

I hoped that the clerk would not notice anything unusual about me as I signed in.

"Did you have a reservation?" he asked officiously, in the manner of Europeans who work for Americans.

"No," I said evenly. "I'd prefer a room with a bath."

"All our rooms have baths," he said.

He looked down a list and pushed a pad toward me. Meantime, he kept up a conversation in Italian with another clerk. He rang a bell.

"No bags," I said. Already a bellboy was approaching. "You won't need to show me up," I said. I reached into my pocket for a hundred lire. The coin I fetched was only fifty; he accepted it with contempt. It is a different league, I thought.

When I sat down again, Vittoria placed her hand upon mine. "Gianni," she was objecting. But she did not continue. Instead her eyes rested in mine.

"Shall we," I cleared my throat. "Shall we order a drink?"

"Yes, Gianni. To celebrate your return."

We did not feel like drinking. We could not sit apart. We tried helplessly to invent conversation, to pretend there was no urgency. Nor could we be scrupulous in finishing our drinks; I paid the waiter and helped Vittoria rise. Her perfume, her hair seemed suddenly more intimate, more mine, than they ever had.

I held my arm around her on the elevator. The operator, it seemed, perceived. I was sure he leered as we left. We walked down the carpeted hallway to 634. The key at first didn't seem to fit. We stepped inside and I closed the door. When I turned, we fell into an embrace. For many seconds it sufficed to push our bodies as close together as we could. But then I began to wonder how to preserve the mood, the urgency, while undressing and moving to the bed; a thousand missteps lay in front of us.

I began to lower the zipper on her back. She stiffened, then kissed me harder.

"Let's do this slowly," I said, trying to be mirthful. I had felt her heart beating as hard as mine.

We moved nearer to the bed, and I threw back the spread and took off my coat and tie. Vittoria slowly set down her beaded handbag. I came to her and put my hands on her cheeks. Slowly she kicked off her shoes, and I helped her to undress—belts, straps, light things—and she helped me. We embraced, cool body to cool body, pulled together like two magnets. I lifted her and we lay silent, breathing on the bed. I was determined to proceed as slowly as I could, sensing that I would explode instantaneously; self-control never seemed more important or more delicate. Like two children, we explored each other. I took her fingers to me. She came suddenly and we kissed, teeth to teeth, wildly. Then we pushed apart.

"We must laugh a little," I said.

She could not speak clearly, either. "Then why aren't you laughing?" she said, biting my nose. We fell to kissing.

It was becoming more difficult for me. I tried to keep our loins apart. I caressed her thighs with my fingers, moving slowly. She was already warm and moist. The sweet odor of musk began to arise, and we tumbled together. I could not find her. She understood, and lowered her hand to guide me. She shuddered at the first impact and bit my shoulder. The honeyed, spasmodic warmth overcame me, and my frame shook and I fought away, spilling upon the sheets.

We pressed as closely as we could, though scarcely moving. When speech became possible, I said, "I'm sorry. I wanted to wait." She could not answer, and I stroked her hair upon the pillow. Gradually I became aware that she was sweating and that her hip was hurting my side; I became aware of my weight upon her. We pulled apart, caressing each other, kissing. I wished urgently that I could do more. The ardor grew; the flesh was weak.

"Oh, Gianni!" she said happily. For a long time we played together.

When it was time to dress for dinner, she asked me to close my eyes.

"Why?" I laughed.

"I know it is silly, Gianni. Please."

I turned my back and she arose, picked up her things, and walked barefoot toward the bath. I lay watching the far wall until she emerged radiant.

"You don't have to close your eyes," I said.

"I will."

I kissed her as I walked past into the bath. I showered, marveling at my joy and exhilaration. I had done what I had chosen. And now a shower, dinner, conversation; no vulgar wrestling in the back seat of a car.

We ate dinner by candlelight. Her pearls mirrored the colors of the room. Her eyes were filled with merriment and love. The steak and wine restored us.

During the long drive to her home, on the farthermost hill of Rome, she lay back silently upon my arm. I ran my fingers slowly over the fine hairs of her forearm. Occasionally we touched our lips together.

From her home to the Nazione, I basked silently in deep contentment. I felt very proud and free. Finally, practical thoughts made their presence felt: the evening had cost me so much money that I would not be able to fly from Rome to Paris to catch the charter flight for New York. I would have to travel by train again. That meant I would have one less day with Vittoria. I didn't want to recall how brief the hours allotted us, and shook my head.

Arriving at the Nazione, I couldn't bring myself to climb to the dismal cheap room awaiting me. I walked into the Piazza di Spagna, where I could sit on the steps watching the illuminated fountain and lean back to look into the inky sky. Even then, my heart was full of song and I found it necessary to walk; I walked the darkened streets for at least two hours, in the soft warmth of an August night, before it seemed possible to sleep.

The days passed speedily. We met at every opportunity. Rome in August is lovely and soft; we went to evening concerts in the Forum, walked the sparsely illumined lanes of the Villa Borghese, visited the Piazza Navona for ice cream, walked interminably. We made love at my hotel, transforming the small metal cot and unpainted walls; we noticed only our joy. We could not keep separate; our need was as deep as our affection was serene. At twenty-four, she had been properly brought up; she had never slept with a man. Vittoria loved with a fierce Latin love; she pressed her teeth into my shoulder and moaned and tossed.

She asked me lazily, one day, about Sarah. I was reluctant to talk. It was difficult, but she listened. She told me then about the cousin her parents had picked for her to marry. He had just acquired a position with an American oil company; she said that she despised him.

"But he loves you?"

"Love! What does he know about love? All he loves is money. He wants me because I speak English. It will help him with the Americans. He does not want me as a wife."

"Then you will not marry him."

She was silent.

"How could you?"

"How can I avoid it? Oh Gianni, let's not talk about it. It is too awful. I have sworn I will not marry him. I am determined. But there seems no way."

I said nothing.

I felt uncomfortable. Surely Vittoria knew that the two of us could never marry. We were too different, as we both had understood from the beginning. An affair of the heart, bounded by the requirements of reason.

We ended our discussion by coming together a little sadly, in yet a different way than before.

On another occasion, Vittoria corrected something I was saying in Italian. I had never learned to use the familiar *tu*; when I unconsciously addressed her formally as *Lei*, she countered: "*Io sono 'tu.'*"

The words alarmed me. She had to ready herself for our parting. "I'm not you," I pointed out slowly. "You're not me."

For a moment she was puzzled. Then she laughed. "I meant you must call me *tu*. Not *Lei*."

She invited me to use *tu* for the sake of tenderness, and I took refuge in it. My embarrassment reverberated in our silence: "I am not you; you are not me."

In the end, it proved possible to swap places with someone else on a Columbia charter flight, delaying my reservation from Paris to New York by one more day. And I decided to fly to Paris so that Vittoria and I could have two more days together, one of them for a trip to the beach at Fiumicino. Once more we sat in the broiling sun. We built an enormous castle. We swam in the crystal water. And, hidden in a dune, upon her large white towel, we made love to the rhythm of the sea.

On the last day, she had said she could not come to the airport. But as I was closing my bag, Paolo came to my door and told me that a *signorina* was awaiting me. I hurried down behind him.

"Vittoria!"

"I couldn't allow you to go." She pressed a white flower into my lapel. "Do you mind if I go with you?"

"Do I mind!"

In the taxi we kissed and tried to pretend that the fare box was not ticking off our time together. Each turn of the road to the airport seemed familiar; twice we had passed this way to the beach. The sun beat down upon the waving green fields and the dark trees and flashed from government houses painted deep maroon.

Inside the huge airport Vittoria seemed lost beneath the great clock as she waited while I had my ticket cleared. We had half an hour. We walked up and down, often in silence or speaking of frivolities, her high heels marking time on the terrazzo. My eyes were fixed on the rising and falling of our legs. It seemed incredible that we should never meet again.

We embraced one last time, next to a kiosk full of the latest newspapers and magazines. I turned and passed through the gate, unable to look back. At the last possible moment, on an impulse, I turned. She was still standing there in her white suit. She saw me. It was useless for either of us to wave.

Seated on the airliner, I was too far away to distinguish her. I waved a handkerchief up and down and then across, in an unusual manner, so that she might guess it was I. As the great jet lumbered down the runway, I was so choked that I longed to cry. I had never cried since childhood. A hostess was approaching, and as I looked up, a heavy woman across the aisle, her face expressing haughty curiosity about the tears streaming down my face, glanced away. The hostess leaned across toward me.

"Chewing gum?"

6

THE PLANE RIDE seemed interminable. The seat cushions were hot and hard; shifting from buttock to buttock no longer helped. I dozed, slept, awoke, in recurrent cycles. Constantly the hostesses were feeding us or offering us drinks.

At last we landed in New York. The wide, sweeping expressways and huge cars seemed strange to me. The sound of English in the terminal was harsh and grainy. The airline bus driver seemed vulgar by comparison with Italian drivers; no love or tenderness crept into his manner, only hours of pro football on television, a shrewish wife, stacks of beer cans on the carpet, and an ash tray burdened with Tiparillo stubs. I took a cab from the East Side Terminal and settled in a cheap room at a hotel on Forty-fifth Street; I had sublet my apartment near the university for the summer. I intended to spend two or three days in New York visiting friends. A knock at the door: a bellhop brought the tall Tom Collins I had ordered. My shoes off, my tie loose, head back, I sat in a straight line, half reclining across the edge of my chair. Finally I bestirred myself and put in a call to California.

"Sarah? Jon. Greetings."

"I thought you were supposed to come in yesterday."

"So I'm a day late. You could at least say hello."

"Hello."

"What's the matter?" The connection was not clear, and I wasn't certain I could understand her tone of voice.

"I'm angry about something here."

"About me?"

"No, I said something here. You called me at a bad moment."
Her voice, with effort, brightened. "Sorry to be a wet blanket.
It's really good to have you back in the glorious U.S.A. When will
I see you?"

"I wish it could be tonight."

Silence.

"Will you be coming east with your father?"

"He's not sure yet. You can't come west?"

"Darling, I'd like to, but I'm broke. I spent everything I had."

"I'm sorry."

She asked me to tell her about the trip, but I was afraid of
boring her. Sarah always hated to talk by telephone. "You have
to have someone in front of you," she'd say. "A voice is an abstraction; it isn't a person." After a few more moments of small
talk, we hung up.

I sat and sipped my drink. The image of Vittoria had not been
dispelled. It was stronger than ever. The conversation with Sarah
depressed me. Pursue her? I decided then and there it was impossible. She was too far away. How did I know what she was
doing, let alone thinking? She lived easily without me. Yet it would
be fun to see her, now that I had changed my way of life. For
a long time I rolled the ice in my drink around and around in the
glass.

Finally I picked up the phone to call home. The line hummed.
The ringing began, and the phone was picked up slowly. My
father's voice sounded weary. He had retired from the mill on
medical disability several years ago. Most of the people in our
neighborhood were college-educated, professional people; Dad had
not completed high school. Every passing year he seemed to feel
less sure of himself. His bluff, physical, optimistic manner had
given way to an injured, vulnerable, self-deprecating uncertainty.
His emotions often seemed to be those of a backward child in
need of a father's strong hand, affection, and encouragement. It
was painful to deal with him. I wanted him to be strong. Instead,
he needed me.

"Hi, Dad. It's Jon. I'm back."

His voice hesitated. "I have bad news, son. Your mother is dead."

With great effort I kept my voice steady. "When, Dad? How?"

"Evening before last. She wasn't sick or anything. The high blood pressure. She was at a church bazaar and she just—fell. Dead immediately. There was nothing to do. How come you're late? We were expecting you yesterday."

"I—I just decided to stay an extra day."

He interrupted. "Can you come home? We'd like to see you."

"Sure, sure. I'll leave right away."

"You're at a hotel? Get a good night's sleep. You can fly in tomorrow."

"When—when's the funeral?" The word fell like a stone.

"Day after tomorrow. At ten."

"Is David there? Can I speak to him?"

"He's here, and Frank and Helena. Wait a minute."

Soon someone else picked up the phone.

"Hello."

"David? Jon. I feel terrible. How is Dad taking it?"

"Where were you yesterday? He could have used you. You know how he likes you. He was really hurt."

"David, I'm sorry. But I didn't know."

"Are you coming home tonight?"

"Tomorrow morning early. Dad said to get a good sleep."

"You'll need it. Relatives are coming in from everywhere. It's a pretty lousy time."

"How's Edna?"

In an irritated voice, he said: "All right. Look, I have to go now. More people are coming in. Dad can't manage them all."

"I'll see you as soon as possible."

We hung up. I picked up my drink and walked slowly around the room. Then I dumped it in the sink and undressed to take a shower. With the hot water streaming down my face I realized what Mother, whom I loved, would have thought if she knew about Vittoria. I could hear the adjectives: sinful, shameful, vulgar. My focus on the last three weeks shifted, and I knew I could explain nothing to anyone—nothing about why I was a day late, nothing about what had been so important and so beautiful to me in Italy. I could hear David say distinctly: "Three weeks living with a broad! Jon boy, when are you going to grow up?" Growing up to David meant marrying an attractive and cultivated woman,

having exactly two children, working in an office on the way upward, and belonging to the Thursday Club. I shut off the water and
toweled myself vigorously. As I finished combing my hair in
front of the mirror, a word escaped my lips with great forcefulness:
"Vittoria!"

I sat down and composed a long letter to her. Before it was
finished, I knew I would have to tear it up. The long effort
exhausted me, and the sadness I had been avoiding overcame me.
I went to bed praying for Mother, or to her, or wondering whether
I believed in prayer, or if anything made sense at all.

The small, two-engine airliner circled over the hills I knew
so well. I hadn't remembered that Conemaugh spread so far in
so many valleys. The vast green hills seemed primitive and
untouched, silent and wise; the city, belching orange smoke from
its mills, cut into them like a small gray scar. Mother will soon
be at rest in those hills, I thought; the forest overgrows the
cities one by one.

I could not shake the depression that had settled over me. My
stomach was empty, and the skin of my fingers was so cold that
I was afraid I couldn't grip a glass. Images of hundreds of by-
gone days fled elusively through my mind; I could not make
myself believe that my childhood had been lived in these hills,
that this horizon had once bounded my awareness of the world.
Mother squeezed my hand white and dug into the skin with a
burned needle. Mother was approving the Class Day speech I
gave in the fourth grade; her single comment: "You dropped the
last words of every sentence; your voice trailed off." She used to
reminisce about her own childhood, and I used to like her to
tell me again how, at the age of three, I spilled soap suds all
over the kitchen floor and she slipped and fell coming to turn off
the overflowing water.

I hardly knew my mother. She was a stranger—more distant
than most of my friends. I had never thought of her as a woman;
I never thought of her as one who made love with my father.
What had she feared? What had she desired? Had she been happy?
The arguments we had had in the last four years had grown in
intensity. Now it would be impossible to explain myself to her
or to comfort her.

I remember the cumulative shock of noticing, as I came home

from college or seminary, how much grayer and quieter she had become. She tried to be gay for my arrivals—she never had to try when David was coming home—and would bake a graham cracker pie every time, since I had once praised the pie at dinner. She made sure the candy dish was full of Hershey kisses; I had had a craze for them when I was eleven. I could also vaguely remember her in her thirties, one of the youngest and prettiest of any of the mothers of my classmates. We had even been, I would say, very close, comrades almost, and sometimes she would tell me things she would not tell David. I first surmised that I might have a capacity for listening, a certain sympathy, when she told me how she hated my father's job in the mill, how she had never said a word to him but hated it, and had been afraid every day for many years. But she did not confide in me often, nor, as far as I know, in David either. Her letters to me at college were full of household details and conventional sentiments. Only when I was in the seminary did a more intimate, more ardent personal note break through her prose, but even then hesitantly, except once or twice when she became meditative and the whole letter seemed like a hymn or a prayer not quite addressed to me alone.

The creaky, chunky airliner hummed in over the tree tops aiming at the runway on the top of Redstone Hill; the flight had been bumpy all the way and now the cross currents in the valleys shifted us like a pillow's feather.

The pilot fought us down; we bounced, bounced again, and taxied to the cyclone-wire fence. I could see David waiting for me. The airplane rested at a steep tilt, and I pulled myself reluctantly from my seat.

David was wearing a dark blue sport coat and perfectly creased black trousers. He had a black handkerchief in his breast pocket. He drove the big Oldsmobile with fingertip control; he was thoroughly relaxed. It was as though he was imitating a full-color ad in a magazine; he was tall, rugged, handsome, and at ease in the knowledge that other people admired him. I always thought of him as what every American male should want to be.

"Good flight?" he asked casually. There was just enough indifference in his voice. I watched my brother squint ahead at the highway.

"Yes," I nodded.

"We're glad you're home. Dad was worried you wouldn't make it."

"Well, I'm here."

"You shouldn't have worried Dad. It—"

"I'm here. Let's not fight today."

We drove in silence awhile. He looked into a rear-view mirror and spurted ahead. The thickly grown trees that crowded in upon the narrow highway were already turning brown. I had always seen them a luxurious green. It must have been an especially dry summer.

Our descent into the valley was flanked by unpainted wooden homes, red-brick housing projects with blue work clothes and gray sheets slung between them, and store fronts with rusty 7-Up signs. The faces of the few people we passed were weary and blank. Yet I could never help being stirred by the sharp green hills that rose above the valley and the red dust-covered mills along the bracken river. It was ugly. But it was also a miracle that here in these mountains an industrial city had been born and begun to die in the space of a hundred and fifty years.

Birth, yes, and death. My mother's corpse would be the first I had ever seen. One doesn't often face death; it is as though the millions simply disappear, lifted away at night by great, black birds.

"We may not get to talk too much," David began in a sober, reasonable tone. "I wanted you to know that we've decided I'll run."

"Run?"

He mastered his irritation without effort. "For Congress. Edna agrees with me that it's a good idea and that now's the time."

The car sang steadily over the rough pavement.

"Where will you get the money? You have enough support, I'm sure."

"Uncle Walter is going to help me. I've been talking to lots of people. I know I can do it. Quite a bit of enthusiasm, in fact. Considering I'd be the underdog."

We waited for a stoplight; there was silence in the interior of the car. I asked: "What's your program?"

He laughed lightly. "Youth. Young people are moving away from Conemaugh. You don't see anyone around any more. If

we don't stop them from going away, we're dead. I'm a symbol of
young people who stay; we are, Edna and me."

"Will you get party support?"

"With Marella as county chairman? Don't be funny."

"What then?"

"Independent. Marella is finished, the crook." He ground his
teeth a moment before continuing: "The lifetime of a machine is
twenty years. He's been running his since 1938. He's got plenty of
enemies, and, besides, the state house is Republican. He's been
cited on five counts of bribery in connection with his trucking
business. He's finished. He's dead."

"So you think you can win the Democratic nomination without
the machine."

He nodded confidently. "Wouldn't try if I wasn't absolutely
sure I could win."

"But can you beat Soldier? He's been in—eight years?"

"Fourteen. Too long, much too long. Besides the Democrats
hold Washington now. The businessmen in town can't get anywhere with a Republican in Congress. It's time for a change.
Last week the city redevelopment director told me, 'David,' he
said, 'Last time I was in Washington they told me, send us a
Democrat and we'll see what we can do. Until we do that, the
door is locked. So Davey, I'm with you, two hundred percent.'"

"You really think you can win," I mused aloud.

"Absolutely sure of it. You're talking to the next congressman
from the fourteenth district of Pennsylvania."

He was so pleased with the thought that I suppressed an unkind
rejoinder. Instead, I said evenly: "I wish you luck. I really do.
Are you going to want me to help?"

He looked over at me with a condescending grin. "Yeah, stay
away. You think a professor of literature from a Communist Ivy
League school is going to help? No sir, I'm the people's candidate.
Why, do you know," he suddenly became concerned, "that thirty
percent of the people in this county are below the federal
standard for subsistence wages? And that's not to mention the
other two counties, which are worse off."

"And also Republican."

"And also Republican. I think we can break that. Rip Carter—
he was on my debating team at college—is a lawyer over in

Kittaninni. He's going to help me there. With this poverty
program, I think there's a new factor in the hopper. Sonny boy,
I think we can win!"

"I'm sure you will," I said calmly. But I was thinking about
Mother as David nosed the car down Oak Street to the funeral
parlor owned by the husband of one of the women in Mother's
bridge club. David seemed to guess my mood and fell silent, too.

"I just wanted you to know," he said. "Dad's waiting up at
the house. He can't bear to be here all day, though he wanted
to be. Edna and I made him stay home. I told him I'd bring you
up after we paid our respects."

He eased the car up into the driveway. It crackled over the
gravel and stopped. I put my hand on the cold door handle and
slowly got out.

It is not true that the Catholics around me during my boyhood
lived in and through the hereafter, *sub specie aeternitatis*. Our
monsignor drove a dark blue Pontiac with a green-tinted wind-
shield, and he ate very well; his taste for linen, wine, and well-
turned roasts led him to think of himself as a humanist. All the
Catholics I knew seemed at home in the world, content with
their lot, grateful for earthly pleasures. The Protestants I later
came to meet edified me by thinking of the suffering and the
poor as they sat down to eat; they always seemed to drive themselves. All too spiritual. Catholic grace at meals, by contrast, is
thanks for the present, perfunctory, merely a prelude to the
enjoyment of the soup.

Death is as Catholic an experience as praise for womanhood.
How can God resist his mother? Mary is the Catholic's "justifica-
tion by faith." A woman who menstruates, gives bloody birth,
pushes her nipple toward a child, Mary humanizes Latin law
and Irish authority. The Catholic sins boldly. Some of the people
in our parish, it was widely assumed, had connections with the
Mafia. Some were certainly involved in what *The Advocate* spoke
of as "rumors of corruption in city government." There were
stories in our town of Jewish doctors who preferred to choose as
mistresses young Catholic nurses. Catholicism provided a terror
of sexual sin, which heightened every dalliance into eternal drama.
At Columbia, I heard grisly jokes from staid professors about the

pleasures of seducing nuns and countless stories from men—in busses, in bars—about how much fun it is to score with girls from Catholic colleges.

Catholicism, in brief, is a constant flirtation with animality. Why would there be confession if it were not assumed that man is weak? I was not sure, as I walked across the porch of the funeral home, that I believed in eternity. I had never seen it. I knew I was an animal. That I knew. A dead rabbit rots beside the highway, is worn away by sun and rain, and becomes again a part of earth. I felt very close to Mother, somehow. What did I expect to see?

David and I walked through the dark hallway of the funeral home. Several old Slovak ladies halted their whispery gossip and looked at one another. The sick scent of too many flowers penetrated to my stomach; I could feel muscles tighten and my mouth went dry. David tugged my sleeve and nodded forward. I pushed gently past persons standing in the shadowed doorway of the last parlor.

The inside of the casket lid was pink. Banks of flowers reflected the flickering candles. I stumbled forward almost blindly to the prie-dieu before the casket and knelt looking at my mother. They had put a green dress on her. Rouge and powder had been applied too thickly to her unresisting features. For what seemed many minutes, neither thought nor sentiment came. I could hear the candles sputter and feel the rotating air of some discreetly hidden fan and absorb the murmur of voices from the other room. I could not swallow; it would violate the stillness. My emotions did not move; I was in tune with nothingness. Mother was plainly clay, plainly putty. The knowledge that hour by hour the inward cells were collapsing and generating odors met no counterknowledge. Before the irrational, silence. Tedious and unpleasant silence, in which one stifles the impulse to scream.

During the requiem mass, Dad began to shake. His heavy stomach moved up and down and no sound came. But then his long, painful whines rose chokingly above the murmur of the ceremony. David and I grabbed his arms. David said imperiously: "Grab hold of yourself. You've been great up to now. *Grab hold of yourself!*" Slowly the sobs began to subside.

The man beside me seemed like a child, and when I offered

him my handkerchief, he showed me a face that was anguished and maudlin and silly. He no longer seemed like my father! I didn't know this man.

David and I were pallbearers, and Edna took Dad's arm. The drive to the cemetery was silent and remote. Six of us carried the heavy casket step by step over the hillside lawn to the mound covered with blue artificial grass. To my furtive glances the circle of blue hills in the distance was sharp against a tranquil sky. The air blew cool and fresh. Mother, I thought, will command a view of the entire valley and look upon life and death in calm. Across a narrow ravine the foliage was luxuriant. Somewhere a wood-pecker was knocking on a hollow pole and the melody of sparrows leaped from place to place across the banks of graves.

Our footing was treacherous on the felt-covered planks beside the grave. Gently we laid the black casket upon the thick-webbed belts; I let go last for fear the belt might give way and the casket go plunging prematurely into its narrow slit. Inside, the shovel blades had wrested brilliance from the damp cloven earth. The soft cheeks, the hands, the woman would here return.

The monsignor recited Latin prayers which no one understood in a rapid, stumbling, bored tone of voice. He clanged the golden water sprinkler in the bronze bucket, raised it and waved it toward the coffin several times. The newspaper photographer David had summoned raised his camera. Columns of silver droplets fanned out sparkling in the sunlight and splattered in the stillness upon the casket. I watched one of them gather and trickle down the side, a long lonely black rivulet slowly losing its momentum.

We went soberly and without a word to David's new home, having determined that at all costs we must keep Dad out of the house for as long as possible. Edna's two daughters had remained behind with a babysitter; a friend of the family had come over and prepared a luncheon. She was a petite middle-aged woman whose face I knew but whose name I couldn't remember. She grasped my hand; her eyes were moist and understanding. I didn't want to talk to anyone and excused myself to go looking for a bathroom. I opened the first upstairs door. Inside was four-year-old Ann, in a room almost totally dark, sitting about two feet away from a glowing blue television set. She hardly turned her

eyes away long enough to see who was interrupting her. Dismally
I closed the door and walked, somewhat lost, down the hall.

7

How IS IT one can grow to love a city as ugly as New York?
Where else is there to live? A certain asceticism is required: the
water is rationed; the subways and newspapers go on strike; when
it rains taxis are as rare as policemen; and when it's hot cross
ventilation is impossible unless your neighbor across the hall
props his door open with his Bronx and Queens directories.

I returned to New York with relief, even though the temperature stood at 97 and the harsh grit blew fitfully down the avenues.
My second morning back, I bought a Late City edition of the
Times and wondered, reading it at breakfast, which stock I should
buy with part of the thousand dollars my father had given me
from my mother's insurance. It had not been pleasant at home.
For the time being at least, my father was bewildered and lost;
we feared at first for his emotional stability. He had always assumed he would be the first to die; two of his friends had died
at fifty just when their wives, their children grown, seemed to
be beginning life afresh—they wanted to travel and to find jobs.

I no longer felt at ease in Conemaugh. I had been away too
long. The accents and colloquial expressions—"spicket," "red up
the house," "younse"—seemed now like a foreign language. Besides, everybody wanted me married, and they couldn't imagine
what I was doing in school for so many years. At the funeral, a
friend of my grandfather's asked me how many years now I had
been in school. I told him twenty-one. He asked me then what

more there was to study, after all those years. Was I trying to learn everything? "When you gonna get a job, Jonny? When you gonna come back home?"

New York is freedom, and if you are willing to trade loneliness for freedom, you come to love the city. I sat eating my breakfast at Tony's Luncheonette on 117th Street. I was a regular customer, so Tony gave me a discount. A dollar-twenty-five covered breakfast and lunch: cereal and two eggs or else pancakes, and soup and the hot dish of the day, with dessert. He gave me dinner, when I came, for another dollar. I could eat for under twenty dollars a week, which I did until I got a larger apartment, alone, with a dirty stove and ancient half-sized refrigerator. The lease on the apartment I had sublet for the summer was about to expire; I had already paid a month's advance on a room nearer Riverside Drive.

I had found, on my return, a notice from *The Liberal Catholic* accepting an article I had sent them just before leaving Europe, attached to a check for forty-five dollars. Two of these a month and all I'd need money for is rent, I thought. I felt unusually well placed. The fan was blowing wearily over Tony's head as I counted out twelve dollars for the forthcoming week. He kept a checklist of meals I took with him on a greasy blue card taped to something under the cash register. By my calculations, he always threw in a free meal or two before asking me for another payment.

"You back for good now, Gianni?"

"For the school year, at least."

"Look good. Europe must have agreed wit' you, huh?"

"Sure did."

"Like those Eye-talian dames, huh!"

"They're the best, Tony."

"Didna I tell you! You don't have t' tell me about Eye-talian dames. You hear that, Carlo? Gianni's tellin' me about Eye-talian dames! He *liked* it over there. Didna you, Gianni!"

Two old fellows at the counter looked up at me; I recognized one.

"Oh, yeah, I liked them all right. You should see the bikinis on the Riveria."

Tony's huge brown eyes were glowing. He was a huge man, bigger than my father, and his apron was always covered with streaks of food even though he mostly stood behind the counter and shouted orders to Carlo, his son, who attended the grill and served the tables. Tony plunged his hands under the string tied in front of him and tapped his fat thumbs on his belly. "Still, not like in New York, eh kid? Nothin' beats New York. You see all those young babes on Fifth Avenue about five o'clock, there ain't nothin' like it."

"Nothin' beats New York. It's good to be back. See you later, Tony."

"You bet. Take care. Don't study too hard. It's bad for the juices."

"You keep the saltpeter out of those eggs, I'll be all right."

We went through this routine on the average of twice a week and Tony laughed every time. "Good kid, Gianni, I like him," he said to people at the counter every day as I went out. "A brain. Goin' to be a philosopher." He made it sound like some sort of engineer who understood the stars in a special way. Once I overheard him say, "He'll be famous some day." I thought, how right you are! But the exultation faded when a girl told me at a party: "Listen, there are four hundred thousand budding young writers in New York. They work at Macy's and Marboro's, and never even write a letter home."

Classes didn't begin until the last week of September, and I had almost a month to myself. I intended to get seven or eight days of solid reading done in the libary. Once classes began, I had two sections of freshman English to teach and a seminar with my thesis adviser. The main task of the year, as of the previous half year, was to get the damn thesis written. I was comparing certain themes in John Henry Newman's theory of ideas in history—especially from the *Essay on the Development of Doctrine* and the *Essay Toward a Grammar of Assent*—with notions of Whitehead about the relations of experience to language. For background, I was also reading Ortega y Gasset, Polanyi, Sapir, Durkheim and Marx, Weber and Sartre, on the problems of ideology and relativity. It was a fairly heavy thesis for an English major. The main point was that Newman's description of the "Illative Sense" called for a theory of intelligence that would identify those factors that enter into human judgments—factors

like a "feel" for things, hunches based on past experience, sensual
perspicacity, and the powers of infantile emotions—remnants, long
suppressed, of the prehistoric animal still alive in us—to discern
the truth of human situations more precisely than our analytic,
pragmatic judgment could. I wanted to argue that what young
Americans are taught to call "reason" is only a pale fire compared
to powers of the soul neglected in our civilization—not only
neglected, but systematically repressed. My evidence for such
large assertions was based on records of the actual working
practice of artists, scientists, academicians, and intellectuals gen-
erally. Their best judgments, I tried to show, arose from unconscious, contemplative, playful, and fantastic powers of theirs
which, unhappily, it is the habit of philosophers, psychologists,
and other theoreticians to neglect and the business of most
American education to search out and destroy.

The only difficulty was, of course, to get such a vast thesis to
be entertained at Columbia or anywhere. A Ph.D. curriculum is
not an arena in which to float ambitious balloons; it is no place
to question fundamental assumptions. I was, however, young and
reckless. Unlike a colleague a few years my senior, I had no hopes
of making it. Life is short, I told myself. Think your own thoughts.
Do what you wish. Let the chips fall. I made a little sign on an
orange 8x4 file card and taped it to the gray plaster wall over
my desk: "IT IS IMPOSSIBLE TO BE BOTH A PROFESSOR AND AN
HONEST PHILOSOPHER.—L. WITTGENSTEIN."

It was very clear to me that a Ph.D. thesis is primarily intended for at most six readers: three thesis advisers and possibly
another three examiners at the defense. So far as a thesis' truth
goes, their minds and sensibilities are the Absolute World Spirit.
What they find unintelligible *is* unintelligible. Objections that oc-
cur to them must be explicitly taken account of. Books they have
written or read with special devotion are, if one is wise, brought
to bear on the subject matter. Distinctions they have thought of
had best be made. Moreover, since an acceptable thesis ought to
contribute something new to the field of scholarship, one proves
one's brightness by advancing positions that help one's readers
to feel open-minded; professors like nothing better than to be
brought to revise views they have long held, on matters that do
not touch the center of their own work.

But I was constitutionally unable to proceed within the frame-

work of my mentors. For one thing, I did not have the intellectual
roots they did. I was neither Jewish nor Protestant Establishment.
The world of Marx and Freud, so dear to the radical Jewish
tradition, and the more genteel, hard, clear literary sense of the
Anglo-Saxons were foreign to me. *My* world was not like that;
they did not speak for *me*. How was I to express myself? I felt
inarticulate, confused. Little that I thought or experienced was
expressed in their categories. They judged too harshly works that
made my heart soar: Gerard Manley Hopkins, for example. I was
not only Catholic, I was Slav, and I grew up in western Pennsylvania. Somewhere I had to find a tongue to speak my word.

The categories of socialist criticism baffled me. I did not feel
put upon by a capitalist society, nor alienated. Freud's sensibility—
severe, scientific in an old-fashioned way, Viennese, afflicted with
conscience, duty, and devotion—was not exactly mine. The Jewish
attachment to Marx and Freud escaped me. But the relaxed style
of Anglo-Saxon scholars, brought up in families who for two or
three generations had been writing books and advising publishers,
did not express my own sense of relaxation either. I had my own
quiet spring to unveil, a pool hidden by a labyrinth I could not
yet penetrate. I sought to find my source. My thesis was an
attempt to make some tools, to topple a few constrictions, to
gouge out some breathing space. It was like calling for a workman-
like off-tackle slant from within one's own one-yard line, with the
minutes of the last half ticking away and the score tied. Not
desperation, but room to maneuver, and hopes of an open field
ahead.

The thesis was personally valuable, then. Every minute spent
upon it was for the sake of my own soul. The only trouble was
that the opposing linemen were very big, professional, and intent
on smothering freshmen quarterbacks. It seemed to me, after
four years in graduate school, that my energy was flagging; the
opposition had already made me pay a heavy toll. So I was
beginning to devise a fake. Gamely, I would fade back as if to
flip a daring pass, meanwhile slipping the secure football to my
toughest halfback behind my toughest tackle. He would not
advance my soul very far. But if he earned us a few more feet of
green grass, I would come back later with the pass I really wanted
to throw—a surprise to electrify the opposition, to teach them
some respect, to elbow a place for myself in that dreadful game

in that dreadful league. My hands trembled as I called the play; I hated a thesis that was only an off-tackle slant. And yet I wasn't really sure I could come back with the pass. So the weeks got longer and longer. I couldn't bring myself to put so many energies of my youth into so petty a play. Why, I groaned in fantasy, do graduate studies have to take place so entirely within one's own five-yard line, when even the regulations call for a field of a hundred yards?

Except for the city, except for the blood I could feel pounding in my fingertips and the stray, strange, exciting thoughts which, like sparrows outside Noah's ark, had no place upon which to rest, I had often felt like a zombie. That is why I had decided to go to Europe. The pretext had been that I would improve my French and visit libraries and scenes of importance to my thesis; there were some good books on Newman in German and French, and certain European authors might become instruments of my liberation. But gradually the trip became, in my heart if not in my mind, my own version of the grand tour, and I drifted like a lead ball in oil to the southern part of Europe—toward what Camus calls the region of the noonday sun, away from the cold earnestness and ideologists and history-building of the North. There, where the brilliant Italian sun makes even fence posts gleam in stark, clean clarity, and draws one's blood taut to the surface of one's skin, my soul expanded. There I discovered my body. There I began to live.

It was with joy, then, shortly after leaving Tony's on my return to New York, like the release of a prisoner of war at the Liberation, that I unfolded and read a surprise letter from Sarah, briefly offering condolences for my mother's death and wondering when I might come to see her. I had the money. I had the time. I had never been to California. I began to feel love for her again. "I'll go to California on Tuesday," I thought, and the preposterousness of that decision incited me to jump in the air, cry "whoopee!" and land resoundingly upon the thin tiles of the apartment floor. It was noon, no one was home downstairs, and no one protested.

Karel Karazov was the Czech travel agent who had set up my trip to Europe. He asked me about my Czech name—Slovak, I corrected him—and we became friends, more or less. I invited him

once to a party at my apartment; he didn't come but invited me
in turn to meet some of his friends at his place. They were a
sober yet loud group, mostly Czechs and other Europeans, and
they mimicked Americans, argued violently about de Gaulle, and
danced nervously up and down as they stood and drank. Their
dark suits had continental cuts, their ties were unfashionably
wide, and most wore pointed black Italian shoes. There were
hardly any women present; I remember only three in the entire
crowded room.

Once more, I went down to see Karazov at his office on Broadway.

"May I help you?" a new girl asked.

"I'll wait to see Karazov."

"Okay!" she replied in a cute European way and turned to the
heavy girl who came in behind me, eating a large éclair.

Karazov didn't look up until he was finished on the phone.
He was prematurely gray, or else I underestimated his age in
placing him at about thirty-seven. His hair was clipped close
and he had a shiny indentation along the right cheek. He looked
like a man who had once been an athlete and then later, with a
keen sense of strategy and organization, had set himself up in a
thriving business. There were now at least five people working in
the office; he had opened up three years earlier with two.

"Yes, please?" he began mechanically. "Ah, Svoboda. Did you
enjoy Europe?"

"Very much."

"Everything went all right?"

"I had to change my reservations coming home. Everything
else went like clockwork."

"Good, and what can I do for you?" He seemed slightly pre-
occupied but, as ever, self-controlled and calm. I often felt that
he could tell me dozens of stories. There was a rumor around
that he had been in Dachau for two years. European politics
fascinated me—the first radio broadcast I ever remember hearing
was the announcement of Hitler's invasion of Poland in 1939.
I grew up, it seemed, not with nursery rhymes but with inch-high
black headlines announcing defeats, beachheads, and air raids. My
imagination lived in Europe, though my body was in the United
States.

"I want to go to California. Is there an excursion rate?"

"Seventeen-day," he said, "if you avoid Friday afternoon and Monday morning."

"I want to go on Tuesday. I'll only stay a week."

"This Tuesday?"

I nodded.

"To visit the girl?" he smiled slowly. He was already dialing the phone.

I remembered then that I had brought Sarah in when she was flying home the past spring. Karazov's memory for faces reinforced the image I had of his efficiency and reliability. In a short while he had my tickets made up and I wrote out a check.

"There you are!" he said, flapping the packet into my hand. "I saw another friend of yours yesterday," he said. "He came in here as a priest before. You know which one I mean. Mister . . . Mister Flanagan." He ran his finger over the active file.

"Eddie Flanagan?" I asked incredulously. "I thought he was supposed to be in Europe."

"He said to say hello if you came in."

"I didn't know he was coming. . . . Do you have a number where I can reach him?"

Karazov pulled out the card. He gave me an address on Amsterdam Avenue and a phone number. The card was headed "Mr. Edward Flanagan."

"Thanks, Karazov," I said. "I'll look him up."

I had the sinking feeling that frequently precedes true intuitions. Catholicism grabs your emotions very deep, and many feelings which your intellect does not accept reassert themselves in surprising ways and at surprising times. But maybe Eddie has not left at all, I thought. Maybe he has been reassigned to Harlem. But the order, so far as I knew, had no projects in Harlem. I resolved to telephone him.

Eddie Flanagan came from a small town where one-third of the town was Catholic, one-third Lutheran, and one-third Methodist. A new high-school teacher who admitted to being an atheist fled after one year; his wife had been made to feel distinctly uncomfortable. The Catholics in the town supported a parochial school that was so small most of the grades were doubled up, two to a room. Eddie always grinned about what an important figure the town had made him out to be—he was only the second boy from his parish to become a priest in a hundred years. (The first, he invariably added after a pause, is now a bishop in California.)

Eddie had been slow and reticent when he first came to St. Benedict's Seminary. On the first day, someone called him "Hayseed" and he flushed scarlet. He played a mean game of football, and in his sleepy way became an excellent student. He loved to read. With every passing year he became more radical. Classical music, painting, cinema—he moved from one enthusiasm to another. His first love had always been politics. He wrote his thesis at Fordham on Don Luigi Sturzo, founder of the Christian Democratic Party in Italy. Eddie was liberal on every point but one: he remained adamantly anti-Communist. I vividly recall him defending Whittaker Chambers. But in the teeth of a pro-McCarthy class, he also argued that Alger Hiss, intelligent and suave, exemplified the deepest illusions of the better people of the United States, and Joe McCarthy the illusions of the lower middle class.

"I'm not a fanatic," he said, gazing calmly through his innocent Nebraska eyes. "I'm hardheaded. There are people whose view of the world is quite different from ours. And they don't mind killing people to enforce it."

"Are we so different?" I would argue.

"Totally different. We're no angels. The welfare state is mostly for the welfare of the rich. Don't get me wrong. But there's no comparison between their ruthlessness and ours."

I could see in Eddie why Iowans and Nebraskans make good soldiers: hardheaded, quiet, serious, inured to the acceptance of hardship, inheritors of moral passion. I always wondered what would become of him.

Later that evening I found myself walking up Amsterdam Avenue to the address Karazov had given me. I had not been able to get through; a recording kept announcing, sorry, that number is out of order. Since I was leaving in two days and since I had nothing to do, I decided to walk over.

I had not often walked through Harlem before. As the people on the sidewalks became predominantly blacks, I became conscious of my white skin and of the gold watch on my wrist. Was I dressed too well? Too obviously a stranger? Why would white men come to Harlem? It's a free country, I kept thinking, but I

had seldom felt so out of place. Europe is more mine than
Harlem is.

The black men leaning up against the taverns and grocery stores
eyed me coldly, and I began to listen to my footsteps. Skinny,
active kids played on the stoops and sidewalks. Yellowed pages
from newspapers blew up against the buildings. The store fronts,
the dirty neon tubing over the taverns, and the battered white
marquees were like those of a dozen other neighborhoods. Maybe
there were a few more boarded windows. The litter baskets along
the sidewalks seemed more futile. The windows above were darker
and the interiors, as far as could be seen, more depressing. But
mostly a sense of quiet, a suppressed energy, frightened me. How
did you know which were the pimps, I wondered, and the pushers.
Supposing that one wanted either, what would one do?

As the address I was looking for came within range, I began
to wonder whether I could enter the building. My fingers were
already lightly doubled up, almost clenched. Does a black man
feel so threatened in a white neighborhood? It was a hot evening.
I had been walking steadily and was perspiring. I was hoping the
address would mark an office of some sort. It didn't. It was a drab
red-brick apartment house like all the others. What in God's name
was Flanagan doing here? I studied the black numerals above the
door; the "2" was hanging at an angle. I mounted the stoop past
two preschool black girls who looked quizzically after me, and
studied the buzzer tags at the entrance way. I recognized Eddie's
scrawl on a new white tag torn from a calling card, "E. Flanagan."
I pressed the button, but the hall door was open—the lock obviously broken—and slowly began to climb the stairs toward 3A.
The air was rancid. Candy wrappers and gum and three tin cans
lay silently on the narrow unswept stairs. There was no light. I
didn't want to touch the rails and climbed slowly so that my eyes
might become accustomed to the dark.

At the third turning, I could see 3A just in front of me. I
knocked. At first there was no sound; then Eddie's voice: "Who
is it?"

"Jon Svoboda," I said.

Silence. "One minute." But he was at the door in seconds,
buttoning his trousers, barefoot and bare-chested. The silver chain
and cross were gone. "Come in," he said, as if with resolution.
"Glad to see you. You got my message, huh? Come in." I stepped

inside. "This is Cindy Lou." He pointed vaguely toward the cot. Cindy Lou was black, about twenty-five, firm, composed, and nude. It was my whiteness, I think, that made her reach tentatively for a sheet, but it was too hot for that, and she simply said, "Hello."

"Hello, Cindy Lou," I said, and turned my eyes to Eddie. "Good to see you. Didn't know you were in town."

"Here, sit down." It was a very small room: the cot, a table with Eddie's messy suitcase on it, two wooden chairs, a small refrigerator, a hot plate. The streaked window was raised as high as it could go; it overlooked the avenue. The dusty air that blew through it was cool by comparison with the room. "Yeh, I got into town about a week ago." We were both sitting at the corner of the table. Cindy Lou sat in front of us and began pulling a slip over her head. "Cindy, let's have some cold drinks." She nodded and rinsed two finger-printed glasses at the small sink and pulled another from the cupboard, which she blew on before rinsing. Soon we were drinking Scotch and soda—Eddie always drank Scotch.

"What are you doing for a living?" I asked. I had decided I would skip questions about the past, letting him fill in whatever he cared to.

"Nothing yet," he looked down at his knees. "I'll have to start looking soon. Teach, maybe. They say there might be an opening at the New School. I've applied to the poverty program."

"You're over at Columbia?" Cindy Lou asked. "That's where ah am. Was." It is difficult to render her accent; it was slight and elusive, and she spoke softly, surrounding her vowels with quietness, as if to protect them.

"Yes," I said. "What department were you in?"

"English," she said.

"I was telling her about you. Wasn't I, Cindy?"

She was sitting on the edge of the bed and looked down at her glass. "He said you think too much and don't live enough." She raised her eyes from her glass and smiled in a teasing, mocking way.

I liked her and began to relax with the two of them. "Don't feel too sorry for me," I replied. "Did he tell you about our time in Europe last month? How many secrets did you tell her, Eddie?"

"Oh, not too many," Eddie shook his head in a boyish way that made him look especially handsome and innocent. His hair was blond in the harsh light of the unpainted room, and his pink, hairless skin shone. His nails had been bitten close to the tips of his fingers. "We did have to fill each other in a bit, you know."

"Where did you meet?"

"In a brothel, of course!" Cindy Lou flashed.

I protested.

The two of them roared with laughter.

"Well, you did look a little shocked when you came in," Cindy Lou countered.

"Jonny, for anybody else but you I'd have hid her in a closet."

"If you had one."

"Well—" he shrugged. "Anyway, Jonny, it's good to have you here. Cindy Lou and I met in the Village. We'll take you there for dinner."

The two of them dressed and we went out merrily for the evening. The black men on the street glared at us sullenly as we waited for a taxi. We watched a black comedian at a small coffeehouse after dinner. He made painful jokes about honkies—a new word for me—and black men. Cindy Lou enjoyed them; they made me uneasy but I laughed.

I had a chance to talk to Eddie briefly afterward. He had decided in France that he had to leave, and once the decision was made he saw no point in delaying. He had flown back to Cincinnati, consulted with his superiors, and left. He was given a temporary leave of absence, to cover him until the process of laicization could be completed.

"I feel much better now," he said. "A little scared. I'm hurting for cash. I'd sure as hell like to break in with the government, anywhere: Peace Corps, poverty program, I'm itching to get to work. Friend of mine, a Baptist minister, has this parish in Harlem. I'm helping him out a little. Doesn't help pay the bills, though."

"Doesn't seem to me you're eating very much."

"Costs even more to drink."

"Well, I'm glad you finally decided."

"So am I."

By the time I came back from California, Eddie had left Harlem. There was no message. I suspected that he wanted some time to find himself. He no doubt cherished anonymity. It is almost the only freedom left.

CALIFORNIA

◆◆◆

*". . . it is well for young men in a young land
to proclaim their attachment to those few
essential and perishable possessions that
give meaning to our lives: the sun, the sea,
and women in the sunlight. They are the
riches of the living culture, everything else
being the dead civilization that we repudiate.
If it is true that true culture is inseparable
from a certain barbarianism, nothing that is
barbaric can be alien to us."*

—ALBERT CAMUS

8

A HURRIED STEWARDESS set the green plastic tray in front of me. I picked up the sealed knife and fork and pushed the cold metal with one thumb; the cellophane resisted, stretched, was punctured. I wrestled my thumbnail under the lid of the white plastic cup of salad oil; the lid was stubborn but finally cracked. I poured the oil on the cut lettuce, the slice of egg, the wilted slice of tomato, and the single cold stalk of asparagus. The bun was too cold and dry to eat. The faint odor of metal, upholstery, and artificial air afflicted the food. I hardly cared. An airplane trip is my favorite narcotic, my time of contemplation and reflection and reverie. It brings back to me an attitude I learned in the seminary: quiet, restful, more an attitude of the will than an activity of the mind. Thoughts, images, and remembered sensations flit through

consciousness without censorship; one's attention is not on such
mental contents but on the fundamental act of ease, willingness,
and openness that makes them possible: shifting, sliding fragments
of color in a tube held lazily to the light.

Today, however, contemplation was impossible; vivid contents
were in view. Almost two weeks had passed since my last evening
with Vittoria. Sexual urgency pounded in my veins. For years it
had been relatively easy to be celibate, but now the dam had
ruptured, a new need had been created, a hunger as elemental and
necessary as hunger for bread. I could feel the seat cushion pressing against my thighs, the armrests upon my elbows; my body was
alive to every touch. The flaxen hairs of the stewardess' arm excited me; I watched the movements of her breast. I was eager to
see Sarah, and a thousand fantasies of love flickered through my
mind. Amoral, sensuous, experienced, she would be surprised about
Vittoria.

For five hours the jet soared smoothly over thick, lacy, gleaming
clouds. Occasionally the strata parted upon the dark red humps of
the Rockies. Streaming through the plexiglass, the sun pressed
upon my face. Its heat squeezed the muscles of my thigh. Flashes
of silver burst from the wings when the jet dipped or rose.

Sarah was waiting in the airport lounge in San Francisco, sunburned and lithe, her blond hair tied in a ponytail. Her arms were
bare and her bright smock clung closely to her. My heart bounded
when she smiled. I was so glad to see her that I bent to peck her
cheek with a sweeping kiss; she seemed self-conscious, hesitant but
pleased. Her breasts bounded like deer, hardly haltered by her
low-cut dress.

"My, you're looking great. It's wonderful to see you."

"You look sunburned. Europe was good to you."

"It was great. You look marvelous."

"You keep saying that. I'll become self-conscious."

"That only makes you cuter."

"You're a real ego-builder. I had to park illegally." She blushed
guiltily. "Late again. Do you think I should get the car while you
pick up your bag?"

"Probably."

We fell silent as we walked together up the long, shimmering
ramp, whose colored tiles were set in patterns that failed to dis-

guise its length and narrowness. You long to meet people you haven't seen for a long time and then in the airport there is only small talk.

"Down here," she pointed to the escalator. I watched her thin bronzed ankles, registered inwardly her soft flesh, and checked a wild desire to pat her buttocks.

"What's the time?" I asked, adjusting my watch.

"Twelve twenty-five. Guess what?" she said.

"What?"

"We have the whole place to ourselves. Daddy's gone away for the day. He took mother and they won't be home until tomorrow morning." Her tone of voice was plainly naughty.

As my fantasies came closer to reality, my old habits reasserted themselves and I could feel myself drawing back. "Great!" I said, but my tone of voice gave me away.

Her tongue flashed; she enjoyed baiting me. "Of course, that means I'll have to cook for you, or else let you take me out for dinner."

"No cooking. It's our vacation."

"How are things at dear old Columbia? Sometimes I miss it."

"Not the same without you. But getting along."

"I didn't expect it to fall to pieces. I didn't exactly set any records there."

"How do you like Berkeley?"

"Haven't really started yet, but it's almost like staying home. I'm trying to get Daddy to let me take an apartment. He doesn't want me getting mixed up with any radicals," she laughed.

"You've got the sandals. All you need's a beard."

"Small chance! I like the rich too much. My car's out here. Be waiting for you. Don't be long." She squeezed my hand, then hurried through the glass.

After a short wait I picked up my bag and walked awkwardly outside. Sarah was waiting in a white Ford convertible. It was good after so long to sit beside her on the red cushions. The sky was clear, the breeze mild. She had tied a yellow kerchief around her head, and I was looking forward to a long, leisurely conversation. It seemed so long and I was remembering how I had loved her.

Suddenly, however, Sarah was slowing the car and moving toward the curb. "Where to, boys?" she called.

Two tall, fair-skinned, brush-haired sailors ran alongside. "San Francisco."

"Hop in!" She waited barely long enough and shot away. As the conversation became four-way, I found myself growing increasingly silent. She couldn't have understood my feelings if she did that. A free spirit, I thought, her own kind of girl: take her or leave her.

We dropped the sailors somewhere along Van Ness Avenue. One of them winked at me as he got out. They were heading, they had said, to Vietnam, quartermaster duty. We climbed and descended the impressive hills of the city, past clean stucco buildings of a beauty surpassing that of any other city; the feeling was that of Madrid or Rome. Soon we paid the toll for the Golden Gate Bridge, and the cool sea breeze whipped across us; painted deep rust red, the cables and supports seemed to float from the azure sky. A gray destroyer, its white numeral clearly visible, was heading seaward. We climbed then into the harsh, eccentric mountains of Marin, turned off the throughway for San Rafael, and wound back into the narrow valley, lush with hardy foliage, where Sarah lived.

Her home was sprawling and white, Spanish style, set in the trees, beyond a pear-shaped pool and a tennis court. Banks of flowers were in bloom. Dark green leaves from trees I didn't recognize dipped and swayed. There was a stillness in the valley, a loneliness, as if far from civilization. In the cool, flagstone living room Sarah poured us each a drink. "Hungry?" she asked. "I'm famished!" and she brought out a tray of cut shrimp and crab from the refrigerator. She showed me to my room casually, as though she hadn't really thought much about it. "How about a game of tennis?"

"Okay. I'm not very good. But if you're willing."

"Fine," she waved an indifferent hand. "Daddy says I'm getting better. I'll change and be with you in a jiff."

"By the way," I said, "I brought you something." I lifted the suitcase onto the royal blue bedspread and snapped it open. I lifted the lid and reached into the side pocket. "I picked it up in Rome."

She opened the tiny box with delight. "How beautiful!" she squealed. "How perfectly beautiful! I love presents." It was a golden circlet in which a half-dozen peach-colored stones were set; it was trim and elegant. "Thank you!" She held it against her sun dress and leaned over to kiss me on the cheek. "How nice!" She pirouetted from the room.

Her pleasure was exhilarating. I rummaged in my suitcase to find shoes and suitable shorts. I wore my red bathing trunks and a new polo shirt. I practiced a few motions, forehand and backhand, with an imaginary racquet and then walked down the three stairs from the hall to the living room. Sarah breezed in still buttoning her tennis skirt.

"I'll lend you Daddy's racquet. Treat it gently, though. He's proud of it."

"Maybe I shouldn't—"

"He won't mind. Now let's see. The balls? Yes, the balls. Okay, let's go. Beautiful sky, isn't it? See why I love it here?"

"Compared to New York, it's pretty lush."

"You serve. . . . Hey, bring it down! Not out of the court. . . . That's better. Try another one. . . . Good!"

She proceeded in her easy, graceful way to demolish me. I concentrated to my utmost simply on getting the ball to clear the net and stay within the lines; she returned my shots with ease and effortlessly placed them wherever I happened not to be. I tried to keep grinning. Sweat was rolling down my back; it rolled from my brow and fell, burning, into the corner of my eye. The red clay from the court colored my white sneakers, and my new white polo shirt developed random patterns of rusty smudges. The ball ponged back and forth in the sweet air. Occasionally I managed a good rally and she cheered me on. Once or twice my hardest serves stayed in bounds and she couldn't play them. Once I ran to catch a blooper she had placed in the far corner and at the last second stretched too far and fell upon my stomach. I don't think she perspired at all.

"Say, you're pretty good!" she smiled afterwards. "I particularly like your dives."

"You mean the one I tried to save in the corner?" I laughed. "In football that would have been a diving catch for a TD."

"In tennis it was pretty funny." She enjoyed laughing at me, so I joined her. "You're going to need a shower."

"Don't you want to swim?"

"I'm too tired, I think. You go ahead. I'll be showering."

I dove into the chlorine-green pool and luxuriated in the warm water. It lapped against the smooth blue cement. I churned for two or three turns in the short pool, floated on my back, and then pulled myself out to go inside. I knew exactly what would happen. How quickly one advances down the broad boulevard of love. Chaste Jon Svoboda. There are some things one has to learn. Experience, a rule of life. I dried myself as thoroughly as I could, and entered the cool, silent house.

"Jonny? . . . Jonny?" she called as I walked down the hall.

"Yes?"

"Come on in. Last door on the left."

I walked down the hallway looking right and left and stopped at her door.

"Coming?" she called, the voice much clearer now.

"I'm here."

"Come on in." When I stepped inside, I heard the shower still running. "Come on. I want you to wash my back."

I swallowed and walked slowly to the bathroom door, knocking on it as I entered. Warm moist steam coated the mirror and billowed into my face.

"Step right in!" she called. She wore a naughty smile and held a yellow washcloth at two corners as a screen in front of her. "Here it is." She handed it to me, turning around. "And here's the soap. Scrub hard, please."

I stepped into the shower and began to rub a film of soap over her shoulder blades, her spine, her ribs, her waist. Then I rinsed and began again, this time including her bottom.

"Hey! No fair!" she giggled. "What is this?"

"An assault," I said.

She half turned. "To be an assault I have to resist, don't I?"

"You're thinking of arrest."

"I don't want to arrest anything," she said. "Go on." She turned fully around. She put her arms around my neck and let her nipples barely touch my chest. Then she began to press.

"Ummm, it's good to see you," I said. There was, after all, solace in defeat.

"Now turn the water off," she suddenly said. She spoke a kind of baby talk. "Time to dry ourselves. Oh, Jonny!" She tsked and began to pull my trunks down. "What a pretty little train Jonny has! Naughty little Jonny! Getting big! Naughty, naughty!" She stepped out of the shower and wrapped herself in a large white towel.

We dried ourselves.

"I think I'll take a little nap," she said, padding into the other room still wrapped in the towel.

"May I join you?"

"I didn't know Jonny went in for so *many* sports!"

"It's a better game than tennis." It amazed me that I could talk as I was talking. It was a bluff—an adventure, I thought, I owed myself. A duty.

"Well, just for a teeny nap." She sat on the edge of the bed.

I stood and held her cool face in my hands. My fingertips massaged behind her ears. She pressed her slender nose against my stomach and her lips tried to bite it.

"Take it off, Jonny!" she said, pulling at my towel.

"And yours," I said. I pulled and her towel fell across her lap.

"One moment!" she said solemnly. "Mother always says, when you make love in our beds, take the bedspreads off."

I helped her fold the golden spread. "It happens often?" I asked.

"It's what my mother always says."

She dallied with the spread and, when she was ready, returned and threw back the sheets. Her breasts were small and pointed. Her hips were rounded, and as she bent over a diamond of light appeared high between her legs.

"Come!" she commanded puckishly.

She wanted to roll and be kissed and touched. The sun dropped from its zenith as we played. Then, our hearts pounding in the silence, she finally motioned for me to sit up, on the edge of the bed. She sat in my lap, her legs tight around me, and pulled herself up and down until she shuddered and I, shuddering, joined her. We held each other tight for several minutes without movement. Then she pulled away and asked, "Pretty good?" She pulled herself free and padded to the bathroom. I sank back upon the pillows and she flung in a towel. The water ran in the sink for two or three minutes. "Besides," she said, "it all runs down that way. It's safer."

"What do you do?" I asked. "Take the pills?"

"Christ, I'd like to. But they make me sick. I have to wear creepy things like this. And lots of douche." She threw me an extra diaphragm. It was made of hard white rubber. I ran my fingers over it. "It's a damn nuisance. I don't see why women have to . . . why don't they experiment on *you?* Why throw everything on us?" She shrugged.

"Hey, wait till you see these!" She opened a drawer of the heavy walnut dresser and pulled out something white. She stepped into them and pulled them up, swaying her hips from right to left, and stood before me in thin panties with roses painted on them. "Hand painted! Hand painted for chrissake. Wouldn't you like to make a living painting roses on ladies' panties! Aren't they lush?" She snapped the elastic and hunted for a bra. She fastened it in front of her, spun it around, pulled it up, slipped her arms into it, and adjusted it. "Come on, cowboy, didn't you promise me a dinner?"

The cool blue-striped sheets were comforting; it was seven o'clock New York time and I had been up since six. I kept wondering how I had gotten here: New York, the humming, buzzing plane, and now in Sarah's bed. To be lying naked there seemed unreal; it didn't seem like me. Yet through some strange alchemy it seemed also like a truer me.

We drove to Sausalito for dinner. The restaurant was built on a wharf jutting over the water; a small yacht was tied just beyond our table. The sky was streaked with orange and pink, and the evening air was fragrant with the dry-season foliage of the hills. The surface of the Bay heaved under the motions of the breeze, a violet and blue and silver sheen. Small boats streaked in the distance toward the San Francisco shore or toward the bridge. Sleek, fat gulls hovered and dove, their lust stirred by the champagne and crab and steaks being served in the open air below. The women wore deeply cut cocktail dresses; the handsome men at the nearest table wore powder blue jerseys under tight-fitting jackets.

We drove back slowly through the night and slept together, like old sweethearts. She whispered, several times, "I love you."

Her parents returned the next afternoon. Roderick Douglas was tall and wore his graying hair cut close; he looked like a splendid tennis player, and skied, Sarah told me, two weeks every winter.

Priscilla Douglas was slight and pretty and elegantly dressed and smoked one cigarette after another.

"How did Suzy take care of you?" she asked Sarah in a dry, ironic voice.

"She went home yesterday morning."

"She did? I thought I told her to stay and cook dinner for the two of you."

"You did, but I told her she could go. Jon took me out for dinner. No use paying her for a useless day."

"Now, Sarah, you shouldn't have done that. You know the trouble I've been having with that girl. She doesn't take me seriously as it is. I wish—"

"Must you girls always trouble guests with gory domestic details? We usually have a cocktail before dinner, Jonathan. What will you have?"

His certainties made me uncertain; I hesitated. "Gin and tonic," I replied.

The Douglases were very white, Anglo-Saxon, and Protestant. He was the president of a small chain of banks. I felt as if they couldn't possibly take to me. I wondered what Rod would say if he knew I had been laying his daughter, on her own bed. Probably, *Be careful*. All the time I spoke to Rod or Prissy I felt I was in a sort of reverie, distant, not quite tuned in on their reality. Even the glasses Mr. Douglas served his drinks in were thicker and more substantial, more decorative and ornamental, than any I had ever had in hand before.

That night, of course, it was impossible to sleep with Sarah, but she came into my room wearing a white mohair, sleeveless sweater. She wanted me to hold her in my arms, and we rolled quietly on the bed. I slid my fingers under her sweater and under her bra and rubbed gently as she hardened. Then my one hand raised her skirt and slid under her silken panties and searched out her wetness for the tender spot. She groaned lightly and through a continuous kiss said, "I wish I could stay. I wish I could stay." She left, and I was tense and unhappy. I tried to pick the strands of white mohair from my green jersey. My fingers smelled of musk. I washed them, brushed my teeth, and lay upon the bed.

I didn't like all this. I really didn't. Sarah and I weren't hitting it off; what we had in common was the bed. Except for diversion,

she didn't like me; except for adventure, I didn't like her. Making
love with her was fun; the emptiness came afterwards. I felt guilty
as I hadn't with Vittoria. There was something wrong, and it
stifled something in me. It made me dislike myself.

I tried to figure out how I could leave; I was supposed to stay a
week. But then the image of Sarah's little, slender figure returned;
I saw her across the bed, throwing back the new fresh sheets. She
had said, "I love you." Perhaps I was misjudging her. I'd have to
adapt to her ways; she couldn't throw off her background overnight.

The next afternoon, after a morning's tennis and swimming, we
were—it's difficult to believe—lying on her bed again. Her parents
were away; Suzy was far across the house. Sarah's skin was fair,
like satin, rough and pebbly only on her buttocks. She was not
heavy and her hips and ribs made her skin shine very white. I was
curling her thin mat of hair around my finger. Vagrant silvery
hairs climbed toward her dimpled belly. As we lay resting and
playing, the white phone beside the bed rang softly. Sarah's eyes
concentrated a moment before she answered it.

"Bill!" Her voice expressed guarded, genuine pleasure. "What
brings you back? I thought—"

I pulled my head away to allow her to pull herself closer to the
phone. Her small breasts were almost flat as she lay upon her
back. I tried not to feel pain gathering in my stomach.

"I see—well, didn't it work?"

I touched the purple nipples gently but they were slack and relaxed. I was deciding not to seem defensive. One has to learn to
be mature.

"Not today. . . . No, I can't. Tomorrow? I'm sorry it went so
badly. . . . No, I'm fine, everything is fine. . . . I do, too." She
hung up slowly.

"Boyfriend?" I asked.

She was annoyed. "Bill Thompson."

"Like him?"

"Sort of."

I forced myself to ask a question I wished would have no
answer; my maturity was thin. "Were you arranging a rendezvous?"

"If you must know, yes."

"Do you often arrange them from your bed? With other men holding on to you?"

"You have a dirty mind."

I nodded. "I'll bet you sleep with him tomorrow, too."

"Of course, I will. He's had a—"

"Don't you set any limits?"

"Don't talk to *me*. You've slept with other people."

The accusation shocked me. "Not all at one time," I said drily, to cover my embarrassment.

"Bully boy! No one owns me, see." She was sitting up. "I'd take the two of you at once if I wanted to."

"Not me you won't!" I was already standing; it was time to show decisiveness. The indignity of stepping into one's shorts, however, injures one's decisiveness.

"I want you!" she laughed, throwing herself into a waist-high tackle. She took my maleness in her mouth. Dignity began to fade. I slowly lay down over her, turning her, using my tongue in the salty regions between her legs. The pressures of her tongue upon me did not relent.

The next day, she left for the afternoon to "have her hair set," and firmly let me know: *no further questions.* I sat restlessly in my room. I was studying the suntan on my arm. Suddenly I said aloud, "I can't live like this!" I packed my suitcase and asked Suzy if she could drive me to the heliport. I left a short note for Sarah. I wanted to hurt her; I wanted her to feel a little pain. At first I wrote: "Don't you have any standards at all? You taught me a lot. Like stay out of certain holes. Jon." I tore it up. Finally, with strict self-control I wrote: "Thank you and good luck. Business in New York. Affection, Jon." I missed the New York flight by thirty minutes and had to sit for three hours pretending to read paperbacks. I half expected Sarah to come bursting into the lobby.

Then we were rocketing down the runway and airborne for New York. The plane banked over the Pacific, swung around the Golden Gate, and strained for height over San Rafael heading eastward. "I'm not in your league at all," I told her from about eight thousand feet. "You'd beat me every time."

I was beginning to hate airplanes. How many good-byes is a man going to have to say? The future seemed to me to promise an endless series. Too much to ask! I cried out, to the cosmos I suppose. The plane leveled out over Sacramento. *Too much!*

9

IT WAS COOL before a rain, and the wind was whipping thin black dust into the air. Grit leaped toward my contact lenses, caught, and rubbed against my eye. My hand shot to my face. I stopped and blinked until the tears flowed. At last the grueling pain was cleansed.

Ever since leaving California, I had been miserably lonely, and my nerves were screaming for comfort. Laura Thompson, a teaching assistant in my department, was by reputation an easy lay. The wind blew my clothes against me and made my cuffs crack. Anyone who was looking could see that I was hard. But I couldn't telephone Laura. She wouldn't believe I was serious; she would laugh. I needed a girl very badly, needed one like air, and didn't want it to be anyone I knew.

I walked aimlessly, not knowing how to reach a girl. I half desired, half feared, that a girl would approach me, some short, dumpy, pockmarked girl of thirty-nine. What if she were diseased? Or took me to buildings I didn't want to enter? One by one, I went through the list of casual acquaintances I knew—a good-looking student, girls I'd met at parties. Almost everyone would still be out of town. I told the man at the bar to refill my Schlitz, and stared blankly at the television set as the Mets played far away in San Francisco. The sight of the slender narrow light posts: Sarah! I disliked intensely, hated—because—because I loved her. She had stirred a wildness in me. I imagined her long white legs around the darker legs of dozens of different men. Her laughter rang out so vividly I had to close my fingers around my cold, wet glass and focus hard on the snowy gray ball game to bring myself back to New York.

What was I, after all, but a hunter hunting the streets? I could no longer live at peace with myself. My self-image demanded something nobler, more restrained, calmer, more dignified. "Life is more than sex." I couldn't place the accent of the voice calling out those words to me, sadly, sweetly.

How do you break down the walls of inhibition when you cannot even see them? How do you break out of a self-image that is narrow and false? I hated myself and hated my frustration.

I concentrated on the wet ring left by my glass. I set the glass halfway across the first circle to make two, interlocked. Then I made a third. I couldn't believe that sex is as neutral as eating and drinking. The central expression of morality, the delicate encounter, not of bodies, but of persons. That is what I had been taught and what my emotions had accepted. To make love consciously and knowingly is to tamper with personality. I wanted to explore. I wanted to try everything I could. Guilt feelings, of course, couldn't be prevented. But they could be turned to fruitful use. Whatever I felt guilty about, I must do. Guilt leads to integrity.

Even as I sat on the bar stool, one toe dragging in the sawdust on the floor, I knew there was rationalization in my thinking. But through fear of rationalization, I had often tied myself in knots. I stepped out into the warm midnight air at 118th Street, looking confidently at the neon lights and the red taillights of passing cars. I had made a resolution that would change my way of life. The feeling was good and clean and I drew a deep breath of the warm night air.

My first attempt, there is no way to lie, went badly. I went down to Washington Square Park the next afternoon and waited. A mangy collie walked lazily to my bench and sniffed my crotch. Even the dogs know, I thought. *Go ahead, bitch, leave!* After a tedious hour my emotions were worn and the juices of my stomach were out of harmony. Anger. Hostility. My fingers drummed on the flecking green paint. Two girls went by, looking over their

shoulders. The tall blond one was wearing a white dress; the figure
of the stocky one was packed into blue silk.

"Can I help you?" I asked. I was on my feet walking with them
before I had time to think about it. They looked me over quickly,
one taking the arm of the other.

The blond girl said, "Thanks."

The chunky one was righteous: "Those boys tried to snatch
my purse."

"Where?" I asked.

"Around the corner." She pointed. The boys ducked out of sight.

"They won't bother you."

"I don't like New York."

"Where are you from?"

"Minneapolis. St. Cloud. It's a kind of suburb. A town."

After a few silent steps, I asked, "Do you mind if I walk with
you?"

"Please. Until we get over the shock," the blond one said.

The chunky one had a harsh, musical voice. "It's been one
thing right after another ever since we got here. First our baggage,
then . . ."

"When did you arrive?"

"Last night," the blond one said.

"Yesterday afternoon." The righteous voice.

"My name is Jon Svoboda," I said. "I'm studying English at
Columbia."

"Very happy to meet you," the blond girl replied. She offered
her own name: "Barbara Carver. This is Jodi Andrews." Barbara
had alert green eyes. Affectionate, too. But St. Cloud? She had
showed too much relief when she heard I was a student. I felt
trapped in my old self-image: Aloysius Gonzaga the Third.

I took them to my favorite restaurant in the Village, Alfredo's
—spicy Italian sauces, buttery fettucine, lasagna, reasonably priced.
Alfredo was an enormous man, six-two, three hundred pounds.
His mother ran the restaurant. Barbara and Jodi warmed to the
smells of sauces and spices, the sawdust on the floor, the deep blue
bowls of candlelight, the crisp cold Verdicchio. Jodi lost a contact
lens in her lettuce. I was sifting through the sawdust when she
found it in the oil and vinegar. The romantic dinner led to a
movie, and the movie to a taxi ride. I had an arm around each

girl, squeezed the brassieres of each—felt each girl tense a little, and began to hate myself. It was not going to be possible to separate the Minnesota twins, and I was not quite ready to take on two at a time. Two regrets: I had insisted on paying for the dinner and had wasted an evening.

Unconsciously one tends to suppose women less willing than men to slide between the sheets. That supposition is the first hurdle I learned to jump. The second was the supposition that rejection is embarrassing, rather than an early move, a parry, a counterthrust, and if delivered harshly, better to accept anyway. Thus, by and large, if one supposes that a woman really wants to go to bed, one can't be far wrong. One may not get her there but, then, not even Notre Dame scores every time it gets the ball.

I had vaguely imagined that sleeping with a woman requires a businesslike approach: bing, bang, dust your hands. Where did I get such outrageous views? From James Jones, I suppose, and from indistinct ideas of bawdy houses, pimps, and casual liaisons. From magazines. From the fact that the female equivalent to "male" is "nymphomaniac."

I feel sorry, now, for the first girls I encountered. They endured quite a lot of innocence. I had set myself a target: fifty-two girls, one for every week—my novitiate in masculinity. Meanwhile, my sensibility absorbed the use of words like "pussy" and "cunt."

When I had all but given up, Cindy Lou helped me. I met her by accident on Broadway, outside a laundry. At first she didn't recognize me. When I asked her about Eddie, she remembered. I asked her if she felt like a drink; I said I was lonely and glad to see her. Eddie, it turned out, had left the city. She didn't know where he was. He had been having trouble with his papers. "Or something," she said with a gesture of her hand. "I don't understand it all." Her voice had a hushed fullness.

We had a long, cool gin and tonic in a cocktail lounge near the corner of 112th Street. We enjoyed talking together. She said that for some reason she felt tired. I suggested we go up to my apartment. I had an air-conditioner and gin. We could keep cool.

The room was up three flights of stairs and my heart was beating pretty hard as I opened the door to show her in. I hoped she was thinking what I was thinking. We sat near the window overlooking the river. I was very proud of my view, even though it was partly cut off by the brick building at the corner. The pane was grimy and gray. We could see the trees bend lightly in the sulky breeze, and watch a stretch of the thick, shiny river slide by in the heat. Cindy Lou kicked off her shoes and I brought her another drink. We talked about a prominent essayist for a while.

Suddenly she said: "Jon, we goin' to bed? 'Cause if we are, I'm tired just waiting here."

"Y-yes," I said with all the assurance I could manage. "I'd like that." I stood holding my glass in both hands, releasing one hand in an ambivalent wave toward the other room.

She looked at me incredulously, and I could see a judgment forming in the hazel of her eyes. Deliberately she lapsed into dialect. "Man, you sho don' sweep a lady off her feet!"

In the bedroom, whose narrowness would have embarrassed me had I not seen the tiny room she and Eddie shared, she calmly began to undress. It was a swift process: dropped sun dress revealing long, lean legs; white bra released and falling with a forward shrug of the shoulders; black panties caught by a thumb, jerked downwards, swayed over the hips, falling. She stood there, and I realized my mouth was dry and I hadn't opened more than a button of my shirt.

"You never seen no black pussy?" she mocked again. She leaned forward and waved her hands in front of her knees in a kind of dance. "African," she said. "Savage! Wild!" She straightened up and laughed, holding her sides.

She knew she had a woman's power, and I feared she was going to sit down on the bed and wait for me; I was paralyzed. She stepped out of the heap of clothes and took my hand. "You concentrate on lookin', lookin' an' enjoyin', an' I'll do the res'." She began unbuttoning my shirt. "My!" she said, as she slipped down the zipper of my fly. "Look at this. Tsk! Tsk!" She beat a finger on the hardness, and then her fingers slipped inside the elastic of my shorts and brushed them down over my hips. "C'mon, boy! Give Cindy Lou a hug." We stood there pressed together in the heat and the coolness, and she lifted herself until my hardness was between her legs, wet and warm. She rocked undulantly from side to side. I could see that her eyes were looking out over my shoulder, but then she felt my glance and leaned back to catch me in the

eye. "C'mon, lover boy, hold me tight." I lifted her and walked
awkwardly to the bed. We fell with a laugh. "Slowly, boy,"
she said.

When we awoke, it was evening outside, hushed, peaceful, red
and purple skied. I kissed the nipples of her pointed breasts. She
had been lying quietly, and unmovingly accepted. "C'mon, boy,"
the hushed mocking voice began. "Buy me dinner now." She was
gentle and quiet as we bathed. But she tried to let me know with
unmistakable signals that this was not the beginning of a liaison:
it was finished.

The valves were slow to turn, however; I was not yet used to
thinking in terms of solo appearances. I asked her what she was
doing until school started and, later, where she lived. She waited
for the mood to pass. When it didn't, even at dinner, her voice
became unusually hard and grim: "*It was a good afternoon, Jon.*"
The silence afterward furnished a period finally able to penetrate
my dreaminess. I felt my neck redden. Her voice resumed its
hushed serenity. We said good night outside the café. She insisted
on going home alone. She put both hands in mine but her eyes
were already distant and her brow was furrowed. My apartment,
when I opened the door, seemed unpeopled and vacant. For three
or four weeks, until it was replaced by other presences, Cindy
Lou was as present in my apartment as my books, as solidly
there as the humming air-conditioner. Without her, the sheets
made me shiver, and in the space inside the door where her clothes
had fallen she stood, if not eternally, then in my memory, like
lithe Egyptian marble. *Nigra sum sed pulchra!* we had chanted
at Vespers in the seminary. Memories of high-pitched Gregorian
chant, of mountain air and holiness; the shortness of breath I had
felt on first seeing her.

Slightly on the heavy side, bright, bored, brought up to treat
sex as a thirst to be satisfied, and convinced that two rational
people should be mature enough not to romanticize intercourse,
Laura Thompson was at first pleased by my conversion. She wasn't
certain of the source of it, but she had known Sarah during Sarah's
one year at Barnard and knew, vaguely, that I had been out to
California to see her. Laura had green eyes and straight black
hair which she kept cut in bangs, "to hide my ugly forehead." She

was so pale her skin was a little on the pasty side, and she was so
cerebral—she seemed to meet people chiefly through her eyes and
in those eyes were calculation, analysis, penetration—that it was
sometimes hard to find out where her instincts were. She was
compassionate, could even be gentle and loving, but the tender
side of her was unattached to the primary, analytic side. She did
not live through her body; she lived in it. She experienced it like
an instrument; a true child of the Enlightenment, of generations
who thought of themselves in the categories of Kant and Hume
and Russell. Wit was her salient point. The fact that she had
soft lips, rounded white thighs, and modestly ample breasts was a
sort of refuge, not even at the second line of consciousness, an
aside, a part of herself not to be repressed but, on the other hand,
not subject to analysis or theory. The mode of dealing with the
body was to keep the intelligence away from it, to let it go its
own way. But, of course, her intellect—trained to be aware—was
smoothly, hummingly in gear during almost every waking hour.
It could hardly help hovering over the hours left to the body.

Laura's father was a professor of psychology at Ohio State, and
she herself had gone to Vassar. Her younger brother had recently
entered Milton Academy, heading for Yale probably, and Harvard
Law. One day in late September I met Laura at the English office
when I went over to pick up my mail. She told me about the
beauty-parlor murders up in Michigan: nine people laid out in
pinwheel fashion and shot, one by one, through the head. I
hadn't read the morning papers. We were supposed to meet with
five other T.A.'s to plan the freshman scheduling at three. Two of
the committee weren't in town yet; the meeting was off.

"Can I buy you an iced tea?" Laura asked. A feminist, she
always paid her own way, at least. I was feeling restless and agreed.
I said I had some in the refrigerator if she cared to come over. We
could read in the cool of the air-conditioner. Desire was making
me eloquent, and I met the quizzical look that stole into her
green eyes with an added burst of unusual generosity: "I might
even ask you to help me finish off the roast I made last night.
And I'll open a bottle of—Châteauneuf-du-Pape?" We had gone
to the movies alone once or twice—usually four of five T.A.'s
went together—and had not so much as pressed elbows on the arm

rest. Until now, our relation had been strictly business. If she was suspicious, she masked it. Her curiosity got the better of her.

"What is all this?" she quietly asked some time later, admiring the last two inches of the deep red wine in the light.

"What is what?"

"Come on, Jon! I can feel the change. You've never been like this before."

"Like what?"

She was silent, but pursed her lips.

I was wondering what the strategy ought to be. The road from the kitchen table to the bedroom is strewn with obstacles, and sometimes mined. One never knows what women are allowing themselves to think. ("Men's minds," I can hear Laura counter scornfully, "have absolutely only one single track.") With Laura, I figured a direct approach was better. Also, it ought to be cerebral. To pounce on her with kisses and a hand in her crotch was as apt to anger as to soften her. She needed help in disengaging her mind. What should it be? Music or books? Charades? *Look, sister, strip! Get the hell into bed, and spread your legs.* No, that wouldn't work at all.

"To be truthful, Laura. I've decided to seduce you."

"You seduce *me?*" she laughed. She wasn't sure.

"I have become a great lover."

Questions raced back and forth under the skin of her face.

I sat almost in a straight line, my feet outstretched and crossed, my butt on the edge of the chair, and my shoulders against the back of the chair. The small wooden table bore the remnants of the roast, a half loaf of French bread, dirty plates, an oily salad bowl, ash trays, and two half-empty glasses.

"I thought it was about time I got to know you a little better."

"And me you?"

I nodded. "First we finish the wine." I rose noisily to pour it.

"Where the love comes out of."

"Where the eloquence comes out of."

Her green eyes began to calculate.

"I toast your green eyes, your black bangs—"

"—my ugly forehead—"

"your ugly forehead, your unseen bosom, and your holy navel—"

She opened a button of her blouse. "Better?"

"Coming along nicely." Continuing: "Your hairy crotch, your smooth thighs, and your eloquent ankles."

"Wow! All out of a bottle."

"Shall we dance?" I took her hand—it was moist and warm— as she quickly drank off the last of the red wine. "Music!" I snapped my fingers over the hi-fi, let Laura stand immobolized a moment, turned the switch, and set the cartridge arm in place. I had been playing a raucous twist earlier this afternoon—my thesis went better when I played music with a wild beat—and now the hi-fi hummed and the turntable began to spin; the needle loudly sought its path and then music exploded into the room.

"I don't really want to dance," she said.

"What?"

"I want to undress!" she shouted.

"But don't wake the neighbors!" I moved my lips emphatically.

We began throwing aside garments as we danced. Near the end, she kicked her panties and I caught them and hung them on the nearest peg; it dipped and they slid to the floor. She rushed toward me and tipped me onto the bed. We tumbled and, though she was in a hurry, I couldn't hold out for her. I felt wretchedly about it, and the memories of what we had been to each other began crowding back. We spent the night and parted gently. But we were forcing, and knew that we had better quit.

It never quite came to hate. We tried to sleep together once again, about three weeks later, but again the emotions refused to come. We were perfunctory, somehow, even when we tried to please each other, and the effect was dismal.

"It just doesn't work," she said.

"We better go back to being friends," I replied. "I'm sorry."

"It's no one's *fault*. These things happen. Mature people get used to them." She touched my chin. That school year we worked together as if nothing had ever happened.

10

I LIKE TO TEACH. I like the first days of school. After twenty-one years as a student and two as a college teacher, I was still excited. The ambitious breeze of autumn along the river, the scent of new clothes, the fresh ink of newly opened books, the tactile ecstasy of ivory pages print-impressed; girls in first rows, legs still crossed in summer ways; suggestions of softness never touched by sun. Summer is the wild time of the American spirit; winter belongs to Puritans. The juices come to thickest ripeness. Everyone is bronzed. Memories burst with romances of the summer. The iron round of duties has not clanged down.

I look over my class and know that I will like them. Freshmen, facing their first college teacher, size me up. They expect me to be precise, to exhibit "amazing factual knowledge," to excite their minds with theories, insights per quarter-hour, x revelations per class worth buzzing over as they walk into the sun. My hands are moist; I walk up and down. To them I look calm and self-assured, and it surprises me to feel as self-possessed as I do. My mind today is as clear as mountain air, and I perceive myself teach, operating on at least two different levels—teaching them and observing myself—and sometimes three. I feel cocky, complacent, possibly contemptuous—daring them, telling them I *know* and they, not I, have to measure up because I've been through this before. Then I try to get that tone out of my voice; they are a fresh group, and we are both starting over from the beginning, equals. Insidious, slow, calm, I want them to see things as I do, and I prepare surprises for them—booby traps—and walk them along the road until *boom!* they feel Fourth-of-July shock, delight, and they are all

awake: ideas bursting like slow, phosphorous, shooting stars at
night, more lasting, nutritive, linked to each other like roots of a
forest.

Teaching is dangerous, I think, if you care how students respond
to you. Learning occurs where there is love or its most intense
opposite. It is not what exams are made of: how much information
you've absorbed, how well you can analyze it. I tried to let my
students come live inside me, and tried to live in them a little; in
my opinion, teaching is a shared way of life. Intimacy is treacherous. The teacher is exposed, the students, too, and inadequacies as
persons are in danger of discovery. Learning is judging: evaluation,
appreciation, repugnance for what is not true, intense attraction to
integrity of mind and heart and eye. The bright and alive, octupi
testing their tentacles, go to work first of all upon their teachers,
whom they must devour in order to gain their independence. The
student becomes a judge. He sucks nourishment from every experience and memory and feeling; it is not the mind alone that
makes a student. The myth of the laboratory expert in a white
chasuble has misled us all; it is not objectivity we want, but passion
and sensuality and bold, creative judgment. My thesis and my
teaching went together.

So going back to school was fun. I loved the sweet-sour smoke
from leaves burning near the river. I liked the heft of new books
in the palm of the hand, the excitement of fresh titles and chapter
headings. I liked new people. I liked facing a new and different
class, feeling the need to improvise to find a route to their special
state of soul. Coming away from class I felt depleted, like coming
down from a marijuana high, worn out, a little sad. (I had tried
smoking pot after reading Coleridge, and still do, from time to
time.) It was impossible for me to work on my thesis on Tuesdays
and Thursdays, the days I met my two sections, one at eleven and
the other at one. The morning was lost in preparation, the afternoon in long, slow, unpleasant unwinding.

Cardinal Newman, however, remained fairly interesting to me; I
was enjoying my thesis more than most. I got turned in his direction—one of those queer turns that guide the selection of theses—
by the passages in *Portrait of the Artist as a Young Man* in which
Joyce acknowledges his debts. No one controls the English sentence
as authoritatively as Newman. Yet his sentences require a time of

confidence and peace, the stateliness, ease, and leisurely pace of
aristocracy, the assurance of empire. No one today can use such
full-bodied sentences—run them on, yes, as Faulkner did in the
sleepy-violent South. Yet if a man can learn to master the elements of Newman's prose, then he can manage any other. In the
twentieth century, writers dare use only half the power of the
English sentence; a civilized sentence would be a lie.

There were other suasive reasons for choosing Newman as my
thesis topic. First, no one at Columbia had touched him for at
least forty years. Secondly, the director of my thesis committee—
director not by choice but by a process of elimination arising out
of professional sabbaticals—was currently intrigued by Catholic
themes. It had become something of a departmental joke that X
was trying to seduce a bright nun in our department (he was a
notorious, if highly cultivated, philanderer in his life as in his
fiction) and the T.A.'s were taking bets on his success.

Newman was the texture of my nights and days, especially on
the days I was not teaching. I learned how to waste extravagant
amounts of time. I hated the actual physical labor of moving my
hand across the paper, hated the thinking and rethinking necessary
to avoid the mistakes and weak assumptions that thesis readers,
peering down the sentences with powerful telescopes, commonly
find. I drank too many cups of coffee, kept all my files in scrupulous order, read newspapers thoroughly, answered letters immediately. I used the telephone frequently, spent hours reading
magazines, and had many long discussions with Mario Moro and
Jacob Goldblatt, my two best friends among the T.A.'s. I did
everything but write.

Mario was handsome, black-haired, suave, and an incisive critic;
he had been born in Italy and came to this country, age twelve,
when his father began to teach law at the University of Michigan.
He was already a favorite book reviewer for *The New Republic*.
Jack Goldblatt was tall, shy, witty, sensitive—in brief, a poet. His
work had appeared in the *Partisan Review* and in *New World
Writing*. He was very good, and I was proud to be his friend. The
modest notoriety the three of us received in graduate school made
us confident of our future—we wanted to be "literary figures." We
had idle dreams of taking over from the generation in power whose
views, we felt, were too conditioned by the cold war. We wanted

to reintroduce a moral sense into critical discourse. Mario had his reviewing; Jack had his poems and had completed a version of a novel; I was the only one of the three with no defined image of how I would become a "literary figure." I flirted with philosophy too much.

"You could write the world's best biography of Cardinal Newman," Jacob used to tease me. "Then you could move to Richelieu. And Spellman. You could know more about cardinals than any man alive."

"You can be our resident Catholic intellectual," Mario added. "Every institution needs one." Mario pretended to be an Italian citizen—he was actually an American—and affected cynicism toward America. "Jewish novelists, Catholics-in-residence, WASPs as university trustees." He pinched his nostrils.

Apart from moral consciousness, our literary aim was narrative; we wanted to tell stories, to bring the human figure back into painting, to create human archetypes and myths. We predicted before it happened that major novelists would turn to journalism, since the human animal craves stories about himself. The old stories are exhausted, and artists for too long have pursued pure form, like seekers of the Grail. Each culture has its archetypes: imitation, voyage, descent, nothingness. In our culture, we felt, the modernist quest for subjectivity and abstract form was, after all, an honest mistake. The alternative is not naturalism. It is story. Scientists are unafraid to invent regularities and lawlike "stories." It is impossible to cope with the overwhelming flood of experience without myths by which selection, definition, and action are accomplished. An "age without myth" is impossible, for human beings cannot attend to everything at once. What they select from the primal flood as "real" defines their myth; their sense of reality is only one selected story. The problem is to tell the story of the modern age. The solution is for each man to tell his own, leaving cues by which others can grow through sharing it. Unless the race develops empathy, survival is not probable. The ear is the organ of communion. Through it lies the only route to another's sensibility. Images and definitions are shallow; music is more profound than philosophy. The ear is the organ through which the illative sense is chiefly nourished; it is the most personal sense. The university is not a library, but a place where

persons hear one another, where judgment can be learned. Certain
heavily laden emotions, to be sure, are generated only in the
range of sight and touch; the ear alone will not suffice. The prehistoric animal requires bodily presence, if its instincts are to work.

The literary problem, of course, is that tones of voice—the
qualities the ear discerns—are unheard in silent lines of print.
Readers ingest signals through the eye, but only signals they are
prone to see. The voice of the other cannot insist on being heard.
The author feels new helplessness. He contrives. He cannot suc-
ceed, I think, until his story is in some way about himself—apart
from his story of himself, there is no shared myth in which the
reality of others is truly touched. Men in a brotherly darkness call
out to one another, sometimes hear, and sometimes go unheard.

Jack Goldblatt was living with a Jewish girl from Italy, from
the colony of *ebrei* on the hot Adriatic coasts, a smooth-skinned
dusky, gentle, smiling girl, closer to nature than American girls, of
more fire and temper and stubbornness, a sharper, stronger personality, willful and determined and loyal to a man in a wholly
continental way. There was power in Olivia that forced one to
confront what growing up in America means, the limited emotions
one is allowed to share and to manifest, the petty self-determina-
tion and willfulness life here teaches one to develop. The American
girl is taught to move within a very narrow range of emotions and
accomplishments. The male is trimmed and whittled for a pro-
ductive role in a technological economy: not too much ecstasy,
not too much despondency; a dependable and affable regularity,
attuned to the schedules of machines. An Eastern Airlines pilot in
ecstasy as he descends into La Guardia? Idiosyncrasies on the
assembly line? A despondent Walter Cronkite, voicing despair?

Mario had a steady string of girls. He called himself "Italian
lover," and "Casanova Two." He changed girls almost weekly. If
he went out with the same girl two weeks in a row, we promised
to hire an organ.

Mario once received communion on first Fridays for nine months
in a row. The priest promised that anyone who made the nine
first Fridays would never die in the state of mortal sin. "So it is
very simple," Mario concluded. "As long as I stay in the state of
mortal sin, I cannot die." He still wore, in his mature atheism, a

Lady of Lourdes medal around his neck. The white silver set off
his dark shoulders and hairy chest.

I wish I could explain my own state of soul. I was born a
Catholic; moreover, for many years of my life belonging to that
people was the supreme reality of my life. I would have traded
anything—anyone's respect or love—for sanctity. I wanted to be
as thorough and simple a Christian as it is possible to be. *Limpid,
Lord, in thy sight,* I used to pray, *a clear pool, still and deep.*
I used to imagine myself seen through and through, utterly
known, without secret, in the eyes of the Lord. I still do. But
there have been so many changes in my attitude! How can I
begin to state them?

First, it is possible that I do not believe in God at all, that I
regard Jesus as no more admirable than Socrates and Camus, and
that I do not count upon eternal life. On the other hand, something has happened inside me which I cannot shake. When I
am silent, when I am alone, my heart burns with a love and an
attraction that I cannot still. I feel overwhelmingly at one with
people I meet—there has never been anyone, no matter how bitter
our arguments or how hostile our encounter, in whom I have
not felt the same God living as in me. I suppose that I do not
have the normal westerner's attitude toward the world. I feel so
united to a white, winter-weakened twig lying in the spring grass,
dark and wet on its lower side, its living substances dried out
inside, only a shell of its former self; so united to a sparrow
crying out in the elm overhead; so united with the dark, jagged
clouds from which the brilliant sun suddenly breaks forth, that I
do not think of them as separate from me. They are not objects.
I am not a Cartesian consciousness. The power of consciousness
and life that lives in me lives in them: I look into them as in a
mirror. More exactly, we converse, this spirit of life and consciousness and I—we see each other in and through our diaphanous
world.

Perhaps I write confusingly. I would not dare to speak of this,
even to my closest friends. One must take each precious object
in the world seriously, *in itself* and *for itself*. The twig is not a
"sign" of God or a "trace" or a "reminder"; it is a twig—precisely
the twig it is, no other, in its own time, in its own place. And
yet. And yet. A consciousness lives in it, a spirit that also lives in

me. Am I insane? Am I an animist? I *do* talk to twigs. Sometimes the flash of sunlight on pine boughs waving in the wind gives me such ecstasy I have to look away. I am inhabited by spirit, and sometimes the joy that gathers within me seems about to push out my ribs.

But the favored manifestation of God within me—if there is a God, for the usual words do not describe the experiences I have—is a lingering dryness, a brokenness, a darkness. It has gotten so that I rejoice in rejection and misfortune. "In the darkness *and* secure," St. John of the Cross writes. It is when I feel insecure that I know I am secure. Insecurity, I reason, is a truthful image of the human condition, and I rejoice to be in harmony with truth. There is nothing I desire more than that. I don't know whence the appetite for honesty has come; it is the deepest drive in me that I can recognize; no other gives me peace. I would prefer honesty and truth to God, if there is room for preference. My image of God, the imageless, is derived from the fire of honesty I experience within me; God is more like honesty, in which I strive to live and move and have my being, than like a man. If that is not to be called God, then I do not believe in God. The word is unimportant to me. I would not mind being thought of as an atheist. St. John: "Where he—well I know who—awaits; *the place where none appears.*" My God is like the void, where none appears. Atheism-theism: the opposition is meaningless.

I have learned to seek experience, to widen the range of all that I can see and do. Religion, I have decided, is not a system of taboos, restrictions, boundaries, but a thirst for voyaging. I know that there are commandments, and I suspect they have a point. But my responsibility is to experience life, to find out who I can be. I found out with Vittoria and Sarah that I am afraid of my sexuality, that I am almost passive—I put myself in situations, almost, where they would have to seduce me. I needed to experiment. I needed to find out. I am glad for all the "mortal sins" committed; before God, I know I am not guilty. Eye to eye, face to face with the honesty within me, he cannot accuse me of fault. I am seeking; every day I seek. And in each search the thirst grows greater. Farewell, I always seem to live through nothing but *farewell.* Always it is further on, up ahead. *What? Where?* I keep searching, knowing that at any moment the thread will be snipped and what may be yet one more life without meaning will fall into an abyss inscribed "OBLIVION."

I have no fear of death; often it has been so immediate I felt its breath: two near auto accidents, a plane tossed while landing in a storm, a moment yet to be recounted in Rome. In all four cases death flashed before me a second away; in no case was I afraid. Cold, shaken, disappointed—so much yet to do!—but unafraid. I feel death inside me; I have never counted, New Year's Day, on living out the year. If death is oblivion, what else do I deserve? If it is nothingness as God is nothingness, the unseen communion of eternal life, oh, happy chance! Total honesty, unfeigned love, and humble charity may well resemble, as Dante and Dostoevsky saw, more the sun and all the stars. Yet what are we to imagine after the Nazi concentration camps? After Hiroshima? Committing myself to honesty, love, and humble charity, I wait.

I cannot believe the old certainties; I cannot disbelieve them. In my guts I am living out a new way, struggling to find an image of man able to bear the truth of our time. Not for others, but for myself. The task is too heavy to undertake it for anyone but oneself.

I love Jesus Christ with a quiet passion I cannot shake. For four years I have lived without him, without the sacraments or church or concentration. High in an airplane, looking down on rusty mountains or, in the dark, on the strings of greenish pearls across America's cities, jewels of the night, I encounter a movement of my heart which forms his name. *In him, by him, with him were made all the things that were made.* Perhaps it is not the historical man I love; perhaps that name merely gives shape to the small compassions and the large unities of my experience. In any case, no one can know me who does not know that I speak his name from the profoundest emotions I have felt, from the widest range of my consciousness.

Do these facts make a Christian? I am certain that I am a Christian, but most of the identification tests of Christians in history do not apply to me. Many clergymen, no doubt, would reject me. But, then, I regard few of them as Christians. Has not mankind itself changed in the last two generations? It there not very little continuity anywhere with what has gone before? In the lifetime of my father, since 1905, whole cities have been transformed, destroyed, or come into existence; the face of the earth is unrecognizable. And will there be an earth much longer? Will I, or my children, live out the normal course of our lives before the man-made cataclysm? Yes, I am a Christian, in my own terms, working out a way of life under pressures never seen in the history of the race.

I go to mass regularly again, not because the symbols are meaningful to me. They aren't. The liturgy is neither American nor ancient; it is a pitiable nothing. Yet it is my connection with my ancestors. The pilgrimage of the human animal has been a long one, and since the days of Abraham my people have attended this sacrifice. They have not come so far to allow the chain to break with me. I am not a solitary consciousness, but an evolutionary animal, and the memory of the race lives in me. Its vestigial rituals must be nourished like the embers of the fire Prometheus brought to earth; from them alone new flame can spring. Myths, symbols, rituals cannot be invented by one generation alone; their purpose is to carry forward tribal memory, the possession of no single time. In "eating the Lord" in the eucharist I feel primitive and true, prehistoric and part of nature; I do not wish to be a merely modern man. The crucifixion in which I share is my feast of the absurd, the direct contradiction of all hopes and dreams, cruel and bitter and ironic. The mass is a passage through blood and degradation. It is also a metaphor for pilgrimage, for odyssey, for a long march to an unknown land— ever ahead, ever demanding false starts and detours, as Mao Tse-tung went north and west six thousand miles in order to go east.

For a long time, what I hated most about the mass—what made me cease going once I left the seminary—was the bored, indifferent, apathetic people present with me. We had nothing in common, I thought, but the times to stand, to sit, to kneel: a mechanical unity, spiritless. The sermons were appalling. In the parish in Manhattan after I left the seminary, the pastor, a white-haired man of sixty-five, put on a false, droning voice for his sermons and announcements. The sermon was always shorter than the list of announcements; he had nothing from the gospels to

say. Every Sunday there was at least one denunciation of communism, linked with "secularism" and sometimes with "the cheap,
dirty, filthy garbage of so-called best sellers." Even the grammar
and coherence of his remarks were spiritless; the sermons revealed
neither care nor thought nor conviction. His vocabulary was
grubby, narrow, small, vicious, sarcastic. In the three years of
sermons I was privileged to suffer through, he never once voiced a
phrase that had not long been a cliché. His sermons were identical
each year, in cycle.

It is pointless to describe the three assistant priests. With more
or less fervor and intelligence, they each seemed to be en route
to becoming like the pastor. They were incapable of speaking of
the concrete life of the parishioners so mute before them: of
dirty dishes, of lack of time or space for making love, of the
desperate need for forty dollars to cover a loan, of garbage in the
passageways, of children in stunting and debilitating schools. Their
sermons were, like the Latin mass, remote. Yet the people returned
Sunday after Sunday, unhearing, beaten down, back and back
again.

Still, my responsibility as an intelligent man is to understand
that even if every priest in the world misuses his responsibilities,
even if every parish becomes an ever greater mockery of Christian
community than this, still, the power of creation is present in the
eucharist. Jewish and Christian testaments constantly predict the
indifference and apathy of large numbers of believers. My life is
not governed by what other people do. Even if one were the lone
Christian in the world, still one must go on; what others do is
not decisive. Catholicism is my birthright. It is not something I
can "leave." What would be the point? If I became an atheist
like Mario and Jack, I used to ask myself, what would change?
In my outward way of living, not very much. I didn't see God
any more than they did. As for immortal life, yes, somehow I
still had the instinct; it felt right to me. But no more than
they could I describe it, count on it, or guide my life by it. The
thing I concentrated on was now: the task at hand.

"What does your confessor say about those chicks in your
apartment?" Mario asked me invidiously. His light blue eyes
flashed.

I shrugged.

"He doesn't like it, huh?"

"I don't tell him."

"You don't tell him? What kind of a Catholic are you?"

Jacob seldom joined the mocking; his parents were orthodox, and he himself had wanted to be an orthodox rabbi before the world suddenly exploded before him and he changed. He came to my defense. "Mario, who made you Inquisitor?"

"In Italy it would not matter," Mario rebutted, "but in America the priests keep their hold. Don't get the wrong idea. But I think the priests are losing hold on you."

"I inform them of every fuck by mail," I said.

My understanding of the word Catholic is that it means part of a historic people, various, open-ended, risky, independent. I want to explore the meaning of my life. I am a man. The freedom is man's; being a Catholic does not take it away. The people called Christian—indeed the people called Jewish—are my people. I do not wish to be anything else, even if I could. For the church with its long history, the Christian way is presented *a priori*. For me, it is an experimental method; I accept the consequences of my acts. I don't expect confessors or theologians to understand that. But mine is the more or less instinctive logic of the layman, and always has been. Chaucer wrote his retraction *afterwards*. His lascivious miller was a good man among the faithful, delicious and delightful maker of pilgrimages, and kisser of buttocks. If you see things as they are, not as preachers picture them, the pilgrims are, always have been, and should be a pretty lusty crowd. When, if ever, Catholicism begins to or falls into decay, the sniffer for heresy should look for those who do not delight in the human body, do not love the human animal, have never eased genitals inside another in the hay, and consequently have no idea what the resurrection of the body means. Catholicism needs the fuckers, as most Catholics have always instinctively confessed. Rising from the dead, the first thing erect is not the tongue, but the instrument of manhood and progeny and piercing pain. The prick is restored in paradise, by breath once blown upon a fleshly rib.

11

MY PARENTS WERE surprised when I entered the seminary in 1953, just after my high-school graduation. My mother was delighted. My father was at first dismayed, but then became so pleased at the thought of having a priest in the family that, when I finally left, he was more grievously disappointed than my mother. Meanwhile, David had gone into the service and we worried a great deal about him while he was in Korea. He was a second lieutenant, and in combat second lieutenants did not have a high life expectancy. One winter he was wounded and suffered frostbite; a few weeks later he was back in action in the desolate hills. Later, he was hit at short range and lay under fire for twelve hours before being pulled to safety; his heavy armored vest had protected him. He came back from the service something of a hero, with battle stars and a bronze star for bravery. He had an ugly violet scar on his left side where the machine-gun bullets had shredded his flesh and cracked one rib. I often wondered what terrors he experienced as he lay there, whether he had watched the stars, or accepted death. He never talked about that night. The experience gave him a superiority I could never hope to attain. I longed, sometimes, for exposure to an equal violence.

I could not have gone into the army, in any case; very poor eyes and an injury had caused me to be classified 4-F. It was a dubious blessing and in our environment a source of shame. St. Benedict's Seminary, meanwhile, taught me a discipline perhaps equal to that of the army. The remote, quiet, gray-stoned building sat upon a hill at one end of a small college campus. We arose at five every morning. Our "monitor"—a fourth-year student in charge of the dormitory—was addicted to oxygen and every night threw every window open wide. One night the dormitory in which thirty-three of us slept, in rows of eleven, was so cold that the radiators froze. There were snowdrifts under the open windows, and dry flakes slid in flurries off the covered radiators. It was not unusual for us to sleep under eight or nine thin blankets, most of them army surplus, doubled over; one boy from Alabama had twenty-two blankets on his bed. The meals rivaled meals anywhere for plainness and, above all, regularity. The weekly menu was varied so seldom that every slight difference at a meal—brown bread instead of white—was cause for celebration. Four German nuns cooked for one hundred and thirty of us, not counting faculty (who ate at a separate table and had separate and better meals). The oldest nun was seventy-six; the youngest—the superior—was sixty-one. Every Sunday evening, with only one exception in three years, we had frankfurters and beans; I still shudder when I see them, even at picnics.

I learned a good many basic habits. "Recollection" was perhaps the most useful one. Recollection, in our usage, meant control of mental attention, but especially of the eyes and ears. We practiced recollection during meals, while walking in the corridors, and while studying—during everything except recreation hours—and the trick was never to raise the eyes beyond immediate necessities. We did not look into each other's faces when we passed in the corridors: eyes straight ahead, gazing downwards slightly. We did not raise our eyes from the quadrant shaped by the edges of our desks or the plates in front of us at table. We kept count of the times we violated recollection and confessed these faults publicly at a weekly session in the chapel. It was hard to learn to ignore a loud noise or a bustle; some fellows were rather flighty, others didn't much care, a few simply had too much common sense, and most of us violated recollection almost constantly. We confessed our lapses by working out an average—estimating eight, nine, or ten times a day—but it would have been as easy to count the times we *kept* it. The practice, like the absolute silence we were to maintain during the same periods, derived from European religious orders founded since the Reformation; it had a precedent of a different sort in the earlier monastic period. There was some common-sense value to the silence—it

certainly allowed concentration during study periods—and a value
to the required discipline of will.

Recollection tended, however, to put too much emphasis upon
the will, teaching us to suppress our instincts and spontaneous
movements, making us somewhat cold and oriented toward abstrac-
tions like the rule instead of to people and concrete, changing
situations. It was understood, of course, that real needs took
precedence over the rule; in emergencies or demanding situations
we assumed normal attitudes easily and with relief. As Americans,
we were not favorably inclined to such disciplines, not because
we were weak-willed but because we valued instinct, experience,
spontaneity, novelty, the concrete. We did not admire persons
of severe and dominant power. When I read *The Lonely Crowd*,
I recognized immediately the conflict I felt between the European
inner-directedness presupposed by the seminary rule and the other-
directedness we had been taught in dress, manners, and behavior
through all the instruments of American culture: the open sport
shirt, the clap on the back, the studied easy-goingness. I set myself
to working out in my life a kind of synthesis.

I was lucky to have as a spiritual director a man who had been a
psychiatrist before his young wife died, in Mexico City, and then
had fulfilled a lifelong ambition by becoming a monk. He wished
to explore the relations of mysticism and psychotherapy. He had
small, intense, black eyes; his head was totally shaved; he spoke
so softly I could hardly hear him; and his movements were so
gentle he scarcely disturbed the air. His name was Father Alfares—
his first name Juan—and he reminded me of John of the Cross,
for whom he, too, had a passion. Before he agreed to take me on
among those who sought his advice—he was the most popular in
the seminary, but also the most feared—he made me write up
my life's goals. I wrote: "I want to be a saint. To say so frightens
me. The saints suffer so much, and act so irrationally. I also want
to write, and other things, which I am afraid will be taken from
me. Still, what are all these things by comparison with living in
God and He in me? I understand sanctity to be love of men, and
listening carefully for the will of God."

He was silent when he read my statement. His room was painted
an ugly institutional green of many years' standing, and the dark

brown bookcases were overflowing with books and recent period-
icals. The October sunlight was pouring through the window
beside me, warming my arm uncomfortably; I was afraid to move
it and break the silence.

"And how do you know the voice of God is speaking?" he
finally asked.

"The rule, the commandments, the voice of superiors, the bell,
the—movements of my own heart," I replied a little nervously.
Father Juan seldom went outside the seminary, although he kept
up his therapeutic practice, calling it counseling, on a limited
scale. Visitors were always arriving by automobile. He talked with
people, older seminarians said, fourteen hours a day, a steady
stream of seminarians and others. I hated to take his time, hated
to add to the burdens that must, day by day, be burning him out.

"Why do you put your own heart last?" he asked quietly. "Does
God?"

"No."

"Why should you? Tell me. If the rules forbade you to do
something you felt you had to do, would you obey them?"

"That depends on the feeling."

"How?"

I shrugged. It was hard to sit back in the easy chair he provided,
and still more awkward to sit forward and erect. "Sometimes I'm
impulsive. Not all impulses are good."

"What do you mean, 'good'?"

"When I have time to think about it, I'm not happy I followed
them."

He touched his fingers together in the silence. They were short
and surprisingly white, for his arms and head were very dark.
His hard chair creaked. "What if," he began, looking slowly out
the window and into the boughs of the great oak that must have
been, just then, shimmering gold in the brilliant sun (I wondered
if the glance gave him occasion for a mental prayer of praise),
"What if you can't trust the feelings of happiness that tell you
which impulses to be happy with, which not?"

"Then the problem goes much deeper."

He nodded. Then he slowly rose. "There is one more thing I
want to show you before going on." He took a short blue birthday
candle from a box on his desk, showed it to me, white wick

toward me, lit it and set it in a drop of its own wax in a saucer. Its light flickered up toward a Spanish crucifix standing at the edge of the desk blotter. He sat down and gazed at the candle. We watched it burn for many minutes, no sound but our breathing in the room. My mouth was dry; I didn't know if I should speak. The tiny yellow flame seemed to have a center of blue; it flickered hardly at all, burned tall and straight. The blue wax swelled into clear liquid, gathered, ran down into the dish, whitened. The black burning edge of the wick moved steadily downwards. A light black smoke climbed a few inches above the flame before disappearing. The smell grew stronger in my nostrils. Finally, swimming in its own wax, the wick silently went out.

Father Juan fixed his burning black eyes on me. "Those he loves the Lord exhausts." His hand pointed, palm up, toward the dish; it was like a gesture at the mass. "There is nothing left."

I tried to swallow as I nodded.

"Are you willing to be emptied?"

I summoned up my courage, not quite from the bottom of my soul, for I did not then know how to find it. "Yes."

"You need to agree only to the first step," he said gently. "None of them, one by one, is very hard. You will make them with joy. But I wanted you to see quite clearly what you are asking for. The flame burns everything away."

I checked an impulse to cry out in joy. As I walked down the dark corridor afterwards I almost bounded. This man would be honest. He would not let me lie. He was serious. At last in America I had found a man of spirit.

I took the rule seriously, and imagined that every single detail, no matter how silly, had some psychological truth behind it if I would look hard enough to find it. Under Father Juan's guidance, I read the Psalms and the wisdom literature of the Jewish Testament carefully, studying the way in which the Prophets spoke of "the Law." The law, I found, is inward-pointed; it built up habits and made me sensitive to the nuances of the heart. Silence and recollection enabled me to cope with myself; they directed my attention away from objects, events, and persons outside. Instead of concentrating on the stimuli, I studied my responses. In the ocean of silence on the hill, I found that I hated myself; I was, in that disagreeable word, alienated from myself. I did not like to be alone, to confront my unpleasant moods, or to explore my inner resources. I deeply resisted fundamental change. The danger in introspection, of course, is an almost total self-centeredness. But the more extroverted seminarians (and priests) were not, I noticed, necessarily superior in other-centeredness. I began to recognize evasions in others and in myself. I did not then know of Sartre's conception of "bad faith," but I was learning every day that sincerity is impossible. A man's inner life is complicated; emotions contradict one another, and presuppositions that I am certain that I hold, daily experience shows I do not really hold at all. Moreover, the instant I thought I had a clear view of what it was that I was being sincere to, that view itself became an abstraction, and my "self," never directly observable, again eluded me. I learned from long hours of silence and reflection a great respect for the inexhaustibility and freedom of the self; tantalizing, squirming, flashing, laughing, more elusive than reflections of light in the ocean. I came to see that self-knowledge is knowledge of the ways in which one does not know oneself: I came again and again to the edges of my ignorance. It was a little frightening to perceive that I did not, could not ever, know myself; even more, that there probably is no such entity as the self. My capacities seemed too infinitely malleable, and I learned to let my imagination roam where it would: no use being frightened. I am, I saw, capable of anything men can do or can become. In a different circumstance, with different aims, with different preparation, I could imagine myself almost any type of man. And thus I came to understand my freedom. To continue being what I was, was, in fact, a choice, just as not to continue was a choice. I could make myself.

My desire was, of course, to make myself open to God's grace. I wished to be as water poured out in his sight, limpid and malleable and pure; be where he wished me to be, do what he wished me to do. But God, I discovered, is as inexhaustible and mysterious and elusive as the self. It is impossible to lay hold of him. Neither the seminary rule nor the orders of superiors nor intuitions of the heart nor the Scriptures themselves confine God's will to channels. I could see, the more I reflected, that God is God precisely because he cannot be confined: superabundant, free,

living. Hence, I tried to become receptive to signs of his operation:
where men achieved acts of understanding or acts of loving, where
greater inner freedom and joy were served, there I said God was
present. *Ubi caritas et amor,* we used to sing (it was my favorite
antiphon), *ibi Christus est:* where there is charity and love, there
—and not in church or in rules or in lines of command or in
pious feelings—there is Christ.

But I also came to realize that, in a sense, such a perception
makes the image of God (Force, Thing, Separate Person) super-
fluous. For if I concentrated on understanding, loving, freedom,
then I could concentrate upon the actions of men. That is what I
came to mean by "Christian humanist," which is what in those
days I called myself. We do not see God directly; all we see are
men. As for the white rocks shining in the creeks near the
seminary or the violet-blue waters of the serene lake or the call of
a yellow-throated warbler in the quiet of the afternoon or the
thick resin on the pines, shiny and runny in the hot sun, or the
silent brilliant sea of stars after night prayer—as for all the
resources of nature that came to mean so much to me, since they
formed the substance of my emotional world—all these things
made me alive to my own senses and my own powers. They
awakened in me understanding and love and patience; they
taught gentleness and magnanimity and endurance of suffering;
they widened my perspective out beyond my own few moments
of consciousness to the eons of evolutionary time; they offered a
vista that swept my spirit like cool air.

In this way, life for me became condensed into understanding,
loving, freedom; these were the power and life of God in history.
But one could just as well speak of them without reference to
God, so long as one had somewhere learned to single them out
from the complexity of earthly experience. For nothing obliges
us to single these values out from others. Even to do so requires
an exercise of freedom. Understanding and loving and freedom
form a beneficent circle: even in discovering them, one exercises
them; without exercising them, they cannot be discovered.

My first few months in the seminary were very happy ones. I
had a sort of honeymoon of the spirit; prayer came easily; insights
were frequent. I disowned my earlier life: I used to snap on the
car radio the instant I swung inside in order never to be in silence

with myself; to hurry from task to task in order to keep busy; to think first of my own desires and impulses; to exercise no control over my contradictory spontaneities and instincts; to drift; to take my ego as a cool center of equilibrium, an electronic eye, registering red warnings when painful stimuli outnumbered pleasant ones; and otherwise proceeded smoothly up the path of life in quest of a pleasurable inward state. I now began to think of myself less as a passive recipient of stimuli; less, too, as a pragmatic agent mastering my environment to suit myself. A subtle conversion took place within me during my four years at St. Benedict's: Father Juan taught me to think of myself, not as a particle of consciousness locked in an extension of skin and moving in an "external world" like a Martian in a hostile environment. I began to think of myself as simply Earth. The planet lived in me and I in it. I was its conscious part, part of the organism Earth, my body's cells its cells, my processes its processes, my evolution its evolution. One night—after days spent lying upon my back in the pine glades in the silence of Easter week, while the sun shimmered on the green needles and almost blinded me when I paused to look up from *The Brothers Karamazov*—one night I lay upon the earth, parted the supple wiry blades of grass with my hand, and saying "Earth! Self!" pressed my lips against the cool dirt until I felt pain. I rocked lightly from side to side and arose with black earth clinging to my lips and to my chin. I did not brush it way until the wonderment, the cleansing joy, had passed. It did not bother me that I was imitating Alyosha; I *wanted* to do it, myself.

But late in my first year and for the next two years the dryness that I looked forward to, the token of seriousness and truth, descended upon me. I lost all emotional contact with God. I no longer felt him or saw him anywhere. At prayer, there were only inner restlessness and nervousness, not a stirring of emotions or affection, not a sign of faith, not a ray of insight. I no longer seemed to be making progress. In conversation, I was impatient, bitter, cynical. In work and at sports I became bossy and defensive. My studies seemed boring and tedious and, even when exciting, entirely independent of my prayer and my attempts at charity. I could no longer remember why I wished to be a priest or why I had opposed my father and insisted on entering.

For he had said to wait until I completed college. He made me apply to Harvard, hoping I would change my mind about the seminary, and with the good record I had compiled in high school, I had been admitted. He thought, perhaps, that I was punishing myself for being rejected by the army or was too much influenced by my mother's secret desires. She had dedicated me to the Blessed Virgin at the churching after my birth; she had held me in her arms before the white, blue-sashed statue of Our Lady of Lourdes in our parish church and offered me. She had always hoped that one of her two boys would be a priest. "One for country, one for God," she had said softly, through tears, the day I left home for St. Benedict's. David was still in Korea then, and the rules of the seminary seemed so strict they thought they would scarcely see me again for the eight years it would take me to become a priest. I began to wonder if my father hadn't, after all, been correct.

I never felt so close to my parents as I did in the seminary. They were my chief link to the outside world. They were the chief sources of my identity and roots. I saw them in a new, softer light, perhaps idealized: plain, simple, humble folk like Mary and Joseph, the image of what a family might be. They had known hardship and some despair. They had no pretenses— or only such as were lovable. They loved each other and were faithful Christians. They lived for David and me, and made whatever sacrifices were necessary for our welfare and advancement. They tried to motivate us so that we would develop beyond what they could attain. My father, whose education was so limited, had lured me regularly to the Harvard Classics, bound in red and gold, by praising Edmund Burke's speeches and the essays of Carlyle. "If you could ever write like *that*, Jonathan. If you could ever write like that!" He boasted of having read the entire set since he had bought it when David was a child, before I was born, and my mother nodded confirmation, but he seemed to remember so little of what he had read and, when I began to read them, they seemed so out of touch with his own speech and interests that I could never quite believe that he had really done it. Still, there the shining books were and they were the source, no doubt, of those desires in me that led me beyond what my high-school classmates had ever imagined. My companions in Conemaugh were always slightly amused by me, slightly suspicious, and it seemed to me more contemptuous than proud when prize after prize, including the first Harvard admission in our school's history, was awarded me.

I turned Harvard down and entered the seminary because of a secret instinct. Perhaps it was fear of the world, fear of my own awakening flesh. Perhaps it was the need of seasoning. I am not really sure of all the reasons. I felt an ardent desire for spiritual adventure, for silence and solitude and strength of will. I felt poignantly that Americans around me were wasting their heritage, were unknowing and blind, were groomed and fed and amused but still barbarians. Justice, truth, liberty—such things, I thought, had little meaning among my friends or their families. I used to look up sometimes from the football field during a lull in the action, my hands on my hips and almost anonymous in my golden helmet and heavy uniform except for the yellow number 12 on my woven red jersey, look up at the crowds beneath the lights. What were they thinking there, gathered like a colony of ants in rows of seats, applauding a futile and silly spectacle which only diverted their attention? What did they think? I saw them rushing toward the darkness unaware.

In my experience, the surest way to reach them, the surest way to prompt consciousness and life and reflection, seemed to be the priesthood. I saw myself as an awakener. I would bend everything else to that—my dark longing for girls, the joy I felt in digging cleats into the turf and showering in the sweaty locker room, the pride and prestige of Harvard, winning fame in some career (I once saw myself as a national politician—to be frank, as President). My father thought I was crazy; he saw his own hopes for me going astray, and his opposition convinced me that my instinct was correct. For he had been bitten by America and coveted the advancement he himself had never attained. He wanted for me a classically American life, and it was precisely that that I was trying to escape. I did not wish to be American and middle class; I did not wish to be like all the others. Somewhere the Harvard Classics had stirred something in my mind—art or achievement or spirit—against the American Dream. For that dream meant betrayal: it meant invention and initiative and mastery and getting rich; it meant technology and hard work and changing the earth.

What it did not mean was human freedom, independence of
spirit, the artistry of shaping the soul. I chose the church over the
American Way.

And in the beginning my choice seemed correct. I felt a contentment I had never known and that joy which comes solely from
the exercise of freedom. It was my life, I had chosen it, and I
would make the best of it. Perhaps because it was my choice, I
took it with a deadly seriousness that again, as in high school,
won me from my companions suspicion and slight contempt. I
affected not to care. Yet after a while, as my own inner life went
sour, I began to wonder whether my companions weren't correct;
I really didn't belong among them.

One day, just before the beginning of a Latin class, Peter Reilly
from Chicago was telling me why the members of my six-man
football team—we had an intramural league and our team was
tied for first place—found it hard to get along with me.

"I try not to give too many orders," I objected.

"It's not that," he replied. "You have a sort of—kind of false
humility. Everyone can tell. It makes it hard to deal with you."

I wasn't sure of the exact meaning of "false humility," but the
pain the phrase caused suggested it was true. I thought about it
all through class. I was called upon suddenly and had to ask the
professor to repeat the question. The accusation made me look
at my recent life in a new way. Yes, I was only making an external imitation of the virtues of the saints; my efforts did not
come from within. I was trying to impose a way of life upon
myself by sheer force of will. I was not genuinely humble—
humus, earth, unpretentious, honest—I was seething with ambitions and images and desires. *The awakener!* I hated that image of
myself. But I was trapped in it. And even to hate oneself is to
evince self-love; one merely proves thereby one's attachment to a
glorified view of oneself and bitter and self-defeating disappointment at one's own reality. Humility is truth. I did not like the
truth about myself, and hence merely pretended to modesty.
Peter Reilly was right.

For weeks and months and years my interior life continued dry.
I could not find God. I wasn't certain that I believed in God.
How, I asked, can belief in God be tested? God cannot be seen
or touched or tasted. He is not a feeling in the heart. Does it

require, then, another belief by which to believe that one has faith? It does not suffice to say the words, "I believe." Anyone can do that. Nor is it enough to say the words with feeling. Feelings can be manipulated. So how did I *know* I believed in God, especially since I lacked all feeling? Perhaps I was an atheist already.

I studied the masters of the spiritual life carefully, especially the Jewish and the Christian testaments. I recognized speedily that the great men of faith invariably experienced dryness, went into a desert, lived in anguish. They had committed themselves to a God whose appearance they could not control. They felt close to him and then bereft. They were left to their own devices. Practically speaking, they were in the same position as atheists. Understanding, loving, freedom, I concluded, are everything. So long as one pursues such things, one follows the only stars available in the desert. Whether there is or is not a God, these are the signs to follow. I gave up worrying about God—atheism ceased to be a threat to me—and concentrated upon my brothers.

That was the second lesson I learned in the seminary: the self is not only earth; the self is others. Consciousness is not single; it is one and indivisible; there is a communism of the spirit of which economic communism is but an echo. Our language is communal and thus our sense of reality is communal; we do not attain to it alone. It is given to us; the main category for understanding human life is that of gift. Reilly conferred on me a part of me when he told me I exhibited "false humility." I had had an unreal vision of myself until he spoke. I concluded that the single human imperative, embracing every necessity, is to help one another to become more real: to be more accurate in our perception of ourselves and others. For we live mostly in dense mists of unreality, far from the truth about ourselves, vague and afraid to see. And it is not only that we are blind; we are willfully blind: there are things we do not wish to see.

I learned the power of such willful blindness when I tried to decide, at the beginning of my fourth year, to leave the seminary. In the summer after my second year, I had almost not returned. I had met a pretty girl named Fran Carney—we walked home after morning mass together, and her brother Tom and I played baseball together. Contrasted with the dryness and emptiness I felt in the seminary, a simple walk with Fran was vibrant, full of innocence and joy, a tangle of emotions and expectations. She had an upturned nose and long, smooth brown hair, a slow smile, a quiet voice. I recognized that, like a sailor in from a year at sea, any port would seem to me like paradise. Fran was not Fran to me: she was Woman. Still, I came alive that summer. Once when I made a spectacular one-hand catch of a line drive behind second base and felt her eyes upon me, my heart almost buckled. It is a powerful thing to feel loved by a woman; there was no such reinforcement in the seminary. Yet a man must be independent enough, I thought, to find joy in the catch itself; the admiration is secondary. I wouldn't want to marry simply to gain emotional reinforcement. I fought my emotions all through that dreamy, evocative, nostalgic summer. One August evening I told my father—my mouth as I began was dry because of the surrender the speech entailed—that I might not return to the seminary. We were sitting on the porch swing; the chains creaked. Fireflies circled in obscure spirals over the lawn.

"That's up to you, son. You know your mother and I will be behind you."

My tongue was loosed; I poured out the whole story, the dryness, the discontent. "I dread going back," I said. "When I think of those buildings, I physically groan. I really do."

"Remember, you said when you were going in you'd give it a serious try. You said you'd stay two years. Well . . ."

"I know. It's hard to decide. I know it's easier outside. All the things I like." In the darkness I thought he smiled discreetly. He had seen me with Fran, and Mother had once asked if I thought I wasn't seeing her too much. "But I knew all that when I went in. I don't have any reason for leaving. It's just that—just that—" the chains of the swing creaked as we rocked back and forth.

"Ummm?" he said, allowing me to say what I wished.

"It's just that I really like a lot of things." Hot tears were burning behind my eyelids. "And I hate that place, hate every brick in it. But I knew it was going to be tough. And I don't want just to—just to quit."

"Not a very good reason for going on with something, though, sheer will power."

"No-o-o," I agreed, beginning to be elated. "No!" Relief flooded me at his words.

The swing creaked. There wasn't too much more to say. By September I was feeling much better, and went back to St. Benedict's not because I had to, even under the command of my own will power, but because I hadn't yet found out who I was and what I wanted to do. As nearly as I could tell, the priesthood still suited me best.

But by the beginning of my fourth year, the old doubts had returned. Ahead a year lay theology, another four-year program. That represented a new, major step and, while I could consider St. Benedict's a kind of preparation for the priesthood, it was also a regular men's college, with about six hundred students besides seminarians. We had minimal contact with the other students, but I could think of myself as basically a college student. Entering theology would be a clear declaration of my goal as the priesthood. Still, I had invested three full years, and now begun a fourth, in one direction; I hated to give up. I liked the life fundamentally. I liked what a priest could do; the scope of the vocation was enormous. The priest's social leverage made him, if he desired, an instrument of change. (I was particularly interested, in a theoretical way, in Dorothy Day and her writings on the Negro in America; I wrote little sermons about Negroes in Conemaugh in letters to my parents.) And a writing career was not precluded. *Jon Svoboda: priest-journalist and revolutionary*. At least, I thought, I have a revolutionary name.

I could think of a dozen reasons for staying on the track I had begun. I had no single good reason for leaving, only dread. I did not believe there was any magic in the priesthood; talk about "holy hands" or "the priest as sacramental" made me faintly ill. But a priest could be, full time and in a rounded way, an instrument of all three of my criteria: understanding, loving, freedom. I could see myself as a priest; I could do it. But I felt, ever more strongly, a revulsion I could not or would not identify. It was this continuing revulsion that finally convinced Father Juan that my temptations were not ordinary ones; it was good to have him nearby while I wrestled in the darkness.

I am sometimes bitter about the seminary—so much life poured out in sand. But I was forced to turn the juices of life inward; I had to go beneath the surface, for the surface was not beautiful. Thus the greatest gift of all was given me. I learned to love the experience of nothingness. I learned to despise the pursuit of happiness and to seek nothingness. My mentor, apart from Father Juan, was John of the Cross; I loved the writings of all the mystics, Suso, Eckhardt, Teresa, Blake, but no one more than St. John. I also read a book by Suzuki, with a glimpse of recognition, and Father Juan encouraged me to look eastward. I cannot define nothingness, but I can name the day and the hour: an October afternoon in my second year, when over the frost-browned corn stalks in a lightly frozen field I heard a crow caw. My shoes pressed upon the crumbling earth; I searched the brilliant sky, sheltering in a joyous heart an icy thrust of fragility, decay, and death. The caw of the crow was gone. No experience has ever equaled in intensity what I felt that afternoon. In a stroke, every-thing I had felt before was altered. I no longer felt *apart from* nature. I no longer experienced myself as a self. There seemed to be an emptiness inside, conscious and in a certain sense full, far beneath the level of mind or soul or self. I could almost taste the fact that I was dying—almost as if I could feel my cells and substances climbing to a peak, declining. It was as though my stomach and my bones made their voices heard, as though for the first time I could hear *myself* speaking. I seemed to see that I was air and field and fire and bird; all the world flows through me, all laws, all connections, all chemical bonds. I imagined oxygen and sun's rays, soils and foods, all the nourishing elements which constantly come into me, constantly come out. I no longer felt separate, which is the way I had imagined myself before, someone walking *on* the earth. I felt for the first time part of a larger organism, a cell within a total element, breathing with its breath, living with its life.

At the heart of that experience was a piercing revelation of my expendability. The organism needed me and then dissolved me. There is a nothing deep down in things. At the innermost tip of me there is no self, but nothingness. The highest privilege is to be conscious of one's place, to share in a consciousness in communion with the shining forms, laws, purposes, relations, which give to trees and flowers and stones and dogs their un-utterable, ravishing beauty. *Splendor formae!* An irresistible impulse overcame me to caress all the things I saw, to treat them gently, to comfort them, since they were part of me but only I (perhaps) had sufficient consciousness to shelter them. I wanted to be gentle because I felt so vulnerable. The law of each particular thing is nothingness; the whole goes on. The community of men, the community of men and things, is founded on nothingness. *The first law*, says the Buddha, *is suffering*. I picked up a gray stick whence life, but not yet shape, had fled.

The caw of a crow. How it has echoed in my life. I hear it constantly. It has become my truest voice. It reverberates to strings in me no other utterance touches.

From that day forward, solitude has become my deepest love. I am not certain that I will ever be able to live with another. The caw of the crow goes deeper than any human voice. If, then, I sometimes seem detached from events, it is in part because I no longer believe in them. I do not really believe in movements, causes, progress. I do not believe in history. The notion "future" seems to me illusory. It is impossible that anything in the future should alter the present nothingness, even if men should find immortality through science. The future is a fresh configuration, slowly perceived, of the ancient and constant nothingness. It is not mortality, moreover, that is at the heart of my feeling; it is human pettiness, self-centeredness, restriction of understanding, of freedom, of love. To live sixty years or sixty thousand, it is the same.

For the next two years I read carefully every writer who seemed even remotely aware of such a voice. My heart became alive because, indeed, the feeling has not been absent from our culture; furthermore, it becomes its own authority. I read others in order to measure them. As the Zen Master says, no one imitates Buddha; to have insight is to depend solely on oneself.

When I seek out the sources of my love for solitude, I recognize that it did not come, as it seemed, by epiphany; it accumulated, like the force of tides upon a bar. There was a solitude in my parents, and between them and ourselves, that was holy and free. They did not counterfeit a myth of "love." Their love was not escape from solitude, but mutuality; it left spaces for breath and independence. In my father's eyes, and in those of my mother, I now recognized a loneliness I sometimes saw, which a marriage does not dissolve. It is a loneliness that moves the heart, and I would like now to run to them; but it is not the sort of loneliness that any sort of love can ever overcome. It is the ground of free community.

I look today for an altered tone of voice, a modesty, a gentleness, in those whose sides have been similarly pierced. The wound cannot be feigned. A note of hostility, of defiance, of arrogance, betrays a Cartesian consciousness, isolated still, unknit, alone. Sartre has not perceived. Camus perceived. Also Malraux. A sense of communion rushes from the one who perceives, his own blood reddening the knife, the community of those who suffer.

The monastery, in that sense, gave me life. It led me along a route I would never otherwise have discovered, a route systematically blocked in almost any other way of life I would have chosen. Who, after all, pursues nothingness? Who commends silence, indolence, or contemplation? I would have been as impoverished as I started out to be, restless unless I jumped into the car, picked up a book, invented something to do. I would have driven myself to death, without ever allowing the voices of mystery to grow strong enough, in silence, to be heard. River of silence, how grateful I am! Church of Christ, had you done nothing else but make silence possible for me, I would owe you what I am.

In the end, praying for longer hours as the months wore on or, rather, sitting in numb silence and merely representing in my will the simple question, "Teach me, Lord, thy will," I decided that I would picture myself outside the priesthood. I began to make plans to leave. With all those around me seemingly content and hardly guessing that I was about to leave them, I felt like a traitor, an informer; I was leading a double life. In the seminary it was forbidden to talk about one's decision to depart; those who left, left silently, without a word. I tested out my new image of myself day to day. And then, gradually, I discovered why I had to leave.

For three and a half years I had learned to practice as profound and serious charity as I could. I learned to speak softly and kindly. I tried to look for the good side of each person, even of those seminarians whom I spontaneously disliked. In fact, I sought out their company and tried to show them that I cared about them and what they did, tried to be available when they needed help— a fourth at bridge, a work project, tutoring, a ready ear. I had begun to feel that there was no one in the house with whom I could not be honest and, quite genuinely, feel empathy. Each had, as I did, problems of temperament and character to wrestle with, loneliness and aridity to endure. We each often did what we most did not wish to do—said words we regretted, acted cuttingly where we wanted to be generous.

Yet, underneath these genuine efforts to come to terms with my real and concrete neighbor, I fundamentally did not admire most of those I was with (Eddie was one exception). Most were essentially nice fellows, a cut above the average intelligence, generosity, and gracefulness, who would be satisfied to help run an immense organization. One thing our "years of formation"—that was the phrase employed—made plain was that we were above all else to be company men, dressed alike, decorous, and always on public display. If we had faith, we would recognize that the church is no "mere" organization; obedience to superiors is not to men but to God in them. Everything about the church is sacred, but nothing more so than obedience and prudence; obedience insofar as the church is divine, prudence insofar as it is human. In exchange for sacred privileges—celebrating mass, hearing confessions—and unarguable social status, the seminarian would become an organization man. My friends and I (Father Juan, at least, supported us), appealing to the prophetic tradition, were determined to buck the system every step of the way, resolved to reform it. Such reform, we know, would be a long-term task, not accomplished in our lifetime. The church, we often joked, is a non-prophet organization. It has marched through history, burning live offerings at every corner and generations later canonizing them as saints. Father Juan seemed to be able to bear all the weight with equanimity, even the harsh criticisms of his brother priests— who said he was pretending to be a saint, was too effeminate, too serious, too lenient in his comments about sexual experience, somewhat heretical in his ideas about the Pope, too European, and more.

When the gates were finally open and I left St. Benedict's, I felt a surge of resentment and hatred for my fellow seminarians and for clergymen in general. I positively hated them. The source of my earlier unknown dread stood naked then: I could not have tolerated such a life; I would have destroyed myself and others, consumed with bitterness. I felt betrayed, as a boy hates a father of whom he hoped too much. For the priesthood was, barring exceptions like Father Juan, another version of the American Way, an organization, a power group, a clubby fraternity. Understanding, loving, and freedom—the conviction burst upon me— are as easy to seek and to nourish outside it as within. Where? I did not know. But I was free at last.

12

THE WELL-DRESSED SEMINARIAN wears a black suit and a black tie. Father Reagan, our superior, allowed me that January to be driven into town to purchase more suitable worldly clothing; he gave me fifty dollars. I hadn't purchased new clothing for myself for four years; I was uncertain what I wanted. I bought a dark brown suit that could serve for both formal and informal occasions and would not represent too radical a break from my recent past. The salesman, a bored college student who kept gazing toward the front of the store, was not amused, however, by my desire to try on as many different colors and styles as I could find. *The new Svoboda!* I was saying to myself. I practiced being rakish and suave and golfy and debonair. I picked out a maroon tie with more red in it than blue; against the dark brown, I thought, it had just the right touch of fire. My mother, when she saw me, was disappointed that from black I had leaped to red; David told me later she thought I was flaunting my change of heart.

For in most Catholic circles it was then something of a disgrace to be an "ex." "He who having put his hands to the plow looks back is not worthy of me." To have entered the seminary was a sign of a vocation; to leave was to turn your back on the Lord's call. To protect themselves against this eventuality, my father had instructed my mother to reply to acquaintances all these years, not that I was in seminary, but that I was in college.

As I entered the house, I studied my parents' eyes for signs of disappointment. They hid it well. They greeted me with embraces; Mother had baked graham cracker pie. It was like my earlier homecomings, yet not quite; a formality, a fear, was in the air.

I announced my plans to leave immediately for New York. "I don't want to work yet. I didn't leave one pris— one job to take another." I tried to keep my bitterness hidden.

My father tried to motion to my mother to keep quiet. "I know what he feels like, Helen. Young fellows have an itch to see the world. I can spare a hundred dollars. But when it's gone you're on your own. That's the only way to do it."

"Thanks, Pop! That's exactly what I want! I'll pay you back some day." I put an arm around his shoulder and pressed it. "I have the best parents in the world. I'm glad to be home."

My mother burst into quiet tears.

New York is a very lonely city. My mother's last words echoed in my memory: "Stay away from Greenwich Village. I don't want you coming home with a stringy blond. I won't let her in." She tried to say it in a mocking tone but she wasn't very good at irony. "I still think you should get a job. By the time you go to college you could have a thousand dollars saved."

"You're such a materialist, Mother. I thought you were supposed to be a Christian."

I was thinking of my parents as I walked beneath the cold cement cliffs of the city. I had never been in New York before. The rumbling of subways under my feet, the purposiveness and harshness of the people, the noise and dust and cold biting air, the smells from open Nedick's and bakeries and Horn and Hardart automats—everything about the city excited me. And the women! Made up with silver hair and yard-long lashes and shaded green around the eyes. Everyone seemed privy to secrets; everyone seemed smarter; everyone seemed to know I didn't belong. I asked a huge Mackinawed man at a dull green kiosk for directions.

"How long you been here?" he asked. "Since yesterday?"

"Two days," I admitted.

"Thought so. I kun really tell."

I had learned to be bolder. "How do you tell?"

"I kun tell." His expression hardened as if he were about to say: "Whatta*you*, a wise guy?" He gave me the directions and I was glad to leave.

I lived for four days in a YMCA, and found a job in a book shop on the edge of the Village, disguising the location in my letters home. I wasn't very good at meeting girls, and I didn't at first want to be. I fell in with a group of Catholic kids who worked as volunteers at *The Liberal Catholic*. We met once a week to send out promotional mailings; we only occasionally caught glimpses of the editors. But mainly I was working on a novel. I worked every night with a concentration learned in the seminary, from seven-thirty to midnight. It was a flop. Nothing went well in it. But I wrote it in a fever of excitement and joy. Nothing had ever made me happier. It takes, I thought, five hundred thousand words to make a writer; well, I would pile up my three thousand words a night until I began to learn. But at first, of course, in the flush of creation, I thought what I was writing was proof of genius; I felt sorry for less-talented writers like Shakespeare and Dickens, Hemingway and Camus; none of them ever showed the excitement that I felt. In the stark, harsh glare of daylight, however, when I reread what I had written, I came close to despair. I began to get headaches. I was lonely and miserable. "I am deluding myself!" I cried aloud, holding my head in my hands one lonely evening and tapping my forehead. I had abandoned something good for something worse.

The food that I was eating was worse than that in the seminary, and more expensive. The room that I was staying in—a fourth floor attic on Twenty-second Street—had a bed with a broken spring, walls last painted during the Depression, and roaches, two or three of which usually greeted me on my gray blanket when I awoke in the morning. I lacked money and friends. I seldom had a good conversation. And the work I had imagined I was cut out for had proven to be beyond me.

The dryness I had felt in the seminary returned. I could no longer pray and I had no confidence in myself. For a while I thought I was headed for a nervous breakdown. I was losing weight and the headaches wouldn't cease; I thought of Nietzsche and Rilke, but the thought of them increased the intensitiy of the headaches. I was deluding myself. I lacked talent and even to be thinking about men like that in connection with myself was its own condemnation. My mother had been right; even my father had known it would happen: reality would force me to my senses.

I hated the job in the bookstore. I dreaded to think of myself spending my life as a salesman. What corporation would hire me if I lacked a college degree? And could I possibly, even remotely, imagine myself selling sewing machines or house paints or encyclopedia sets? Becoming a publisher or an editor seemed far more out of my reach than I had imagined. No one comes to you; you must fight and claw your way, by achievement. I was in the city, close to everything, with plenty of time to do my own work, and I was achieving exactly nothing. I didn't know anything—even how to write a novel, let alone how to do research in a given field. I had no expertise at all. I had been living all these years in a world of dreams.

I was determined, however, to persist. Leaving the seminary had cost me a great deal; I was not going to squander what I had gained. It was a thrill simply to eat meals at whatever hour I preferred and to come in at night at whatever hour I pleased and to go wherever my fancies led me, without thought of asking permission. It was a joy to read in bed at night until three and four a.m. I still came awake with a biological shock at five a.m., my head reeling, but now I could roll over and think that only half the night had elapsed. No, I was determined to keep working. If not this year, then next year something good would happen. Art requires an apprenticeship. To create is to make from nothing and in my emptiness I wanted, at least, a sense of not needing illusions. I could have headaches and believe I was a failure and still go on working. I did not need to promise myself success. I chose art as a way of life, and I would accept its disciplines and its aridities. If nothing ever was to come of it, still, I would have lived as I wished to live.

In May, I left New York. I craved a wider range of experience and wanted to fulfill a childhood ambition. More or less illegally,

I began hitchhiking near the George Washington Bridge. I couldn't be certain which cars were heading west, and on the approaches traffic moved too fast. I lost almost two hours and was bitter with frustration. Defeated, I decided to take the subway down to the Holland Tunnel and try there. Almost upon arrival I found a stalled truck. The driver had his foot on the starter and agreed, sourly, to give me a lift. I threw my suitcase on the seat and climbed up. He was a heavy, surly fellow, bald between wisps of curly black hair.

"Where you headin' for?" his cracked voice inquired.

"Points west."

He looked me over suspiciously. I was too well dressed to fit any of his categories. He snorted and drove in total silence until we reached Livingston, New Jersey. Suddenly the brakes squealed and the diesels backfired. "You get off here," he said. He gave no reason, and then drove off in the same direction he had been heading.

Thirty minutes later I was picked up by a muscular, handsome Italian of about thirty-five; he looked like a semiprofessional football player and he was driving a rattling, clanging, empty coal truck.

"Where to?" he asked.

"Anywhere west," I shouted over the din.

"Climb in. Headin' for Scranton."

He stopped sometime later at a diner on the brow of a hill. Green and brown valleys lay serenely in every direction; the air was hazy blue near the earth. The orange and black diner had a rough hand-painted sign out front: TRUCKERS WELCOME.

"Giulio!" the heavy waitress smiled when we sat down. She carried two scratched glasses of water.

He nodded. "How ya been?"

"You're late this mornin'. Little pussy here and there?"

"Don't be jealous, angel. They was late opening the doors. Foreman had the keys come in late. Had to wait two fuckin' hours."

She pulled a green pad from her apron. "The usual?"

He shook his head. "Black coffee. Ate breakfast already. Maybe the kid wants something."

"A piece of apple pie, please. Coffee."

"Pretty educated to be travelin' with you." Her eyes laughed and she moved away with happy flirtatious movements. "Don't let him corrupt you, boy. He's got a dirty mind!"

"Lookin' for a goose!" Giulio said quietly to me, glancing at the ceiling in exasperation and dismissing her. "Dames are all the same. Turn 'em upside once, they want it twice a day."

"See that fella, there," he said later, after we crossed the Pennsylvania line. His chin pointed toward a parked highway patrolman on the side of the road. "Thinks he's pretty fuckin' smart. They try to keep us down to fifty at nights, see. Hell, fifty miles an hour, you'll never make New York. But they got orders, *Stop those trucks.*" Just then he blew his horn and a truck going the other way blew back and the trucker stuck his hand out the window. "Me and my buddies, we have a system. Never catch us. And if they do . . ." He let go the wheel and clenched his fists: square, meaty, and covered with hair. He took the wheel again and watched me out of the corner of his eyes: "Beat the ass off one of them boys last week. Motherfucker stopped me, see, comin' down this here hill. His red light was flashin', so I pulls over, got out the other side of the cab, black as pitch. He comes round to see where I was, *pow!* Jesus, I laid into him. He was still layin' there when I left."

After I had listened to the wind blow through the open windows for a while, I finally asked, "Aren't you afraid he'll turn you in?"

"Hell no! He wants to live, don't he?" Giulio threw back his head and laughed. "Turn me in!"

I left Giulio at a cloverleaf. He turned north toward Scranton; I continued west. I walked four hundred yards in the pale, direct sun, trying to avoid the softest mud alongside the road. The breeze was cold. Cars flapped the air with their swift rush. I maneuvered for a place with a long approaching view and a good shoulder for the pick up. I was hoping that a car entering slowly on the turn from Scranton would find it easiest to stop. I waited twenty minutes, a half hour, forty minutes. The grass on the hillside rippled. I began to think how late it was and watched anxiously as the sun began to fall. When my despair reached its most sour ebb, a beige Plymouth pulled off the concrete and crunched the gravel on the shoulder. I ran to get in. It was a salesman heading for State College. His path would take me north

of Conemaugh, but I really didn't want to see my family on
this trip and decided to stay with him.

My destination was nowhere in particular. I decided I would
stay in the Middle West, driving back and forth, up and down,
for a month or two. It seemed more important to soak up scene
and atmosphere in one place than to try to visit the entire country.
The farthest west I went was Yellowstone; the farthest south
Little Rock. I spent two nights in Denver, visited Omaha, Kansas
City, St. Louis, Des Moines, the twin cities, Madison, Chicago,
Indianapolis—I saw a lot of "the heartland of America," a lot of
stockyards, a lot of corn. I liked the small towns best, and county
fairs and carnivals. Whenever I could, I made a point of sleeping
in small towns for the night, usually in a boarding house for three
dollars a night or sometimes a motel for five. I heard a lot of
plumbing growl and crack, glimpsed a lot of family worries about
inheritances and mortgages and diseases and business ventures.
You would think that with roofs over their heads and beef on the
hoof and plenty of corn, lettuce, radishes, and potatoes in the rich
soil the people of the heartlands would be expansive and free.
Instead, they seemed frugal and worried, calculating and silent,
friendly one by one but in groups suspicious of strangers. Preachers
and Bible music filled the radio waves. News programs were sparse
and brief. Korea was further from Prairie du Chien than from
New York. People described Easterners as clever, liberal, glib.
The Midwest seems to have been scarred by 1929 like the South
by the Civil War. Ads in the papers pleaded in thick black type:
RALPH ("RIP") JENSEN DOESN'T SAY HE'S CONSERVATIVE, HE'S A REAL
CONSERVATIVE. I liked the plates of pie "homemade daily" in the
cafes: blueberry, banana cream, apple, rhubarb, lemon meringue,
with the juices still clinging to the bottom of the pan. I liked the
twelve-ounce steaks you could buy for $1.50; truck drivers could
get better beef than restaurant-goers in New York. It was a different
land, a different country. Grain elevators and sky-blue water
towers, railroad tracks through the center of town and dilapidated
gray train stations with red signs announcing "Railway Express."
As summer wore on, the corn grew rapidly, dark green and shimmering in the sun. Cottontails jumped out alongside the roads, and

traffic had to slow down behind solitary tractors and wagons piled fifteen feet with sweet dry hay.

A memory often recurred. As a child I had stayed at the farm of friends of ours and gone jumping in the hay—gritty particles in the ears and down the neck, sweat rolling from our brows in the oven heat of the barn. And Anita, our friends' daughter, crying out to her mommy that Peter and I had peed on the seat of the outhouse "on purpose, so I can't go." I remembered the rows and rows of chicken houses and the thick black mud at the water hole in the pasture, pocked by cows' hooves and bent wiry reeds, and the cool mud oozing up between our toes as we inched gingerly toward the white rock from which we could swim.

The smells of manure and freshly turned earth, of wheat swayed in the fields by exhilarating ozone, of cut hay, and of sudden rains; the black thunderclouds and the fearful claps of midwestern storms; the twisters sighted in the sky and sometimes touching down to scar trees that had stood for fifty years and frame houses that had been saved from being mortgaged during the Depression —I drank deep of a thousand images. I went to the burlesque show at the county fair in Austin, Minnesota, and watched intently as lanky "Betty Bowman straight from Chicago" stripped off her flimsy clothes and tantalized white-haired, blue-eyed, red-cheeked boys and whiskery men with bumps and grinds and leg splits. A dollar to get in, another dollar to stay for "a look at the real pussy, just like you see down at the club in the wintertime," and fifty cents more for an invitation to "stand right up at the edge of the stage" and let her take your head between her naked knees while she opened up her shaved and softly shifting gates. Betty Bowman enjoyed her work and did not hate the men whose women kept their sacred sex a secret.

I attended a rodeo in Wyoming and watched Fourth-of-July fireworks in Kansas. At the Texaco station in a small town in Arkansas I saw a large sign with three appropriate arrows: MEN, WOMEN, COLORED. Outside of Omaha, I shredded the knees in my jeans helping to bring in bales of hay during a broiling hot week in late July; the cut stalks dug into my clothing and the muscles of my back and neck ached for a week. Alone and fascinated, I watched the weekly stock car races in Ottumwa, Iowa; the brightly

painted, battered new cars roared with deafening speed around the
track, filling the still evening air of the prairie with thin yellow dust.
They skidded in the turns, burned out engines and tires, and, to
the delight of the crowd, sometimes overturned and burst into
flames. A shiny maroon ambulance waited in the infield like a
suburban station wagon at a supermarket.

The three months I spent hitchhiking were among the happiest
of my life: a hiatus, a lost period, during which nothing happened
and yet every moment brought my senses to life. Far from practic-
ing "recollection," I now became greedy for sense impressions. I
learned, quietly and at my own pace, how to become a sensualist.
Paradoxically, the lessons turned my heart to God and sweetness
returned.

I heard a great deal from truck drivers and salesmen about the
sex life of the Middle West. To while away the hours on the
boring, narrow, concrete strips of highway, my drivers talked almost
incessantly of sex. A young man of twenty-one, I must have seemed
the perfect audience: ready but inexperienced—they had no idea
how inexperienced.

One salesman of asphalt and cork flooring wheedled from me the
fact that I had been in the seminary; his son, he countered, was at
St. Mary's of the Lake. He was a short dapper man in a pin-striped
suit. Given that one bond between us, he spun for hours about
his family, his club, his town. "Why we have a woman at the
club—Rosemary, that's her name—she has the hottest teats you
ever saw. For two bucks she'll give anyone a lay and, I tell you,
you just start nibbling on those nipples and she goes absolutely
mad. Don't much care for other things but just that, and it's
enough to up and almost kill her. My God, she'll give a tumble.
Now most women—take my wife—she don't appreciate that so
much—I mean they're just not that alive. But Rosemary, I tell you
bumpers hanging down to here and she'll just about to kill you
when you start on her. Bite and roll. I tell you, boy, I tell everybody, there isn't anything like it in the whole Middle West and,
like I say, I travel a good deal. I been just about everywhere."

He licked his lips and looked over at me with a slightly guilty
smile. It was hard to say if it was fantasy or truth.

I slept that night in a boarding house where there was a pretty
but very shy daughter, who had just graduated from high school.

She was wearing a frilly white blouse, with short sleeves and a low neck. She said very little when she answered the doorbell, averted her eyes later when her mother sent her up to bring me towels, and quickly turned down the hall. The ozone, the tiring ride, hot hanging teats, the pretty high school girl—Midwest abundance was too much for me and I rode the cool fluffy pillow to a poor satisfaction and fell asleep ashamed.

13

THE THUNDERSTORM SPLIT the sky just after I entered Karazov's travel agency. It was August, 1963; I was longing to return to Europe for a second time. After months of grueling routine, the thesis was finished. The defense had been formal but easy. I was sick to death of school. My glands and juices suffered creeping atrophy. The thick rain hurtled toward the hot pavement, shattered, and splashed cool draughts of air upward and through the open entrances. Blue lightning flashed through the street; instantly a rolling thunderclap exploded in the vacuum behind it, rattling the windows. The rain splattered still harder on the steaming street.

"It is ten degrees cooler already," Karazov smiled. Thin beads of sweat had gathered on his brow; his short-sleeved shirt was damp.

"No air-conditioner?" I asked.

"Out of order. I called the man three days ago. What can I do for you?"

"Rome. Leaving on the fourteenth."

"*Roma!*" he laughed, wiping a hand across the smooth scar on his cheek. "*L'amore?*"

"Unattached," I replied. "Purely business." I explained that I

wanted to write for a year and had a four-month contract with
The Liberal Catholic. He began writing out a list of possibilities.

"Look at that rain," I said. The gutters were full and sheets
of water met in the center of the street.

"A cloudburst," Karazov said and then resumed writing. "I'll
confirm you on Pan Am," he nodded, a white phone resting on
his shoulder.

When he was finished, we stood watching the rain.

"Will you stay at the Nazione again?" he asked.

"At Pensione Bianca," I replied. I gave him the street number.

"Castel Sant' Angelo," he smiled. "I lived on the other side of
the river for a year."

"I didn't know you lived in Rome."

"I worked for Radio Free Europe."

"Before you came here?"

"Just before."

"I didn't know that."

"Here you are. Everything in order. *Buon viaggio!*"

"Someday I want to talk to you about Europe. I have relatives
in Czechoslovakia. I often wonder how they are."

His smile seemed forced. "Some day," he said. "Yes, we will
talk."

The heavy rain had stopped.

"Do you think I could visit them?" I asked.

"The Communists want dollars." He rubbed two fingers together.
"Yes, you can visit them."

"Do you go back?"

He controlled his voice. "No. I cannot go back."

"I would like to go," I said. "It's a deep ambition."

Karazov nodded tersely.

"Thanks," I waved the packet. "See you in January."

He began dialing the phone again.

That evening the heat returned and the air was clammier than
ever. Al Koontz, a friend of Mario's, had invited me to a party at
his apartment on Eighty-ninth Street. I was a little tired and
went reluctantly. I hated to leave my air-conditioner. I showered,
splashed on deodorant and cologne more heavily than usual, and
took a cab. The party was a quiet one, drinks and conversation

and not too many people. We sat most of the evening, and
danced briefly around midnight. The apartment was air-condi-
tioned and the liquor was excellent. Koontz was an ad man and
had a lot of money. The girls were invariably beautiful.

"She's a man-killer, broken four engagements," Koontz whispered to me before he led me through the crowd to a girl he
wanted me to meet. "Nadya Masarik," he bowed slightly. "Jon
Svoboda." She was high cheeked and honey blond. She wore a
strapless white dress; the smooth round tops of her breasts were
bronzed.

"Are you Czech?" she asked.

"My grandparents were Slovak," I said.

"Ah, Slovak. My mother's family is from Bratislava."

"But you are Czech?"

"Yes, my father taught at Charles University."

"Excuse me," Mario interrupted. He introduced us to others.
Nadya and I were separated.

I found her powerfully attracting. Her green eyes were innocent
and deep; instinctively, one felt that she had suffered much. She
still allowed herself to be vulnerable, as if she valued pain. She
gave full attention to the person she addressed, in a self-effacing,
quiet way. I was flattered by her attention until I saw that she
offered it to everyone. I took Al's warning seriously and decided
not to pursue her. My eyes, however, kept drifting toward her.
Her legs and knees were lithe, as classically curved at a statue's.
One could catch glimpses of her tanned thighs. She was conscious
of her own sexuality, a little formal, radiating the vitality of her
breasts and hips and hands.

Once at the liquor table I had a chance to speak with her. "Have
you ever met Karel Karazov?"

"The poet?" she asked without interest, dropping ice cubes into
her tall glass. Her breasts, as she bent over, wandered in and out
of shadow; she wore no bra.

"I didn't know he was a poet." My mouth was dry and I sipped
my last drop of scotch before pouring another.

"The travel agent?" she asked.

"Yes, that's the one."

"He is well known in the Czech community." She bit a cracker.
"My father was president of the Czech Academy of Writers when

Karazov was admitted. He has written hundreds of articles. I think he has published two books of poems."

"I didn't know he was a writer," I repeated.

"After Dachau," she said, "he wrote no more poetry."

I wanted to strike a spark in her. "What sort of poetry did he write?"

"I'm not sure," she replied. "I never read it. Patriotic, I think. I was very young."

"I wonder if he still writes at night or something."

"How would he publish? In Czech? A poet cannot learn a new language overnight."

"Have you ever met him?"

"I used to hear of him in Paris."

"That's where you went to school?"

She turned questions about herself aside. "Yes." She looked across the room. "Excuse me." She offered in recompense a gentle smile.

I poured Scotch over the cracking ice and swirled the glass.

"You liked her, huh?" Mario intoned as we left.

"Who?" I pretended. I thought I had given few enough signs of interest.

"Albert knew you'd like her."

"Oh, you mean the blond."

"Oh, you mean the blond?" he mimicked.

"Who was the guy she left with?"

"That's all right, Jon. She turns them all down in the end. You'll get your turn. Don't pay too much attention to her. That fascinates her. She wins a man"—he clicked his fingers—"she drops him." He hailed a cab.

"Sounds like you've tangled with her yourself."

"Never seriously, Gianni. When a girl acts that way"—he slammed the door and we drove off—"I leave quickly. Very quickly." His voice was not convincing.

Jacob Goldblatt and a college friend of his had rented a house on the Jersey coast for two weeks. They invited me to come for a week and bring a date. There was no one around I wanted to invite. I thought of Nadya but figured she would probably say no, and besides I wasn't sure I wanted to get involved with her. The

city was steamy hot for three successive days, however, and the
weather stations kept predicting still hotter days ahead.

Jack was due to report to the army at the end of the month. He
had won high honors in his ROTC unit at Lehigh and, now that
his graduate studies were complete, was ordered to report to the
language school at Monterey for a course in Vietnamese. It looked
like the war in Vietnam would get uglier, and so the beach party
would be a rather sad one. I didn't really want to go, but I had to.
The soaring temperature, moreover, gave me an excuse to call
Nadya.

I hesitated a long time before I picked up the phone. I hated
to receive a no. I didn't know who else to call and it would be no
fun alone with two other couples, one married and the other
living together. The one thing in my favor was that Nadya knew
Jack and Olivia somewhat; she wouldn't be with total strangers.
At the moment of truth, I summoned the nerve to call. A woman's
voice answered.

"Nadya?"

"Yes."

"This is Jon Svoboda."

Silence. "Oh yes."

"Is the heat enough for you?"

"Oh, it is *ter*-rible."

More quickly now: "I have an invitation to go to the shore
next week, at Jack Goldblatt's. You know Jack and Olivia? There
will be one other couple. They would like it if you could join me."

Hesitation.

"We'll be leaving on Friday afternoon. Coming back the following Saturday."

"I had plans to—" she hesitated. "No, I can go. Thank you for
asking me."

"Would you also like to go to dinner tomorrow night?"

"I'd love to. But I'm busy. We'll see each other on Friday
afternoon?"

"Yes, we'll pick you up. At your place." Olivia had a car.

"Great. Thank you. Thank you very much. Good-bye."

"Good-bye. Looking forward to it."

Click.

I held the phone, trying to interpret her tone. I was elated that

she had agreed to come. But was it only to escape the heat? I
arose and walked around the apartment in my shorts. I very much
wanted her to like me. I couldn't understand her abruptness and
directness. Perhaps I was too polite. Or too inquisitive. I shrugged.

The beach at Orr Point was long and clean; the sand was white
and fine, dark and hard where the tide washed over it. The large
wooden cottage lay protected by the first line of dunes. There was
a redwood table on the top of the dune, from which we could
survey the silvered ocean. Jack and Olivia were very much in
love, in the throes of deciding whether to marry before Jack went
overseas; Nadya picked up the signals quickly. I noted that she
was shy in the presence of strangers. She helped the other girls in
the kitchen, but she was neither very knowledgeable nor very eager
to learn. She was willing, and did the simple tasks: slicing, peeling,
dicing, mixing salads. During most of the week she wore very
short shorts, exposing the soft flesh of her thighs and stray dark
hairs between her legs. In the intimacy of cottage living, I found
I could tease her easily; she blushed and seemed to like it. She
wasn't forward or aggressive; I found Al Koontz's description less
and less believable. She walked and sat with a quiet dignity, as if
it were a kind of coolness and distance she would like help to
overcome. Whenever I could, I took her hand or touched her—
discreetly, easily, without forcing her. And she responded: the
physical contact seemed to release her and she smiled. On the
first Saturday she slipped up behind me and grasped me around
the waist. I wrestled, uncertain who my assailant was. She was
laughing.
"What are you reading?"
"*For Whom the Bell Tolls.*"
"I like that book."
"Me, too." I read aloud the passage I was reading. Hemingway
was decribing the attributes of Maria.
We walked down the beach for almost a mile in the thin silver
mirror of the receding tide. She was wearing a white bikini. Her
breasts were firm and round, though not especially large; her
buttocks were soft and rounded and when she walked a few steps
ahead while I bent over to skip a rock on the sea, between her
legs there flashed a triangle of light, a curve of soft flesh. She let

me take her fingers. We talked about our very different child-
hoods, and I wondered how like hers mine might have been, had
my family not fled to America.

I was surprised how many American novelists she had read; it
had been, she said, her way of learning English. She had heard
Sartre lecture in Paris and had, through his famous essay, learned
an especial love for Faulkner.

At the end of the beach, near a dune that ran into the sea, we
turned to walk back. Our earlier tracks wandered from side to side.
I had enjoyed the conversation so much that I wanted to express
it. I lifted her fingers and we stopped. We were sheltered from
sight by a curve in the beach and by a jetty of boulders. I studied
her face and asked, "Do you mind?"

She didn't answer. I leaned forward and, as lightly as I could,
kissed her lips. They were soft and cool. We walked most of the
way home in silence.

The next day, we went to mass with the Ryans. Tom Ryan had
been Jack's roommate at Lehigh; he was a very conservative Irish
Catholic from Philadelphia and now a stockbroker in New York.
His wife Agnes was nervous, somewhat catty, but pleasant; Tom
was big and blustery and argumentative. I was surprised to see the
depth of Nadya's piety; I would have thought that anyone who
looked so good in a bikini would have held the Catholic Church
fairly cheap. She had, she said, belonged to the Young Catholic
Students at the Sorbonne, and made the pilgrimage on foot to
Chartres every year.

We went out in a small boat that afternoon. The hot sun
spangled on the blue shifting water. About three o'clock, white
breakers began to appear. Nadya enjoyed the slap of the waves
upon the boat and laughed when they almost tipped us over. She
rowed bravely and indefatigably. I watched the brown skin stretch
over her spinal cord, and watched the muscles shift in her buttocks
and thighs. The boat tipped over, caught sideways by a wave, just
as we were nearing shore. She came up with water streaming from
her hair. I swam to retrieve one of the oars; she clung to the boat.
We pulled it onto the beach and she turned and ran into the blue-
violet sea, leaping into an oncoming wave. Her brown legs flashed
and disappeared. I followed after her, my legs fighting the knee-
high resistance of the water, dived, and tried to grab her waist. She

wriggled free. I pursued and ducked her. She got her fingers on my collarbone and pulled me over with her.

"You play too rough," she said when she came up. "Too rough!" But the accusation was a ruse, and she used my hesitation to slip free. "You'll never catch me." She dived under water and swam away. I caught her again; we kissed, the clear rubbery kiss of ocean-wet lips, except that we pressed our tongues into each other's mouths.

I debated whether to ask her to sleep with me. We had been assigned to separate rooms—she had a bedroom and I was sleeping on a cot in the lodge room near the fireplace—but no one would object if we ended up together; it was almost understood. Still, I hardly knew her and I liked her and I didn't want to ask something she might refuse. She didn't seem to mind my holding her when we sat around the fire in the evenings. She let my hands fondle her breasts, and allowed them to slip lightly across her thighs and settle on the smooth flesh between her legs; when she had had enough, she'd lightly lift my hand away. She seemed unworried and unhurried, and I had a strong presentiment—which maybe did or didn't square with Al Koontz's suggestion—that she was a virgin. My theory was that, at twenty-six, she was rather careful and tough. She had been very much in love; she had come to America through the efforts of a French student to whom she had been engaged. She gave back his ring before their first Christmas in America. I had the feeling—rightly or wrongly—that she didn't like being wooed too swiftly, as if she had endured someone pawing and pressing her, as if she needed time to breathe. She wanted, perhaps, to come with her head as well as her body. Over twenty-five, girls seem to grow to hate their bodies, to fear their smells, to divide sharply into mind and body, desire and reserve. It is easier to deal with girls who have not taken time to think.

During the past school year, I had slept with eight or nine different girls; their hair hung on my belt (as mine on theirs). I had expelled an evil spirit from my fantasy. I had explored what I had to explore—I knew different bottoms and different breasts. I knew what they could do. I was looking for the girl who was capable of love, not the love that assuages loneliness, for there is no love like that, but a love that strikes the center of the soul, a love that allows you to be free.

I decided not to hurry Nadya. I was willing to take a chance on her. When she mentioned that she was thinking of visiting her mother in Paris for a month, I strongly supported the idea. I couldn't see Vittoria again; done is done. And Rome without Nadya would come to seem bleak. From Paris to Rome was a mere skip across the Alps; we could have such fun in Rome. Nadya was working for an economics research institute in New York, and the project she had been working on was just concluded. She didn't like the work and was thinking of quitting; she had been saving her money to take half a year off.

"I don't know what I want to do," she confessed to me on one of our walks. "I seem so tired of everything. Statistics and numbers and probabilities, it's all a game, a game, a game!" She pulled a piece of grass apart as she talked. "I really hate economic theory."

"How did you get into it?"

"It seemed exciting when I began. I was using it philosophically, to build theories of class and behavior. In this country, economics is a branch of statistics. It makes me feel like an engineer."

"What else would you like to do?"

"I don't know. I just don't know what to do."

"Ever thought of marriage?"

"Don't say anything about that, please. I'm a failure at things like that. I've tried. But somehow I can't bring myself to do it." She flung the remnants of the dark grass to the winds and smiled wanly. "I suppose I'm afraid or something. When men get too close I want to run."

"Are you afraid of me?"

"You haven't come too close. Yet."

"But you might run?"

"I might."

"Then I better not come too close." I was aware of her haltered breasts and her naked legs; I was too aware. "That makes a dilemma, doesn't it? If I don't come closer, we'll just be friends."

She shrugged. "I wish it didn't."

I wondered how confused she was. What was I getting into? Yet her eyes were direct and her speech honest.

"Are you going to leave me?" she asked. Her eyes searched mine. "You should. You really should. I'm not good for men. You've probably heard that. I don't know what gets into me."

I was uncertain what to say. "You can't be a scared rabbit all your life. Let things go slowly."

"You mean that, don't you?"

"Yes."

"I wish I could believe it."

Nadya was a tall girl, not much shorter than I. She liked to tie her hair in a ponytail; almost always a red or blue ribbon was riding on it. Her ears were perfectly wrought; her mouth and teeth were delicate. On her right cheek there was a small black mole, a beauty spot like the red dot the married women of India paint between their eyes. Occasionally when she was nervous, Nadya's fingers touched the spot. She bit her nails, not to the skin but evenly. She often had an upset stomach and kept breath-sweeteners near to hand. While we were at the beach, her period came but there was no noticable diminution of her energy and no complaint; one afternoon she took a nap, a practice customary for most of us because of our late nights but unusual for her. She ate sparingly, vegetables mostly and sweets not at all.

On the last night all three couples sat around the fire on the empty beach. The cool breeze carried in the smells of salt and sun-baked weed, smells through which the human race entered into life. Pin-point, blue-white stars filled the entire heavens. A driftwood log on the fire, translucent as a reddened ingot, heaved and fell, showering sparks into the night. Thin yellow flames broke forth, alternately blue and then a settled orange again. Jack Gold-blatt played softly on his guitar; Olivia sang snatches of Israeli songs in a piercing, sad voice. They had one more night together before he left. It did not seem just, in a world purportedly committed to rationality, that so many young men should still be entering armies sprawled across the globe. We cursed the cold war. We accepted its inevitability as the skeletal structure of our lives; we had never had the experience of peace. I shifted weight and brushed off the sand embedded in my left hand.

"Sing us a Czech song," Agnes Ryan pleaded. "A sad Czech song."

Nadya's cheeks flushed. "I can't. I don't sing."

"Sure you do," Jack contradicted. "We all hear you when you're in the shower."

"You do?" Her hand flew to cover her face.

Jack strummed a polka. "What about that? Can you dance?"

"What about it?" I raised her fingers and we both stood up. Tom, Agnes, and Olivia clapped. We tried to lift our feet and swirl but our feet dug into the sand and several times one or the other stumbled. Soon everyone was laughing even more than they were clapping. Just as we were yielding to exhaustion the ball of my foot struck a sharp rock. We collapsed in laughter, but my foot began to ache and I lifted it to see the gash. It wasn't serious. I rubbed it gently and tied my handkerchief around it to keep out the sand. The bone throbbed. Agnes went into the house to bring out another bottle of scotch and a bucket of ice. I tied a piece of ice in my handkerchief and placed it against the cut.

The conversation drifted into tête-à-têtes between those seated next to one another. Sparks exploded from the fire. I leaned back upon my elbows and gazed into the countless stars, while Tom Ryan talked to Nadya. Soon I lay flat on my back, rested my head on a towel, and watched the stars sweep up out of the sea and into the heavens.

"I hear you're an economist."

"Yes."

"Are you interested at all in business cycles?"

"Yes."

He began to ask her technical questions about the future of the economy. Her answers were impressive; she drew upon examples from France, Sweden, Switzerland, and Germany.

"What precisely do you do?" Tom asked.

"I've been doing a study of the probable effects of optical scanning devices on banks, post offices, airlines, things like that."

Tom's attention picked up. He asked her pointed questions about two or three companies. She knew the companies and the exact state of the art in each. As they talked, I traced a line from Orion's Belt upwards to a brilliant star I couldn't name. The speed of light, the length of time, burned itself into my emotions. I thought of Father Juan. I wondered how he was.

The voices of Tom and Nadya became clear again. The conversation had shifted to politics. All week Jack and I had been trying to avoid the subject because the Ryans were conservative Nixon Republicans who thought Martin Luther King was a racist and a demagogue, and George Wallace a responsible, mis-represented statesman. Tom finally violated the week's taboo: "I hate all the Kennedys." He pulled his cigar from his mouth. "But Bobby is my first choice. I hate him most."

"Why?" Nadya asked.

"Ruthless. Unscrupulous. A dangerous man."

Nadya said quietly: "What difference does it make, Nixon or Kennedy? Neither one has any control over military spending. America is the number one danger to world peace, no matter what leadership you have."

"*You*—a Czech—say that?" Tom sputtered.

"Yes."

"I—I can't understand . . ." he waved his cigar.

"The United States is stronger than Russia and China combined. Who has built atomic bases in every continent of the world? You. Which is the only country that has used nuclear weapons? You. I agree with Sartre. The United States is mankind's greatest threat."

"I just don't understand," Tom Ryan said. His mouth gaped and his eyes were wide. Others, too, were listening.

"Why is Jack going to Vietnam?" Nadya asked quietly. "To defend San Francisco against a fleet of junks?"

The discussion lasted over an hour. Tom Ryan became pro-gressively more shocked. Quietly, firmly, Nadya denied almost every assumption he cherished about human life. She tried to explain to him about the workers' councils in Czechoslovakia, but he could not follow her.

"Was I too hard on him?" she asked as we walked back through the sand afterwards.

"Not at all. You were marvelous."

"There is a certain tone of voice I hate," she said, bumping into me as we walked. "It makes me livid."

"You seemed so calm."

"I was far from calm."

"You were beautiful."

"You're not angry then?"

"Not at all."

The next day Jack drove us to New York and left us off down-town so that he and Olivia could drive directly to Long Island to visit relatives. I took Nadya home in a cab.

"I've decided to go," she said as we stood outside her apartment.

"You have! That's great."

"I'll see you at the end of October."

"Not before?"

"For dinner?" Roguish dimples flashed in her cheeks.

"Tomorrow."

We kissed and she hurried up the stairs of the brownstone.

"Some broad!" the cabbie said.

Not yours. "Hundred sixteenth, please." For the first time everything was working together. I would try out my hand at writing for a year. And satisfy a restless wanderlust. And Nadya would be there too! I didn't feel worthy. In my imagination, I saw her dressed in white: dignity, confidence, talent, beauty. Strong feelings pressed against my ribs. My God, I loved her then!

The evening before I left New York I had a long talk with Karel Karazov. I stopped by the office to pick up my tickets; he invited me out for a drink. I had to leave early to see Nadya, but at least I had a chance to see him a little and to learn something about him. He described what Dachau had been like. He was eighteen when he entered, twenty-one when he walked out the gates and headed for Prague.

"They wanted to take from us the feeling that we were persons." He ran his hand back through his long straight hair. In his neat suit and gold arrow cufflinks, drinking in a black-leather cocktail lounge, Karazov seemed like anything but a former prisoner in Dachau. The smooth scar upon his cheek and the exaggerated caution of his speech came closest to suggesting the truth. "Besides the filth and the dirt, there was organized absurdity. We counted for nothing. Absolutely nothing. Once a guard hit me as I cleaned the toilets. I was never told what I had done. When I awoke I was bleeding against the wooden seat. I was dragged out and thrown into a covered pit. Then they took me back with the others." He pursed his lips in an expression of puzzlement.

"Do you expect to see Czechoslovakia free again?" I asked.

He looked into the distance. He rubbed his bent index finger against his nose to cover a twitching of his cheek. "I?" he asked quietly. "Myself?" He gazed over my shoulder again. "I do not hope to see it. But we must work." Quite smoothly, he corrected himself. "Each in his way. We must hope and we must work.

We cannot abandon the others." He looked me full in the eye. "You have relatives there. You cannot abandon them. You have no right to live as you do while they are in danger."

"I thought—" I wasn't sure how to put it. "I thought there was very little danger. It is not so different from Austria, is it?"

He frowned and tried not to let scorn creep into his eyes. "So long as Russia stands over us. There are right-wing elements in Russia, too."

"And also in Prague."

"And also in Prague."

"Bratislava even more."

He smiled. "In any case, there is little freedom. Anywhere."

When I left him, I was afraid for him. I thought he might be sorry for talking so openly. It was part of my code not to pry. Karel was in and out of the hospital for mysterious ailments, and except for his candor of appearance I didn't know him well enough to be certain where he stood.

mediterranean II

◆◇◆◇◆◇◆◇◆◇◆◇◆◇◆◇◆◇◆◇◆◇◆◇◆◇◆◇◆◇◆◇◆◇◆◇◆◇◆

*"In each period, there is a general form
of the forms of thought; and, like the air
we breathe, such a form is so translucent,
and so pervading, and so seemingly
necessary, that only by extreme effort can
we become aware of it."*

—ALFRED NORTH WHITEHEAD

14

MY THOUGHTS DRIFTED lazily as I watched a heavy American bishop push an envelope into the red postal box on St. Peter's Square. Does grace work even when a bishop licks the gummed flap of an envelope addressed to a building contractor? Despite myself (it was a crisp, glorious day), I yawned and looked at my watch. I had been in Rome for nearly eighteen hours, and had slept through most of them. Signorina Bianca had held a room open for me, a room with a view of Castel Sant' Angelo across the green cypresses.

The sun made the gray stones of Saint Peter's brilliant; the weathered columns of Bernini gleamed. It pressed upon the fabric of my blue suit and made me warm. Part of me longed for a hammock and a lazy afternoon, but another part already sought the delights of Rome. My blood ran faster. The spraying foun-

tains evoked dark, sensuous musings; the air awakened a slumber
in my bones. My eyes were constantly stirred; my ears heard
subtle sounds. My flesh lives a different life in Rome.

I thought of Vittoria and wondered if by chance I would meet
her; I hoped not. It could not be the same. I was not the same
man of a year ago.

I rested my hand upon the wooden barricade; several hundred
tourists had gathered to watch the exodus from the first meeting
of the Council. Far away across the stone piazza, beyond the
obelisk and its slender shadow, beyond the twin glistening fountains, above the wide white steps, the great bronze doors under
the portico hung firmly shut. I had been unable to arrive for the
solemn opening. I was glad enough to be here for the initial
business sessions. Nadya had been hard to leave. We had spent
the last three days almost constantly together.

The Angelus was being tolled by St. Peter's bulb-tongued bells
and echoed by other bells. The bells said that Nadya loved me. I
was sure of that. Yet she also held back. I was drawn to her—I
needed her. But as a challenge? As a test? I didn't understand my
motives or my purposes. I wanted to know why I loved, to measure
the quality of my love, because I wanted my love for her to stick.
I wanted desperately to have a permanent and ever-growing love, a
love without end or limit. I didn't want a "realistic love," satisfaction with an unsatisfactory relationship, a mutilation of expectations and hopes. If love does not mean hope, it is not love. Love
is infinite in possibility.

I longed to see Nadya, to have her near. I longed for the moment
of nakedness between us. At night when I awoke my empty arms
ached for her. Until she arrived, I would have to savor the crystal
October air alone, and try to get my job under control.

Reporters were not admitted into the basilica for the morning
sessions, and all the information of interest, I was informed, could
better be gathered in private conversations and press conferences
later in the day. I could rise at nine or ten, write for an hour or
two, and then have the rest of the day to gather material as I
pleased. My expense account was not large, but I had already
determined to spend my salary as I earned it. A Council happens
only once in a century, and I might never have a chance again to
come to Rome. Shouts from the crowd, like a low sigh, signaled

the swinging outward of the great portals, and a slow tide of black, gray, white, and purple spilled through the doors and down the great steps into the piazza. Fleets of busses began to stir and some pulled nearer the basilica. Sleek black cars sped more important prelates, fingers raised in blessing, from the steps. Then, finally, the loaded busses heaved and groaned through the crowds. Wedged two by two into their seats like awkward and embarrassed schoolboys, the bishops looked a trifle odd in lace surplices, jeweled rings, golden pendants, and colored hats. Some bishops blessed the crowd with one hand and held a wispily smoking Players or Camel or Gauloise in the other. The state of episcopal stomachs and nerves would, plainly, be as important as theology in deciding the outcome of the Council.

"Jon! Jon Svoboda!" someone called. I turned. It had been a woman's voice but I couldn't find the face. "Jon!" she called again. I pushed past three hefty German women.

"Marilou Prescott!" I said, glad to see a friendly face. "What brings you here? I thought you'd be in Paris."

"No," she said, "We came to Rome. At least I did." She looked a little tired, perhaps a little older.

"Free for lunch?"

She calculated. "Yes. I know a place nearby." We pushed through the crowds. She led me to an upstairs restaurant four blocks from the piazza. The walls were whitewashed, the balcony was open, and a large green metal fan kept a pleasant draught circulating.

"Where are you staying?" I asked jovially. "It's great to meet a pretty girl your first day in town."

Marilou's eyes narrowed and she waved the teasing aside. "Jack helped me to find a place. Then he flew back to Paris. In a bit of a huff, I think."

"Oh?" I said to fill the silence. I didn't want to pry. "His thesis is coming along?"

"He's given that up," she said, "Now he's in analysis. Says he can't write on sexuality until he's been analyzed." She swept her eyes to the ceiling, then tilted her soup bowl. "He wants to show that Freud was a misogynist. He doesn't think a man has ever written adequately about the sexuality of women."

"That's probably true."

She was silent. "What brings you to the Eternal City?"

"*The Liberal Catholic* asked me to cover the Council. Paid my way over, plus expenses. I finished my thesis and it was accepted—"

"Doctor Svoboda!" She reached her hand across the table.

"My friends can call me *professore*," I replied modestly. "I finished my thesis, and decided that a year in Europe was exactly what I needed before taking a position. Turned down Berkeley, though."

"Then it's all off with whatever her name was?"

I probably blushed.

"Still a virgin?" she added.

"Trying, you know."

She laid her hand in mine. "Take a tip from Marilou. Go slow."

"Yes, mother."

"Just see you don't forget it." She brushed back her brown hair and reflected. "You're covering the Council. You've got to try to get yourself invited to Joe Metzger's parties."

"Who's Joe Metzger?"

"He works in the Congregation of Religious, and he knows everyone in Rome. He's been here fifteen years and, anyway, you have to meet him. Here's his card. No, I have another one, go ahead. You ought to have your own cards printed up. Take one of mine, too."

"What's this? The *Grand Rapids Witness?*"

"Joe fixed me up as a correspondent. It gives me something to do."

"You used to live in Grand Rapids, didn't you?"

"Originally."

"You don't have to sound so sad about it."

"It's a long ways away and a long time ago."

"Your folks still live there, don't they?"

She shrugged and burst into tears. I never know what to do when girls cry. I couldn't help looking around to the other tables and reached for my handkerchief. I hated to say anything like "There, there." I waited in silence.

"I'm sorry," she said. "I don't know what got into me." She used my handkerchief. The waiter brought our main course. I scratched my fingernail idly on the rough texture of the tablecloth; the napkins, which had been washed overnight, were not quite dry. The waiter set my plate in place, poured more red wine for both of us, and left.

"It's good to be back in Rome!" I said contentedly.

"Good to see you again, Jon." She tipped her glass to me, her eyes still shiny. We drank.

Hesitantly, then, she gave me the name of another priest I had to be sure to meet. "He knows Vatican politics inside out. He's quite a character." She seemed to be studying me to see if I knew who she meant. "His name is Father Georges, George P. Georges."

"George-Georges?" I grinned.

She blushed. "He's a Dominican. He teaches at the Angelicum, but he's really an existentialist. The Holy Office keeps an eye on him."

"They keep an eye on everybody."

"Oh, but he's unusual . . ." She stopped herself and managed to smile. "You'll see for yourself. He knows what's going on. Ask him about the statement on the Jews."

I wrote down his name and number. She gave it from memory.

"I see I'll have to get my own directory."

"Indispensable," she said.

"What—" I tried to be tentative. "What do you see happening at the Council? I'm trying to get a hang on things."

"What's happening?" She made a tiny ball of dough from the inside of a roll and pressed it with her fingers. "Why, it's pretty obvious," she said. "There's a new third force coming into shape. Moscow and Constantinople and Rome—the ancient patriarchs across the center of the world."

I thought she was putting me on. But she was serious. I let her talk a while longer, but she did not add substantially to what she had said. It was a very bold hypothesis and I wondered where she had dreamed it up. It reminded me, crazy as it was, to try various presuppositions. I hoped Jack or someone would read in advance whatever she sent to the *Grand Rapids Witness*.

Afterwards I called a taxi for her.

"I have a Fiat," she apologized. "But I loaned it to a friend who smashed it up." She tried to smile but failed. "I hope it's fixed when Jack returns."

"When are you expecting him?"

"He didn't say." She tried to look warm and affectionate. "Thanks for lunch." She pulled my sleeve. "Do you see that man over there?"

"What man?"

"The one in gray."

"Yes." He was an American, about fifty, slight of build; he looked like a real estate agent or small businessman.

"He used to work for the CIA. He had poison thrown in his face one night in his *pensione*."

I thought she was kidding. "How do you know?"

"From a friend of his. He's retired now." Her face brightened. "It's a great city. See you soon."

Her figure was blurred behind the windows of the green taxi. It roared suddenly away, surrounding me with dry, acrid fumes.

Later that afternoon, when I figured his siesta was completed, I called Father Georges. I was intrigued by the tone of voice Marilou had used in describing him. Besides, stories were already forming in my mind, and I needed a source of inside information; it would be a great coup to have better stories than experienced journalists from *The New York Times*, the *Baltimore Sun*, and the news magazines. I felt new and untried and uncertain of how to proceed. Signorina Bianca helped me past the first obstacle—the Rome telephone system and the slow, casual obstinacy of the receptionists at hotels and colleges. After two tries—she was cut off once—she said *"Qui"* and called me closer to take the receiver. *"Ecco, Padre Georges."*

"Hello."

"Hello."

"Padre Georges?"

"Siiii." The voice was mellow and rich.

"This is Jonathan Svoboda. I'm covering the Council for *The Liberal Catholic*. Do you know the magazine?"

"Oh yes. Indeed. Capital journal. Best in the world, I would think. Of its kind."

"Yes, well—Marilou—Mrs. Prescott is an old friend of mine and she insisted that I call you. I'd be delighted if we could meet."

"Marilou Prescott? Yesss!" The emotional tone suggested that Marilou was possibly just a woman who annoyed him. "Well, yes."

He was thinking very quickly. The syllables came slow, calm, and controlled, and then he began speaking very rapidly. "Yes. Yes, of course. What would you propose? But you see tonight would be out because—I'm not well, really. A bit of an accident. Nothing serious. Walked into a door. A-ha! No, that's not it, of course. Man carrying a ladder swung it around and hit my eye. Ho! Just a bit of a bruise on the noggin, nothing more. Friend of mine calls it my *apertura alla sinistra*, ha-ha! A bullet in the head from the Holy Office. So it can't be tonight. I'm still in bed, you see. Too bloody bad. I should like to see you, really."

"I was thinking about dinner. But we could—"

"It can't really be tonight. Too bloody bad. For I should really like to see you. But this bloody bop on the head gives me a bit of a headache, you know. Doctor says to sleep it off a day or so. You know this fellow just hit me with that ladder—no, that's not it— but it is quite a gash, you see."

"I didn't want to call at this late hour. But I—"

"Say, could you do this? Give me a tinkle in a day or two? I really can't make it tonight. Jolly good of you to call. Do ring me up later in the week. Thank you. Good-bye."

I held the receiver for several seconds after the loud click at the other end. I hadn't been, I was sure, insistent or offensive. I shrugged my shoulders. It might not even have been the right man. Still, there couldn't be too many English Dominicans in Rome. And the accent, the language; he spoke English like a put-on for Americans, like a man falling click-click into a part.

The next day Signorina Bianca called me from my room to take a call from someone at the Dominican house. He said Father Georges would like to meet me for dinner at eight-thirty at Il Buco, and gave me the address. I agreed, though I had made casual plans to meet with Bill Atkins of AP and Jerry Frisbe of the *Times*. I phoned Atkins at his hotel and left a message. I went back and lay down on the bed, wondering what George Georges was going to be like. But soon my thoughts strayed to the honey-blond Nadya and the green irises in her lovely eyes and her limitless energy. I saw her in her white bikini, classic and supple, a slight largeness in the hips—very Slavic, a large-boned girl. I was reading aloud to her; she liked to hear the words against the rolling of the sea.

I had a hard time finding Il Buco. It turned out to be an obscure cul-de-sac in a maze of narrow medieval streets. Two boys in torn gray undershirts were burning sticks from broken fruit baskets against the stone walls; sweet white smoke twisted into the pink sky. The evening stillness had descended on the city, it was after the *tramontana* had passed, and the beams and roof edges of century-old buildings seemed etched in zinc against the sky. The cul-de-sac was narrow and without a light. The doorway was so like the others that at first I walked past it. I returned and cautiously parted the plastic streamers. A white-coated waiter, his black hair shining, waved me inside. The room was cool and small, painted entirely in white. A large painting in the sensuous violets and reds of the ottocento, depicting Bacchus and nymphs and apples and stuffed pigs and classical flowers, hung upon each wall. There were tiny lights at the base of each painting and flickering blue candles on the linen-covered tables. I peered carefully into the corners for a clerical figure; I seemed to be the sole patron of the evening. A young man in a blue cashmere sweater glided in and said, "Good evening," in perfect English. He escorted me toward a corner table—there were only four tables in the first room.

"I'm to meet Padre Georges here at eight-thirty."

"Ah, Padre Georges!" he smiled. "The second room. His favorite table." The table was on an angle that provided a view of the front door without itself being visible. A tiny orange flame leaped from the incandescent red coals of a fireplace. The tablecloth felt damp. Across the two stone rooms, a little electric heater glowed red beside the front door.

"Cocktails?" the young man in the sweater asked me. He looked like a sports-car driver, a gourmet, in the easiest, most disciplined Italian manner.

"A martini," I replied. "Very dry."

"New York dry," he smiled and turned to call a harsh order to the waiter—an instantaneously different tone of voice. He went to a corner of the room, switched on a turntable, and carefully handled a black disc. It gleamed violet in the light reflected from a painting. Soon the strains of American dinner music, played perhaps by the Boston Pops, totally and precisely filled the room. The young man apologized. "Sorry. You will like this better."

He gently lifted the arm of the magnificent equipment, removed the disc, and selected another. "Corelli," he smiled. The sounds of violins raced heavily into the still room. He was as pleased as a discriminating clerk in a men's store. "For Americans," the young man said, "I play Gershwin, Rodgers, Waring. It surprises them. For myself, I prefer Corelli. Please enjoy yourself. The boy will have your martini in a moment. I have taught him how to make it. If it is not dry enough, send it back. I insist." He left as quickly as he had entered, and I was not sure exactly where the kitchen lay.

I had almost finished my martini. Still Father Georges had not arrived. There were so many ways the message could have been in error that I decided to order at nine-thirty. I was restless and impatient. Twenty minutes later, in an ill temper, I was just about to order when a priest in long white robes stepped through the door. He had a bandage on his head. He was shorter and heavier than I had expected, round faced and jolly and cherubic. The robes and the round face made him seem chubby; his torso was solidly built and tough. His hands were soft and pink, and his cheeks were flaming red from the exertion of hurrying—very Anglo-Saxon cheeks, quick to reveal the currents of blood.

"*Enchanté*, Mr. Svoboda. *Enchanté*." He shook hands absently, putting the soft warm flesh out in the air to be shaken while his eyes surveyed the room, clear blue eyes that could be at once ingenuous and clever, limpid yet veiled. He sat down and gazed into my eyes. His thin rimless glasses were proper for a clergyman, a scholar, a gentle soul who would be disturbed to see a moth crushed; but one could also see that he enjoyed life. He ordered sauces whose names I didn't know, and chose a bottle of rare French wine. The dinner was to cost more than forty dollars, almost the whole of my weekly meal allowance, which he made no effort to pay; he graciously nodded when, at last, I took the bill in hand.

He talked for over two hours, almost nonstop. I barely had the opportunity to ask him leading questions. He theorized about the Council in global terms, described Vatican personalities and politics with such gusto that the contradictions which emerged seemed somehow unimportant. I began to wonder how much of what he was telling me would stand up in print. (I was, I soon

realized, using him; I perceived him almost exclusively in terms of
how his words would fit my column.) When I pointed out
contradictions in some of the observations he made—Cardinal
Ottaviani was the leader of the conservatives; Cardinal Ottaviani
was not the leader—he was momentarily irked. His style was not
fact and not fantasy either; it was a mixture of intuitive genius,
alertness to the power of myth and drama, a flair for humor and
eccentricity, an astute judgment of character. He read every
event on three or four levels: what the public was told, what informed people thought, what the principals intended, and what
was at stake. "How often do historical agents," he asked, "perceive
the meaning of their deeds? *'Tis a divinity that shapes our ends,
roughhew them as we might.'* A good reporter must begin with
that," he waved a finger at me. He relished playing spiritual
counselor to journalists. His baby-blue eyes peered at me through
the rimless glasses, over the sauces. "The larger lines of drama are
prefigured, you see, in the unconscious of the race. You have to
know your typology, really. What is *Time* magazine? A morality
play, isn't it? And the communiqués of your Department of
Defense?"

"I don't quite understand that," I said soberly.

"Take the three Romes of the ancient world," he said. *"Here"*—
he pointed downward as if I were especially dense—"Constantinople, Moscow." He lifted three pudgy fingers. "There in a
trinity is the shape of our future, types that like magnets attract
the dust of events into the grand shapes of history. Rome against
Moscow, the central struggle." He bent two fingers downward.
"The synthesis to be achieved through Constantinople. That's the
significance of the Second Vatican Council. That's what a con-
scientious reporter, like yourself, must convey to the people."

He was so patently sincere that the strangeness of the concepts
did not prevent them from impressing me, even moving me—
like the excitement of detecting unrecognized presuppositions and
coming to a wholly fresh awareness. He had such a strong personality that I felt drawn into his own mystical, historical vision.
Only later, at some distance, could I shake myself free and ask
on what evidence did he assert what he asserted; what new facts
did his hypotheses explain, or explain more adequately, than more
familiar views.

In the end, I decided that I liked him but would not print *any-thing* he told me as a fact unless I could find independent verification. He would be immensely useful as a stimulant to my imagination and as a source of colorful detail and mood. And he would be a lot of fun to be around—if not to take to dinner. I recognized now where Marilou's theories were coming from, and had learned a little better how to interpret what she might say. I had a line on several significant Vatican personalities I had not known of, who would be worth knowing. And I had two specific pieces of information: there was a conflict shaping up on the Council floor between the four more or less progressive moderators appointed by Pope Paul VI and other sources of authority within the Council; and Amleto Cardinal Cicobelli, the new Secretary of State, was now (so Father Georges said) adamantly opposed to the passage of the schema on the Jews. Cicobelli was doing everything possible to defeat it, to postpone it, or at the very least to render it as ineffectual as possible.

"He knows, better than most, the importance of the Arab nations in the future. They stand between Moscow and Rome. He is the moving spirit of the Council. He is the one to watch."

"Not Ottavielli?"

"Ottavielli is a serious, sincere man. He is not a conspirator. He is not a politician."

"Cicobelli."

Father Georges nodded somberly.

We rose to leave soon after that, in something of a hush. Father Georges had performed and now was tired; I was unable to evaluate the new perspective he introduced, and many of the questions I had planned to ask were now not germane. I walked through the quiet, echoing streets for almost an hour after leaving him, both in order to absorb the conversation and to enjoy the mild evening. The air was cool and moist. The streetlights of Rome are soft, not harsh, and the bowl shaped by the Apennines seems to concentrate the light of the stars upon the city. "One thing I'm certain of," I smiled to myself. "He is the oddest, least amorous man I know."

I liked to sort out the dozens of smells I could detect in Rome: cold marble and rough granite and soft travertine. Fruits and fish remains. Urine on a wall. The river and the warm breath of the sycamores and pines. The invisible smoke arising from charcoal. Broken pinewood boxes. The heavy choking dioxide of busses. Chestnuts roasted in tin cans by old men in heavy tweed clothing. Horses' dung fresh and steaming on the stone streets.

My head was light and free, liberated by the table wine, the dessert wine, and the Sambuca he had ordered, from too much analysis and careful thought. Associations flowed. Leaning on a balustrade over the Tiber, listening to the backfires of taxis and motorbikes, hearing a young couple laugh as they walked, my feelings grew nostalgic and sad. I was doing what I liked. I was free—free to walk at night, free to do what I preferred. And Nadya was coming soon, very soon. Even the premonitions sighing in the rustling, ancient trees did not disturb my equanimity. I inhaled deeply of the night. In Rome one believes easily that each moment is to be lived for its own sake and that each day has its sufficient evil. The philosophy of the Stoics seeps from the stones their generation set in place.

15

ON OCTOBER 3, unannounced, Jack Prescott appeared in town. I saw him pushing through the lobby as I came up the stairs after a press conference in the basement of the USO building. He said he had to hurry to an appointment on the other side of the city but would call me soon. He had large circles under his eyes and looked like a man who has been driving himself too hard.

Then on Sunday night I met him again at a party at Father Metzger's, a pleasant, three-room apartment in a modern, tree-lined section of the city. I was relieved to find him in better health and spirits than I had expected. He spoke excitedly of his

analysis. "It's really painful," he said quietly. "Makes you as
depressed as hell, sometimes. But I'm getting somewhere! I
really am. You learn a lot about yourself." He raised a hand
from his bourbon glass and tapped my chest. "You really should
try it, Jon. You'd appreciate it." His black eyes flashed. "Do you
some good, too. Remove some inhibitions."

I wanted to tell him that I was a different man. And that it
was no longer a matter of talking but of deeds. But I didn't
have to justify myself to him. I asked him about his thesis at the
Sorbonne.

"It's pretty hard to write anything when you're in analysis. I
write a little, then I see everything differently and want to rip
it up. You'd be surprised what your writing says, when you look
at it analytically. You should try it, Jon."

"You won't finish it this year?" I continued.

"Probably never. I'll do a book instead. I have three volumes
planned, and I've written, say, two hundred pages. I'm never
going to teach. But if I wanted to, a thick book would give me
the credentials."

"Maybe," I said.

"I think so. Have you heard from Eddie? Not to change the
subject or anything."

"He left the order. I saw him in New York. Then he just
disappeared. He went out to Cincinnati last fall to settle his
affairs. That's the last I heard."

"I really liked that guy. . . . Say, this is Joe Metzger, another
inhibited cleric. Have you met?"

Joe Metzger was wearing a blue sport shirt open at the collar,
where a worn, thin T-shirt was exposed. He was of medium
height, about forty-five; his black wavy hair was graying handsomely
at the fringes. He was shaved so clean, his cheeks seemed rosy and
adolescent. His brown eyes were intelligent, and his deep voice
friendly and suave.

"Yes, I met Jon when he came in. Enjoying yourself?"

"Very much. Thanks for inviting me. Impressive group." I
lifted my glass in gesture.

"Where's George-Georges?" Jack ran the names together in a
slightly mocking way.

"Oh, he'll be here. The party's never complete until he gets

here. Everybody's waiting to pick his brain. There's a big battle
behind the scenes, and everybody wants to know who's involved.
George is the only one who knows all the chambermaids and
secretaries."

"He's a slimy bastard!" Jack commented with a smile.

"Excuse me a moment while I do my duties as host." Metzger
nodded to me and stepped between us to go to the door.

"It's a club," Jack said, "a goddam private club." He nodded
toward the room full of priests and bishops. Three or four women,
including Marilou, and five or six laymen, mostly journalists, kept
the party integrated.

Archbishop Stevens joined us. His eyes twinkled as he pushed
his glasses higher on his nose, squinted, and observed: "I say,
Jack, did they tell you what I told McLean?" For my benefit,
his Grace rocked forward on his toes and said, "He's the man
from Irish television. He asked me was I going to keep my ring
if the Pope doesn't confiscate them." He rocked backwards and
again explained for me. "They want to expropriate our episcopal
finery, you see. I told him I hadn't worn it for years but, on the
chance that someone may want to kiss it, for the indulgences you
know, I carry it in a back pocket." He laughed merrily and, as
Jack roared with pleasure, his Grace pushed his glasses up again,
squinted, and laughed some more.

"Pretty good, your Grace." Jack squeezed his arm. "Refill your
Scotch?"

"No thanks, I've had enough. Honored to meet you, sir." He
nodded to me and moved toward the circle surrounding the
freshly arrived George-Georges.

I went to the kitchen to pour myself a fresh bourbon. Then I
wandered to the edges of the circle around Georges. He was
sitting on the floor with his back against a sofa. Marilou was
sitting opposite him, leaning forward, arms resting on her knees
as she held a gin and tonic with both hands.

Clergymen and journalists were sitting on the arms of chairs,
leaning against the wall, and squatting on the floor. George was
talking rapidly, flitting from the Pope to Cardinal Cicobelli to
ecumenism and back again. Laughter flowed in waves and bursts
from the group. On our way out, one midwestern priest called

him "the salt of the earth. He's worth the ticket to Rome all by himself."

The next evening I was sipping a Campari alone at an outdoor café on the Via Veneto, thinking of Nadya and sad that I had not yet had a letter from her, when Jack Prescott, Father Georges, and a girl I didn't recognize came from a side street and turned down the sidewalk toward me. I was just about to rise and wave when George spotted me and pointed. He was wearing a black clerical suit. He wound with the others through the chairs and tables.

"Jon Svoboda, may I present Sylvia Evans," he intoned. "Miss Evans, Jon. I just met the two of them at the cinema. The most marvelous flick, Jon. You must take it in. Marcello Mastroiani and Gina Lollobrigida. Capital!"

Jack was less than happy, but George seemed to be enjoying the situation enormously. "Marilou was too tired to go," Jack said, "so I accompanied Miss Evans. She just arrived in Rome today."

"Today?" I nodded.

"Oh yes," she said. "It's been so exciting!" She had platinum blond hair, poufed high on her head. She could hardly have been twenty-three. "I feel so lucky! I've only been working for *Life* for eight weeks and I never dreamed they'd send me to Rome. I'm just a researcher. I'm so excited!" She looked up and down the avenue. "Is this the one where the movie stars come?"

"Yes," I replied.

"I can hardly wait to write to Sisty. That's my sister. What an exciting day."

"She's already been to the catacombs . . ." George prompted.

"And to the Cola di Rienzo for dinner. It's been a perfectly beautiful evening." She smiled glamorously.

Jack seemed miserable and in exact proportion George was delighted. He made droll comments unceasingly, and kept the silver-haired girl giggling for an hour. "Delighted we encountered you," George waved to me. Then Jack and he took her home in a taxi. I was glad they were gone.

I rose and walked, more lonely than ever and a trifle high, and finally hailed a taxi. The breeze blew coolly over me in the back of the cab. We sped through the almost deserted thoroughfares near the Via Cavour, past the Palace of Justice, and under the glistening and rustling sycamores to the Pensione Bianca.

I lay awake, full of passion and loneliness, longing for Nadya, imagining her long limbs, rolling and tossing on the hard, rough linen, and finally fell dizzily asleep.

In the morning I was awakened by a knock at the door. "Signor Svoboda! Signor Svoboda!" In my pajamas, I opened the door a crack and Signorina Bianca's black, heavily encircled eyes met mine. "A gentleman to see you. Signor Karazov."

"*Momento,*" I told her. "Ask him to wait, only a moment." I threw water on my face, lifted my silver wrist watch to note that it was already nine-thirty, hastily dressed, and hurried out to the reception parlor. It was empty. I turned to the dining room, and there was Karazov, sipping a cup of coffee.

"Ah, Jon!" he said quietly.

"What brings you here?"

"I had your address when I wrote out your ticket. I am on a quick tour of some of our hotels and decided to stop." He was wearing a cool gray suit and a crisp blue shirt, with a dark tie in a Windsor knot. His long blond hair was meticulously in place. "May we talk?" His eyes glanced around the room.

"Yes, the Signorina won't disturb us. She has more or less adopted me." Something began to trouble me.

He sat in his disciplined way and tapped a package of newly opened cigarettes on the tablecloth. He offered one; I declined.

"I don't have long." He lit the cigarette. "I must ask you a very important favor. Can you understand that? A *very important favor.*" He spoke the last words, slowly and quietly.

I poured myself some of Signorina Bianca's thick black coffee, and reached for the plastic handle on the tiny silver pan of hot milk. I tipped the milk into my cup to make *caffè latte.* "I understand," I said, half lightly and half seriously, because I had never heard him use that tone of voice.

"Forgive me for not taking time to ask about your trip. Are you enjoying your work?" He sat back as if to suggest a more relaxed conversation.

"Very much." I looked him quietly in the eye. His eyes did not

waver but I could see that he had not yet come to a decision. I
felt an impulse toward levity and small talk, as if to turn aside
serious requests. The Council and Nadya were quite enough for
now. But something in me propelled me to be ready to say yes.

"Jon, please do not ask me any questions about what I am
going to say." He was leaning forward and paused only to stub
out his long cigarette; it crumpled almost in two. "I cannot say
a word more than I am going to. Not a single word. Clear?"

I nodded.

"You are completely innocent. You are outside all this. That is
why I turn to you. I have something I want you to keep. *It is a
matter of great importance*, you might say *of life and death*."
Again the slow, almost silent tone and a long pause. "Clear?"
When I nodded again, he continued. "It is only a small packet.
I ask you to keep it for me—for not more than thirty days. At
that time I will come and claim it from you and you will never
hear of it again. It is nothing illegal or dangerous in itself, but
it is extremely important." He reached into his pocket for the
packet of Old Golds once again.

"If no one arrives to give you the password," he said calmly,
"then, please, destroy the packet. Otherwise, someone will come,
I cannot say who, and give you the password. Give the packet
to that person but to no one else. To no one else." He waited for
a long minute. "Clear?"

I tried to ask a question but my throat caught. I cleared it and
began again. "And what is the password?"

He nodded. He looked at his knee and brushed a piece of
lint from his pressed gray trousers. When he spoke, it was with a
childlike grin. "It is from a nursery rhyme. Listen. It is: '*Grapes
grapes GRAPES grapes. Butter butter BUTTERfly!*' Do you understand? Can you repeat it?"

I mimicked the accents and the rhythm exactly.

He nodded, brushing his very pale hand across his lips to
conceal his amusement. "You won't forget that?"

"How could I?"

"Once again."

I repeated it.

He was satisfied. "Let us hope you will never hear that again.
In any case, you will never surrender the packet to anyone except

myself or the person who volunteers that password. You will not have to ask for it. He will volunteer it. There is nothing to say in return. Simply give him the packet."

"I understand."

"And are you willing?"

Only one thought was going through my mind.

"Say it."

"Are you suggesting that someone else might try to take the packet from me?"

He shrugged. "Unlikely. No one else knows of it. But to be honest, I cannot promise. A priest named Farina called me last night to see if I had a message to leave with friends." Karazov's brow furrowed. "But it must have been a mistake. No one knows, or even could know. You are perfectly safe if you do exactly as I say. You are, I believe, trustworthy. You are a Czech."

"A Slovak," I corrected.

He shrugged and smiled. "Slovaks have a reputation for guarded tongues. And stubbornness."

"Anyway, I am willing."

"I knew that from the beginning. That is why I turned to you. Here is the packet."

He handed me a package slightly longer, and fatter, than a cigarette case. It was wrapped in brown paper. He seemed pleased by my puzzlement. "Accept my word for it, papers important to me are inside."

As I turned the packet over in my hand I noted that it bore a sales sticker from a jewelry store in Rome.

"Do I need to know anything else? Should I ask other questions?"

"The less you know the safer you will be. You may use a safe deposit box at American Express. I took the liberty of paying for one in your name. Here is your key." He handed me a long, slender key stamped T-836.

He rose and I rose with him.

He studied my eyes a long time. "I will see you before Christmas." There was only a hint of emotion in his voice. "Thank you." He turned and left.

I sat down to finish my coffee and roll. The package was still on the table when Signorina Bianca came in. Involuntarily my

hand moved to hide it. She saw the motion but overlooked it.
"*Slovacco?*" she asked, nodding her head toward the door.
"*Americano,*" I answered.
She cleared the table.
I grew morose about Karazov's visit. I couldn't be sure that
he wasn't playing a trick, but I had heard enough about international intrigue to be a little frightened. I had an impulse to
hurl the package out the window into the sunny stone moat of the
Castello. It wasn't fair to drag innocent people into horrible games.
But maybe it was only a joke. I walked to my room flipping the
package into the air and catching it. It occurred to me that I had
left the key to the deposit box under the rim of my saucer. I
walked back to get it. At first it seemed to be gone. I found it
under the rim of my bread plate.

In the morning mail I received my first letter from Nadya
since leaving the States. It was postmarked Paris: she was already
in Europe, then! She had been delayed a week in New York by a
pilot's strike. She said she was anxious to see me and she signed
the letter—for the first time—"Love." I was so excited I danced
around the room.
Signorina Bianca called from the kitchen. During the war she
had had to manage the *pensione* for her mother who was very old
and ailing. There were few men around and she had been very
busy. She liked to make jokes about lovemaking, and she and
Delia, the sixty-year-old cleaning woman, teased me about sleeping
alone. They told me I needed a girl. I told them about Nadya but
they scarcely believed in her existence—I did not even have a
photograph to show them.
"It is not good to live alone," the Signorina told me. "It is not
good for the nerves. You should find a girl and settle down, make
bambini, and systematize your life. Otherwise it is bad for the
nerves."
"Also for the liver," I added evenly.
The Signorina was puzzled and then smiled. "And bad for the
liver, too!" She repeated it in the other room to Delia, and they
both came to my door to ask if Nadya was coming to Rome.
"She can stay with my sister," the Signorina said. "She has a
vacancy. It is only two streets away."

"She will stay right here!" I said.

Delia clapped her hands and began moving the single beds together. "We will have to tie them. Very strongly. Young men in the bed are like tigers." Then she began reciting a ribald poem, which I could not entirely follow because she spoke the dialect of the streets.

The Signorina blushed and bowled over in peals of laughter. "Not here! Not here! The police would put a stop to me. But later I will make the two boys leave the room next door. There is a connecting door between the rooms. When the lights go out, that is your business!" She and Delia laughed some more and tripped merrily from the room. "You should get married," the Signorina called from the door. "It is best for the nerves."

16

THE NEXT TWO WEEKS passed rapidly. The race from hour to hour was hectic. I collapsed into my bed at night. In the mornings I had to compose my reports, in the face of a major technical difficulty. At best, my stories would appear in an issue dated three weeks after I wrote them; often the lapse was five weeks. *The Liberal Catholic* did not have the resources to pay for Telex; I had to send my stories by airmail rather than cable them. Whatever I wrote one day had to stand up under events I could scarcely foresee.

To help me, I had gathered all of Lord Acton's writings on the First Vatican Council of 1879–80, as well as other eyewitness accounts. The longer one stays in Rome, the more wisdom one sees in doing some things, at least, as the Romans do them. During the first three weeks, however, I didn't nap during the

siesta periods. Instead, I read a great deal. I visited the hotel where
Acton had stayed, and was admitted for a glance into his former
room. It was a joy to sense, for a moment, his vitality and
restlessness. His long account of the Council had become a prose
model that journalists had to meet. I also took the opportunity
to visit the rooms where Don Luigi Sturzo had struggled to
establish the Christian Democratic Party in the dark days before
Mussolini, and the rooms where Dostoevsky had stayed. In such
places I experienced feelings of holiness and awe.

At night I kept a journal. One entry sheds light on the morose
mood events kept reawakening.

I am certain that no one around me fancies me unhappy. But when
I am alone and surrounded by silence I feel empty and useless. . . .
Sometimes I think that murder is as valid as love. I picture Nazi storm-
troopers and imagine that there is no possible way to show that they
were wrong. I have the perception, which everyone must have, that
I . . .
The silence I used to pray in was never peaceful. Now I have no
trust. I used to think that God, a terrible though loving God, was
"hidden." Now I feel, not abandoned, but adrift. . . . Indifferent . . .
I write about the Catholic Church every day, as if I were a Christian
and a Catholic, but I cannot explain why I am not an atheist. Nadya
told me that when my face is relaxed it is sad. It frightened her because
it looks like a death mask.
The word "atheist" does not express my image of myself; nor does
the word "theist."

And now in Rome, Karel had come to me and asked a favor. I
had no way of knowing whether my activity was treasonable or on
whose side. Ignorance, moreover, would not later count as an
excuse; a mature man is responsible for what he does. I decided
that issues of power and *Realpolitik* were at stake. I imagined the
faces of my cousins and decided that some risks were necessary.
I had not been brought up to think of myself as a revolutionary
or a secret agent; guns and plots and battles were for Europeans,
Latin Americans, and Asians.

To be truthful, I grew more and more afraid. I had a feeling
everything would work out badly. I would somehow be embarrassed
or destroyed. Nadya would be hurt. Possibly this action would
lead to my being blackmailed into others. My imagination had

become hypersensitive, and I did not like it. Already the brown package locked in the vaults of American Express radiated destruction.

I spent my mornings writing. The noontime press conference occupied another hour, and either a quick American lunch with fellow journalists or a leisurely lunch with African and German and Australian and other bishops occupied the early afternoon. Then I had an hour or two to myself, times when I walked and thought or sat on a wall in the sun writing in my notebooks. More often, as time went on, I walked wearily up the cool marble steps to the *pensione* for a much-needed nap. At five o'clock there were a multitude of press conferences all around the city, sponsored by national organizations of bishops and other interest groups. At seven I went to dinner, almost always for the purpose of gathering information; dinner lasted at least till midnight, often till one. I was losing a little weight and had begun to worry about my stomach. The food or the water or the air did not entirely agree with me. I was plagued by a very flat, sour breath; diarrhea struck suddenly and often. I took to having scrambled eggs and toast both for breakfast and lunch as often as I could. I took antacid tablets and kept a package of breath sweeteners in my pocket.

I wrote long, intimate letters to Nadya. I wrote almost daily now; I seldom missed. I wrote to her frankly and (I think) unpretentiously. I was beginning to feel a great, warm love for her, possibly a reflection of my loneliness and sadness, possibly a literary love because I scarcely knew her and she was far away. She became the perfect woman of my heart, the distant light toward which my mind turned from the random senselessness of each day's work. (What difference did it make, the Council? Or my reporting? Everything would go on the same.) She learned of all the people I met, the sights, the sounds, the gossip, the conflicts, the anecdotes. The reports I sent her were undoubtedly superior to those I sent *The Liberal Catholic*. I took my time with them and I exposed myself. I allowed the moods to vary— some days I felt businesslike, or tender, amusing or outraged, scandalized, touched, annoyed. Sometimes I wrote brief parodies, sometimes precise and condensed reports. It was a joy to allow myself to create as I wished to create, and to trust that someone was reading with sympathy, possibly with love.

Nadya's responses arrived almost daily, too; they were warm without being passionate, somewhat on the cautious and non-committal side. But I expected that she read great meaning into every sign of affection or concern, every brief escaping syllable of emotional involvement. A girl of twenty-six, I imagined, has been hurt in romantic entanglements before; for her own emotional protection, she holds men at a distance. "Not waiting for a prince on a white horse, are you? Better not set impossible standards. You're not getting younger, after all." I read each letter of hers at least three times: twice right away, and once or more again later in the day. The world of my senses closed in around me as I read. Rome and the Council faded into oblivion. I felt at one with her. The experience of being so overwhelmingly present to each other, so almost tangibly present, when yet hundreds of miles apart, was very sweet.

I found myself counting the hours between postal deliveries. During the afternoon I would think: "Less than eighteen hours remaining, and I'll be asleep for almost half of those." Often I made special trips back to the *pensione* or showed up late for an interview in order to be on hand when the postman arrived. The girls who received the mail downstairs got used to seeing me wait impatiently outside the guardian's window, and knew my resentment when I had to leave empty-handed. They would sometimes greet me teasingly: "The signorina has not written today."

Gradually, Nadya's letters made it plain that she would be coming to Rome "early in November." Her mother wanted her to stay in Paris; I gathered mother Masarik did not entirely approve of me. The reason might have been condescension toward Slovaks, my lack of wealth or title, simply the descriptions provided by her daughter, or journalism—who knew? How could she love me until she met me? I tried to persuade Nadya to come before October thirty-first, since that weekend was to be a four-day holiday at the Council, on account of All Saints' Day. Nadya's speedy arrival would mean that she was anxious to see me; the indefiniteness of her letters had begun to alarm me. I had the unworthy but painful thought that all my valuable letters meant little to her and that my emotions were being played with.

Finally, on Saturday the twenty-sixth, I received the familiar blue stationery with word that she would arrive via Air France about three p.m. on the thirtieth. The timing was perfect. And her closing lines were:

Jon, I miss you very much. Now that it is decided, I can hardly wait to be with you. Do be gentle with me. Don't hurry me. I love you. N.

I was so excited I went for a walk. I did not go far: I sat in the park around the Castello, under the enormous pines, breathing the fragrance pressed from them by the brilliant October sun. Children played ball and drew with soft stones on the pavement. Mothers and nursemaids, old men, two sailors, a bevy of young girls and scores of young men wasting the long hours of the afternoon kept my senses company; my thoughts were elsewhere. It hardly seemed possible to eat or drink, or to make the hours pass fast enough. I had a report to write and to put in the mail before Sunday afternoon—the best, I had hoped, so far—but now it seemed remote and unimportant, and I could think of nothing to make me want to write it. No sentences, no ideas, no viewpoint or structure would come to me. The sun rested upon my face and arms and hands. It made me sleepy and peaceful. I was immensely happy and human life seemed very good. "Why isn't everybody in love? Why can't we be in love all the time?" To my embarrassment, I found that I had whispered the words aloud.

Sunday afternoon, while I was at work typing my article, Jack Prescott telephoned. He wanted to have dinner with me and spend the evening. He was troubled and said there was something important to talk about. I was happy and serene and told him that sounded like a great idea. I told him with some excitement that Nadya was coming Wednesday.

"Oh," he said. "She's the one you met in New York?"

"Yes, she's the one."

"That's nice. That's nice. I'll pick you up about seven."

I hung up. He had no idea that I really cared for Nadya. I shrugged. If I was going to have my article at the central post office before six and be back here by seven, I had to hurry. I settled down and concentrated, in that rare, special happiness that accompanies the union of love and good work, and finished the article in short order. The trip to the post office was hot and muggy; I went by bus but enjoyed even the dry, unpleasant fumes, the dust, and the pushing and shoving at the ticket booth in the rear. I returned, showered, and was dressed just as the bell of the *pensione* rang. I knew it was Jack and beat Signorina Bianca to the door. "I'll be in very late," I told her as she poked her head out from the frosted glass door of her own quarters.

"*Va bene*," she nodded sleepily. Sunday was her one day off and she usually slept through the afternoon. Her sister and uncle usually had her over to their house for a late dinner, and then ended the evening here about eleven with the sweet white taste of Sambuca.

As soon as Jack and I lowered ourselves into the Fiat, I knew something was very wrong. He was dangerously angry. "The Fiat's fixed," I observed easily, to lighten his mood.

"You should know who the hell wrecked it, without paying a cent!"

I tried to speak softly. "Marilou said she loaned it to a friend."

He snorted. "Georgie boy. She's loaned a lot of things to Georgie boy recently. Including our marriage."

I was silent. The car whirred down the tree-lined streets toward the Via Cavour. Jack didn't volunteer any further information and it seemed improper to ask. The startling image of George's head wound leaped into my mind. We drove for almost ten minutes in total silence. Jack was driving too fast and viciously.

Two *vitelloni* in a red Jaguar tried to cut in front of us to make an improper turn. Both cars screeched to a sudden halt. Jack shouted and was out the door in a flash. I slowly got out the other door. An immense traffic jam materialized at once. Turn signals flashed. Hands pressed upon a score of horns. Vespas twisted through the open spaces, wedging in everyone as tight as cement. Fingers pointing upwards, hands behind windows told us of our stupidity, and angry mouths uttered exasperated imprecations. The young boys in the offending car were only half Jack's size. He swore at them in such a stormy fury that they backed down from meeting him toe to toe. The boy nearest him did not dare open his door and kept one arm ready to protect his

head; the other's eyes measured Jack's reach against the sports
car between them. His anger subsiding, Jack heaved himself back
inside our Fiat. He was sweating. Despite the other cars pressing
around, he gunned the motor as loudly as he could and began
to move straight ahead. Somehow the crowd opened up for him
and we sped away, leaving the rest of the Sunday evening traffic
jam to untangle itself.

"You made a lot of friends for America," I said.

Jack's response was a chain of practically unprintable epithets
about Italians, which proved that English can be, after all, as
racy as any other tongue. Gradually, I could see that Jack was
feeling better. At dinner he began to unfold his story.

17

JACK CRUMPLED his napkin in his hand, wiped his lips with it,
and set it down on the linen tablecloth. His curly hair was in
disarray; his usually clear eyes would not focus sharply.

"The point is," he finally exploded, "Marilou is trying to
divorce me. For George Georges. They're trying to get me—committed." He looked me momentarily in the eye, with a weak smile.
"I'm insane. She keeps telling him things, like I don't talk to
her, I leave her alone all the time, I frighten her. Lies. The other
night I asked her to a movie. She wouldn't go. She never wants
to go. Oh yeah. Be objective." He held up a third finger as
though for a third point he wanted to make. "She says I get
furious sometimes and she's afraid of me. She never actually says
I beat her—she knows damn well I don't. God knows I've wanted
to." He added, "I could smash every bone in her body."

I tried to call Marilou's face to mind: sad, tired, unsophisticated.

So the girl from Michigan was suing for divorce. None of it made
sense except that the facts were falling too truly into place. I
felt afraid, sitting opposite Jack, for he was in such a state that
it was hard to judge which was true: that his reactions were
appropriate to the pressures; that he needed serious psychiatric
help; that others were trying, consciously or not, to drive him to
a breakdown. I reminded myself not to sympathize too quickly;
every conflict has two sides. Yet I wanted to let Jack know that he
could trust me. He seemed to be searching for a faithful buoy by
which to chart his own graspings for reality. If I could remain
emotionally independent of him and speak the truth exactly as I
saw it, then he would have a marker. If I tried to comfort him,
I would become an extension of his own perplexities.

"Tell me how it started," I suggested. "Talk it out. Tell me as
much or as little as you like. But I would like you to talk it out."

He stared at the plates in front of him. "It began last summer.
No, last fall, when we came down to Rome to see what was going
on. Mid-November or so. We met Metzger and Weissner and
O'Hare. We had an American colony and it was sort of fun.
We invited them to Paris on their way home, and George Georges
began to visit us. As first he only telephoned once or twice, passing
through. Last spring he came out for dinner once and then,
Chrissakes, he moved in." Jack poured himself a glass of fizzy
bottled water and took a sip. His hand was shaking and his voice
broke: "He made friends with the kids. He used to take Ronnie
everywhere. He even babysat with them. Christ, we couldn't get
rid of him. It was all very nice, very fatherly. But then he started
feeding Marilou this crap about how great a writer she is, she's
wasting her talents, and so on. They read *The Feminine Mystique*
together and he picked it up right away. He doesn't believe a
word of it. He's as continental as hell. But he kept telling her
how unhappy she was, how she needed to realize herself. Exactly
what she wants to hear. She's got the shakes. You know, she's
married and has two kids and lives in Paris. It doesn't mean a
damn thing. I know she's scared. I know that. But he doesn't
help her by filling her with horseshit."

He paused as the waiter came and discreetly removed our
pasta bowls and brought the scaloppine. "He used to go out for
walks with her and the kids. Took them to the parks. I thought

it was a good idea for her to talk to a priest. Paris and flowers and a father confessor. We used to joke about it."

"Was there anything between them? I assume they sleep together?"

He looked miserable but it had seemed a good idea to face the worst and put it on the table. "Not in Paris. Not in Paris," he said quickly. But his tone changed. "I don't think so. Christ! How would I know? Who am I to know what my wife is doing, or where? But I don't think so. Jesus Christ, I hope not!" He lowered his head, and then his eyes filled with tears and he tried to hold them back and was ashamed.

"Go ahead," I said in the stillness.

He shook his head fiercely and resumed, blinking to clear his eyes. In moments his will had reconquered. "I know there's something between them now. When she came down to Rome, he moved in with her. When I arrived, I found razor blades on the sink . . ."

"They could have been left there. They could have been Marilou's," I interrupted.

"Yeah, but that doesn't explain the underpants on the back of the door."

I was silent.

"His all right. I presented them to Marilou."

"What did she say?"

"Oh, she's a systematic little liar. She blushed and fumbled but it was pretty smooth. Pretty smooth. He stopped by once and took a shower, on one of those very hot days. He'd been working in town and was pretty sweaty."

"Plausible," I nodded.

"Yeah, plausible. Pretty good for just the spur of the moment. But the maid told me he was staying there. He tried to lay her when Marilou was away one afternoon."

"Good God, the guy must be sick."

"*He's* sick all right. But the question is who proves it first."

"Proves it to whom?"

Jack shrugged. He wiped his napkin across his brow. "The first thing they want me to do—"

"Who's *they?*" I asked impatiently.

"Metzger, Weissner, O'Hare—all the members of the club. Marilou asked George Georges to go to them as her adviser—

her adviser for Chrissakes—to see if they wouldn't help convince
me to return to the States and enter a clinic, for my own good.
All for my benefit." He paused and took a sip of wine. "She
told them I've been seeing a psychiatrist. According to her, he
said I came to him just in time. She thinks that means I'm
ready to flip, but what he said was that entering analysis just
at this point will be very helpful to my studies. I have great
rapport with him. I'm sure he'd certify my health—at the drop
of a hat."

"What are you worried about then?"

"Oh, they say I don't tell him everything and that it's in
French and my French isn't good enough."

"Is it?"

"It's gotten very good. Honest. Christ, isn't anyone going to
believe me? The goddam psychiatrist understands English anyway; he even takes American patients in English. I've been reading
French novels and talking to people in cafés—my French has
gotten *very* good. I'm not bragging. It's the fucking truth."

"I believe you."

"Well, their line is that I have to have immediate help and
that I need to get it in the United States."

"But why do they need to get you committed?"

"I don't know. I think it's George Georges. Marilou is pretty
squeamish about divorce. A Catholic college and all that. So he's
making her feel sorry for herself. If I'm sick, it's not *sensible* to
waste her own life."

"Doesn't quite ring," I said. Neither of us was eating eagerly;
we barely tasted the food. If we had not been drinking cocktails
and then a bottle of wine, and then another bottle, we probably
would not have eaten at all. Jack drank the wine like water. A
good drunk, I thought, might be just what he needs.

He shook his head miserably. "I don't know. I don't understand
it either. I only know that they're going to advise me I've been
away from the States too long and need a rest. Metzger's already
talked to me. Even O'Hare laid a clammy paw on my shoulder
and said: 'Ex-seminarians make lousy husbands, buddy. They're
too self-centered. I was a chaplain in the navy and if I've seen
it once, I've seen it a hundred times. Nothing personal, Jack. I
believe in talking man to man, face to face.' Christ, I could have
slugged him. I told him to fuck his mother."

"That must have helped your cause."

Jack was silent. "Yeah, they all think I'm nuts. She keeps telling them I'm moody and violent, and the way they act with me, hell, why shouldn't I be? I could wipe out the bastards one by one. It's all I can do to listen to them say a single sentence. Mouths like hen's asses. Christ, I hate them!"

"You're making a good case for Marilou."

"That's not the worst of it. Hell, the whole thing is quicksand. Every time I move, I sink. Remember the girl from *Life* on the Via Veneto? God, it was like somebody goosing George the whole evening; he was so excited he couldn't keep still. He *promised* me in the cab he wouldn't tell anyone, but the next day everybody knew it—Metzger, Marilou, everyone. George Georges told it like he was *defending* me, merely mentioning it before anyone heard rumors. He even admitted I met her accidently—which was true. We were coming out of a press conference at the Dutch Documentation Center and got started talking at the door. She asked me if I could suggest a good restaurant. We were right on Piazza Navona, and I asked her to join me. Bill Strathers was with us; he's one of the guys from AP. Then I told her about the movie—I was tired and I wanted to see it. I'd asked Marilou and she wouldn't come. She tells them I never come in until one or two, and never talk to her. She never wants to talk. Everytime I want to do something, she's busy. It hasn't been a marriage for almost a year. But it *was* great; it was a good marriage. Until George Georges came to Paris. Now he tells everybody he's doing everything he can to hold us together—spending hours at it. He's spending hours all right."

The waiter was standing near by watching us. "*Va bene*," I nodded. He removed our plates and asked about desserts. We looked at the pastry cart, loaded with éclairs, tarts, chocolate cake, rum cake, and cream puffs. Jack winced when he saw them and asked for fruit and cheese. I agreed. "And espresso," he said. "A large pot of it." He measured it with his hands. "A *large* pot." The waiter obviously didn't believe him but nodded, "*Si*."

"Jack, tell me one thing." I waited for his attention. "Do you want a divorce?"

"No!" he responded. "I love Marilou. I really do." His eyes began to fill again and he searched for a handkerchief.

Moments later I broke the silence. "If she gets a divorce, what's she going to do?"

"He's promised her a job in Paris. Working for the Arab League."

"The Arabs?"

"He's some sort of agent. I don't know the story. Something very fishy. I'm going back to Paris to try to get it. He's been leaking all those stories to the press about the hostility to the statement on the Jews. The Jews think he's working for them and the *Times* eats it up. Front pages everyday. Mostly bullshit. 'Usually reliable, informed sources . . .'"

I couldn't quite put it all together, but I nodded.

"You know what's going to happen to her? He's going to break our marriage up and then he's going to drop her. What's she got to offer him? He's a bloodsucker, a pure and simple bloodsucker. And the stream he swims in is the priesthood. That's where his power comes; that's where the pay dirt is. The little bastard's going to ruin things for us and come up smelling like a rose. You mark my fucking words."

Jack was a little tipsy. The high emotions of the evening had left him drained. He had drunk most of the two bottles of wine and was on his third glass of cognac.

"You know the one thing in my life I feared most?" he asked me with an odd, quizzical smile, putting his hand on my arm as we rose to leave. "My parents were separated. Probably why I entered the seminary. Was afraid to marry. My sister married a guy who wasn't a Catholic, and I told her she was crazy, she was cruisin' for trouble. Know what? Got five kids 'n' he's a convert 'n' they're happy as birds! I find a girl who wants to be a nun, good Catholic schools all the way, never been anyplace but Grand Rapids and Omaha, doesn't want to be anything but a wife. I have it as safe and happy as I can. Then, mark it well, baby, a *priest* breaks it up. A fuckin' ordained Catholic priest, in the spring, in Paris. And finishes the job under the fuckin' eyes of St. Peter himself."

I couldn't tell if Jack was playing drunk. I put an arm around him in affection to disguise support. The wine, I feared, would make him pretty sick by tomorrow morning. I tried to take him to my hotel but he wouldn't let me. Outside the restaurant we wandered in the streets.

"I have to piss," he said. Over his shoulder, he added: "One of

the nice things in Rome. They let you piss anywhere." An acid
scent arose from the puddle near the wall. He walked away, zipping
his trousers, appeared to stumble, and began to retch. He was
very sick and vomited again and again, one hand on the dark,
damp wall of the building. We used our handkerchiefs to wipe
away what he had splashed on his trousers. The smells were sour
and we threw the handkerchiefs away.

"Feels better," he said. "Much better."

He needed to walk slowly. After a block or two we came out
upon the Tiber. The *circolare* clanged by noisily. Taxis, their lights
dim and hardly visible, raced down the quiet avenue beneath the
trees. We crossed the traffic and sat upon the stone ramparts,
watching the sad waters of the river slide by in the half-light of
the stars. The breeze from the sea raced along the riverbed fresh
and cool. We hadn't spoken for a half-hour—the silence cementing
our comradeship—when Jack began to shake with the chills. I led
him to the car and drove him to my place to sleep.

18

OFTEN IN THE next few days, perhaps because I felt miserable
and confused, I thought of Father Juan. It was as though he
stood over my shoulder. Would he feel my life had lost purity
and purpose? I had had so many things to learn; the circle of my
awareness had been so small.

I remained in the presence of God. I doubt if five minutes of
my life had gone by without a turn of my heart to God. It
happened as naturally as breathing; I hardly noticed it. Moreover,
my spirit was still open to others. The abandonment in which I
lived was as deep as it had ever been in the seminary, deeper

perhaps in the sense that so few people I encountered believed in God. Since I had nothing to show them, I ceased talking of God and even thinking of him. I had come to like a sentence of André Malraux's: *"For if it is true that for a religious spirit the concentration camps, like the torture of an innocent child by a brute, pose the supreme riddle, it is also true that for an agnostic spirit the same riddle springs up with the first act of compassion, heroism, or love."* I imagined that the only signs of God's presence are human acts of insight, courage, and liberty. When I say I turned my heart to God, I mean that I tried to deepen my desire for such things; I tried to achieve them in that moment at that place. I imagined that life is a full series of opportunities for such acts, but that through indifference, dullness, or hostility I let most of them pass unclaimed. It is as if we live in a sea of spirit and introspection which only occasionally fully shapes, and sometimes ruptures, the inadequate material against which it strains.

I hadn't changed any of these views in the years since leaving Father Juan. I had discovered some ugly things about myself. I hadn't wanted to think of sexual life as a matter of lust; but I had discovered, despite myself, that there is an itch, a self-centeredness, a preoccupation that deserves no better name. Once I had left Vittoria, the memory of entering through soft warm juices stole over me at unpredictable moments; I sometimes hungered violently for relief. I had started out to gain a familiarity with women that would not allow me to think of them as sexual objects. But it was turning out that I needed them in just such a role; I needed release, more even than I needed food.

My preventive experiment was to imagine that I was merely taking sex too seriously, to *treat* it like daily food. But there, too, I was stymied. To make love with a girl every day, or almost every day, solves nothing. The relations between two people struck me as so discouragingly complex that when emotions are out of harmony or pride is injured, the act of love can become heartless, brutal, and cold. It is better not to make love than to make it to get it over with.

I still felt in some confusion about the role of sexual power in my life. One fantasy that I didn't like was that of a harem of thirty or forty women of different kinds and shapes, dedicated to bringing me sexual satisfaction. The fantasy requires women to be slaves, and establishes my penis as the center of my world. I like it to be teased, fondled, caressed between the teeth, left wet by tongue and lips. It sometimes seems that I could live for that.

Men seem to me harsh and unpleasant; a woman's softness, both of flesh and of character, stirs my heart. It was a woman that I was looking for. I dreamed of loving someone perfectly, fucking in delight commensurate with our love.

If I found such a woman, I thought, my life would come together, my work, my health, my joy, my steadiness. Otherwise, I felt a constant restlessness. Nothing appealed to me. I could enjoy things. I could work. But I had not found what I sought.

Another side of me, however, knew that I asked too much. First of all, I often felt incapable of loving a woman as she should be loved—I wanted an adjunct, an aide-de-camp, to help me run my show. The two-centeredness of marriage frightened me. Vittoria, Sarah, Laura, Nadya—every girl I had met—had a life of her own, needs, demands. Women demand so much time! Perhaps I had lived alone too long, and was incapable of changing my way of life. Of Jack and Marilou I thought, that's not for me! I didn't know of any marriages that I admired. Even my parents seemed so matter-of-fact. I could hardly imagine them making love.

Karazov's request troubled me as well. I hated the thought that to be an American is to be part of a worldwide conspiracy. Intrigue and war had always been outside, far away; now in my pocket I could feel the key marked T-836. I wanted in some way to rid myself of it. But I was afraid that too much motion might draw some evil down upon my head.

I had never imagined myself involved in a situation so far outside the range of my character. I was afraid. I didn't want to die, to be disfigured, to have to struggle. For several days I was intolerably restless, until the spell was broken.

Nadya arrived on the most exciting day of the Council's history, possibly the most important day for Catholicism since the Reformation. The issue was whether bishops share in the supreme authority of the pope. The answer determined whether the Protestant and other churches faced a papal monarchy or a kind of constitutional college, and whether Catholicism could evolve away from its autocratic, narrowly Italian tendencies. The question arose on a technical, procedural matter. On October 16 the four moderators of the Council, who were outspokenly progressive cardinals, announced in the middle of the debate on the new constitution of the church that the key issue under debate would be divided into four points, and each point would be voted upon separately by the Council. The commission charged with preparing the exact, final text would be obliged to follow the express mind of the assembled bishops. Thus, the bishops themselves would decide the crucial points, not some uninstructed Vatican commission. For almost two weeks the promised votes disappeared from sight; they were not heard of again on the floor of the Council. Rumors and fears began circulating through the city. Reporters— not to mention bishops and theologians—labored to penetrate the secrecy. Everyone suspected that the conservative twelve-man board of Council Presidents and the Council Secretariat were doing all in their power to preserve the papal autocracy. It was no secret that the Secretariat was much opposed to the new theology, which favored the collegial principle. And it was no secret that most of the Council Presidents were older cardinals, chosen more for the pomp and dignity of their positions than for their theological acumen.

In my article for *The Liberal Catholic* I tried to explain that *all* the bishops, as successors of the apostles, share in the supreme leadership of the church. Before the Council most Catholics, even bishops, thought of Catholicism as a kind of monarchy. Yet ancient and constant practice and Scripture itself indicate that the supreme leadership of the church is not singular but collegial. The pope himself is a member of the college. He is no more a bishop than any other. On the other hand, he has a special role within the college, a role of unity and service. The pope is a member of the college of bishops; but he is also able to act without in all cases consulting the bishops and not merely as their representative. Yet the college itself shares his supreme authority over the entire church. Given centuries to unfold, the implications of an emphasis on the pope alone or, alternatively, on the college of bishops can be immense.

Since Vatican I in 1869–70, the church had been operating on the monarchical principle more one-sidedly than it ever had. Radio and television only served to exaggerate the role of the pope, by making him a public figure in daily view. In earlier times theologians worked at some distance from the papacy, ideas had time to be tested and argued, and mature differences of thought could develop. In recent generations the theology of the papal court dominates even distant churches. Christmas and Easter messages go out from Rome by radio; encyclical letters are published regularly in the press. No local bishops can compete with Rome for attention. One style of theology, the Roman style, has come to be identified as "the Catholic style," and "Catholic" has come to mean, not united and diverse, but uniform.

Questions about the cold war, birth control, revolutions in underdeveloped countries, and other matters would be decided differently depending on who made them; so the issue was important. On October 29, on a less important but lightly emotional issue, the progressive forces in the Council had won a crucial vote by a difference of forty ballots out of more than twenty-two hundred. Thus, when Wednesday, October 30, dawned, predictions of a dramatically split Council abounded. Bishops handing out leaflets on the portico of St. Peter's had been confronted by Vatican gendarmes, and their leaflets forcibly seized. All morning, during the voting, the tension outside ran high. Everyone knew history was being made.

At noon, when the bishops poured forth from St. Peter's, many faces were jubilant. Each of the key votes went in favor of the collegial principle, by majorities of at least nine to one. The Council fathers, in brief, interpreted the role of the bishops in the constitution of the Catholic Church in a far more important and central way than Roman theology wanted to recognize. The bishops are bishops directly through the Holy Spirit, not through the pope. They form a college, and that college is charged with supreme authority in the church, without prejudice to that other locus of supreme authority participated in solely by the bishop of Rome. "The church is now a two-headed government," one theologian said jubilantly as reporters surrounded him. "It is clearly not monarchical." The brilliant noonday sun made his black cassock shine and reflected silver off the threads of its weave. He had removed his glasses and was using them to drive home his points. "The bishops have come of age. A tide of decentralization has begun." October 30 was a watershed date and reporting it

was like hiking into cold peaks and knowing that one stood at a
continental divide, which would be marked as such, the earth
surviving, for thousands of years.

After weeks in a tunnel of discontent and rumor, conspiracy
and argument, the Council like a thundering train had burst out
again into the open and was racing toward open plains, toward
the sea. In my own life the mood was much the same. I had
missed Nadya terribly and now, today, she was arriving. I could
hardly eat lunch and kept looking at my watch. At one-thirty I
hailed a taxi, argued with the driver, let him go and hailed another.
I told the second driver I was meeting a signorina at the airport.
Italians are not disposed to stand in the way of love and, besides,
a drive to the sea just then appealed to him. He agreed to my price,
plus an arrangement depending on how long he had to wait. We
sped off lighthearted toward Fiumicino to meet Air France,
flight 337.

The Caravelle jet arrived precisely on schedule. My heart
quickened as I saw Nadya walking through customs. She wore a
light blue suit and white blouse and seemed more beautiful than
ever. I had no expectation of making love, for Nadya had firmly
settled on a policy of reserve, but I longed to feel her heart pounding near mine, to feel her whole frame soft, abandoned, and at
ease in my arms. I could neither stand still nor move, and time
seemed in suspension, the seconds endless, until at last she came
through the glass doors, and, without too much precipitation,
without too much forwardness, I could fight through the crowd
and stand before her.

"Nadya!" I cried quietly.

"Hello," she said. Her shoulders were drawn back, her two
hands clasped the straps of the white purse she held in front of
her. There was no way to embrace. Her reserve disappointed me
and yet I was moved by the gladness in her eyes and leaned forward, putting my hands on her shoulders, to brush her soft
cheek with a kiss. The scent of the golden hair was the same, the
velvet touch and coolness of her flesh. My heart was crashing
against my ribs but I pulled away and busied myself about her
baggage.

"I have a cab outside. How was the trip? Darling, I could
hardly wait to see you! I'm so glad you're here."

"It was a good trip," her happy, musical voice replied. She walked beside me, carrying her night bag. "I'm so glad to be here, too." She slipped her hand upon my arm and squeezed it lightly as we walked.

She was excited, as I was. The Italian flag snapped in the breeze. Bright orange flowers dipped in front of the fountain. My eyes located our black and green cab; the driver gave me a knowing look, letting his eyes drift from Nadya to me as I helped him lift the bags into the trunk. "*Mamma mia!*" he whistled softly. "An actress?"

"No," I said proudly, and—carried away to extravagance—"my fiancée."

"Blessed you," he sighed and waved the fingers of his right hand downward in eloquent speechlessness.

She let me put my arm around her in the cab, but the day was warm and she did not encourage me. Even the kiss she allowed was broken off a little short. Without saying a word she was establishing her restraint with only a hint that if she was—as she was—expecting such attention and affection, she was not letting it go to my head. "Do not," I read the message, "take me for granted." I was afraid that the message could be even more dismaying than that. Had her mother allowed her to come providing that she would gently, firmly break off with me?

It was, however, so good to be with her that I accepted the quiet and subdued conversation. We rode in silence most of the way, her hand relaxed and yielding in mine. I detected an unmistakable affection, but also a certain nervousness. She was keeping part of her affection to herself; she was not being wholly open. That seemed unfair; I belonged so wholly to her and was, in large part, living for her. I accepted the excuse that she was very tired. She had risen early, she said, and at Orly Field it had been hot—worse than Fiumicino. It might also, I calculated swiftly, be time for her period. When she said she would like to nap for an hour or two before dinner, I was disappointed, but then hoped for a fresher and more cheerful evening.

Signorina Bianca had arranged for a room at her sister's *pensione* until after the two boys next door to me moved out, on Sunday. I took Nadya to the talkative sister, brushed her cheek once more with a kiss of calculated affection and carelessness, and hurried off with some abruptness. She might as well think that I have my doubts, too, I thought. She had better not take *me* for granted.

I walked the two blocks to my own room with rather confused emotions.

After the excitement of the last few days, I was very weary. To stretch my muscles and to be off my feet, to feel the cool breeze slip over my outstretched body, and to know that Nadya was nearby, was like elixir. I fell asleep and arose immeasurably refreshed.

We had, the two of us, a lovely evening. The moon was full— we could see it at sunset even before darkness spread across the silent sky. The evening breeze was alive and full of excitement; yet it also conveyed the sense that the climactic work of the day was done and now was the time for peace and joy. The stucco walls of churches and banks and department stores were mellowed by the shades of evening; the oranges were softened by the sunset and the whitened stucco became a violet-rose. As we walked happily toward a restaurant, the wind turned the crisp leaves of the sycamores over and exposed their silver undersides. Noiselessly, the city's streetlights came to life—the older ones yellow, the new ones gleaming blue and white. A Jaguar without muffler roared under the whispering trees, and taxis purred swiftly over the bricks.

We crossed the Tiber by Bernini's extravagant wind-blown bridge, and walked along the opposite bank. A riverboat that once had been a dance floor was moored, silent and decrepit, across the sluggish green water. We were holding hands and Nadya was no longer stiff or reserved.

"I feel much better," she said.

"There is such a good feeling in the air."

"In me, too."

"Did you miss me, truthfully?"

She nodded. "Truthfully."

"I missed you so much! You couldn't guess."

"That's good." Her chin dipped as she smiled. She wore a white sleeveless dress with a cut that revealed her slender throat, her collarbone, the soft heaving of her breasts. The thin straps of her bra, barely visible, set off her sculptured bronze shoulders, and the skirt's waist fit tightly, accentuating her hips. She was so beautiful I felt no right to walk beside her. Recalling so many years of loneliness, I found it hard to believe that walking here, beside a river across the world from the town where I was born, with a woman as beautiful as she, could be anything other than a dream. It was real and fragile. I wondered how we would end.

And yet Nadya remained elusive. She was protecting something. Perhaps she would never marry, or marry only because she was tired of resisting and would fall, resignedly, into whatever net was then before her, still clutching herself tightly. There was something in her which she could not yield.

And so it went that night. Nadya baffled me. Sometimes I thought of her as hard and beautiful, a woman so warm and sensitive and affectionate that she could not elude entanglements, but, finally, severe and ruthless, watching out for self-interests she could not properly define, whose limits became apparent to her only with the emergence of feelings of panic and threat. At other times I perceived her as a little child, trapped by her own competence—looking out through a bathoscope, her nose pressed against the porthole, but knowing that no one was there to hear a little girl; one saw only an able and competent woman. But she was not either one of these—neither a child nor a hardened woman. She was innocent, though she dressed and spoke like an experienced woman. She had wanted once, seriously, with the determination that characterized whatever she did, to become a nun. She had dissuaded herself because she was so highly educated, and because the manners her education had taught her were antithetical to the disciplines she anticipated in convent life. She was a lady, almost of the old school, in poise and taste and easy manner. She loved—she required—travel and theater and cinema. Her mind was alive and she had sworn never to put it to sleep. She was fiercely proud and determined never to hide lack of self-development behind a husband's career—determined to maintain her own dignity as a Masarik, to retain the name in spirit if not in legal fact, and to be a woman in her own right. She had no particular career in mind—she was not a teacher, an artist, or a scholar. She could find no focus for her proven talents in economics. She was determined only to be independent in reaching decisions, to keep the stuff of Western humanism within her own reach, too, not letting it fall as it commonly does, only to men: the risks and dangers and self-discoveries of freedom.

Her attitude toward lovemaking, I guessed, sprang from such roots. Perhaps she early decided that lovemaking, as she observed it among her friends, was an instrument by which women were made subservient. Not that through yielding in love they lost their dignity or their self-mastery—there was nothing of the puritan in her; she was, I was to learn, childlike in her openness to sensual pleasure. Women were, perhaps she felt, left clinging to men for their sense of identity and purpose and achievement. They were reflectors, mirrors; they were not taken with final seriousness. She did not wish to be even a much-loved slave. And before she "gave herself"—she had told me in New York how she hated most expressions for the most basic human relation—before she gave herself to a man, she wanted to be sure that she remained as free as he did. The test of freedom, she said, is not whether she could be as promiscuous as he, but whether she could pick him and whether she could choose the moment and whether the sign could mean what she wanted it to mean. In her mind sexual intercourse meant not necessarily marriage, but in any case a long-term liaison of equals, desiring to work out together their independence, their freedom, their identity. To men, she felt, intercourse was a matter of biological release or emotional triumph; she did not wish, she said, "to be somebody's sink, just because they need to turn the faucet. I'm not a pawn in someone's march to victory over his mother."

Yet there was something infinitely yearning about her. She did not like her isolation. She was not holding herself aloof. It was not that she was especially proud. "Her trouble is she thinks her tail is a goldmine," Jack Goldblatt had commented with unwonted harshness. She was gentle and in need of help—waiting, looking. What seemed to be sheer rocky cliff was the self-protection of a girl who had been beautiful since birth, in exile since she was seven.

We went, the first night, to a small restaurant in the medieval city that has been in operation since the twelfth century. The entrance is not plainly marked; it stands on a small side street not far from the Tiber. Inside, a narrow cocktail lounge, modern and disappointing, spoils the first impression. But as you wind the narrow stairs to the small loft, you feel reduced to medieval size by the centuries-old beams, the ragged yellow brick, low ceiling, and close walls. The menu is one price—it is very expensive—and the food is exquisite. It was on a journey to the twelfth century that Nadya and I began to find each other.

I was afraid she thought of me as too self-sufficient. Occasionally people had told me I was arrogant, and the word hurt enough to let me guess that it might be true. My goal, on the other hand, was to be sympathetic and sensitive. With Nadya I hated myself for not being perfect. I wanted her to fall in love with me, and yet every fault of character helped to hold her away. She said so little that I could not be sure what she disliked in me, or liked; all I could be certain of was that she had not, so far, refused to spend time with me. I wondered how I appeared to her. There must be at least three of me, I thought: her image, my image, and perhaps an image truer than either of the others. And three of her. Six of us, then, at a small wooden table built for two. Could the two more accurate images, the two unknowns, ever find each other across that no man's land?

Nadya talked freely about her mother. "You will like her. But she is so old-fashioned!" She pressed a long white index finger upon a crumb on the tablecloth and lifted it to her lips. "She thinks she still is in Prague, and that we are still living in diplomatic circles. She does not understand that my sister and I live a totally different life. She can't recognize that the past is past, and begin again." Her clear eyes looked overhead into the distance, then caught mine, and she smiled.

"Is your mother worried about me?"

"Oh yes! You know what she thinks about Slovaks. 'His grandfather was probably a farmer, who left the country to avoid military service.'"

"Exactly," I laughed.

"She does not want me to see too much of you." Her eyes flashed. "That makes me want to see you more often."

"I hope that is not the only reason."

Coyly: "It is one of them."

"What does your mother—do?"

"She goes to teas. She visits with her friends. Oh, she watches her weight! It is a stupid life. I tell her so. She does not like that. But it is. It's stupid. She is wasting her life, living for the past. All those émigrés in Paris." She shuddered. "I hate their life. They are so contemptuous of everybody. They study the newspapers every day in order to find new ways of being horrified. 'Ah, cherie, the world today is full of madmen!' Really! She says things like that, in that tone of voice."

"Of course, it is a little mad."

"Of course it is! But what right has she to say it? Sitting there, sipping tea? Ah! Let's not talk about it." She nervously pulled out a cigarette. I lit it. Her index finger brushed the mole on her cheek.

"Where is your sister Sonya?"

"At the Sorbonne," she exhaled. "I want her to come to America. She would love New York. But now she is very anti-American. She does not want to come. Then there is Raymond."

"Her boyfriend?"

Nadya nodded darkly. "I do not like him. I think he is revolting. He is not serious and he does not care for her. She is only—"she paused but then went on, with a shrug of her bronze shoulders—"young and pretty and impressionable. I am always afraid for her. She does not have good sense."

"Like you?"

She flushed. "Like me. I have too much good sense, they say."

"They?"

"Everyone!" she replied impatiently.

I pressed my fork against the soft, creamy *cannelloni* and lifted a portion to my lips. She sipped her wine—it was Valpolicella; the label had made me think of Verona, of Juliet. "How old is Sonya now?"

"Twenty-two." Her brow darkened. I knew that Sonya had been born several months after her father had died; I had forgotten. "Please, let us talk about the future."

"Have you ever been to Capri?" I had already proposed the trip to her in a letter.

"Never. To Naples, yes. And to Pompei. I love Sorrento. But to Capri, no."

"Are you glad, then?"

"Yes."

"We'll leave at noon. That means we can sleep late and go without hurrying."

After dinner we walked toward the bridge leading to St. Peter's. I wanted to walk through the piazza by moonlight. Nadya drew her white knitted wrap over her shoulders; the October air was cool. The conversation had been difficult, not at all as I had hoped. She had such reserve. She kept at such a distance. I wondered if it was necessary to take her by storm. Perhaps it was a mistake to play gentleman, to entertain her, to open doors for her, to converse politely. Perhaps what she needed—what she was hoping for—was to be swept off her feet. *Pop her in bed and be done with it!* Perhaps.

We walked slowly up the Via della Conciliazione, her white shoes clicking loudly on the almost deserted thoroughfare. The lamp lights on their concrete pillars emitted a soft light. The basilica ahead seemed to float in the air, bathed in a creamy, silvery light. We were sweating slightly from the exertion when we crossed through the arms of the colonnades, into the piazza, our feet falling on the gray stones. We could hear the water of the great twin fountains, throwing their jets of water like bits of gleaming ice into the night air and catching them again. The air was moist with the fine spray. We could see the shadow of the obelisk, raised by the muscles and pulleys of workmen in tense silence so many generations ago; the ropes had slipped and water was applied to stiffen them; had anyone spoken in the moments of suspense, the legend says, he would have been punished by death. Above, in the Vatican apartments, two windows in the papal corner were illumined with yellow light.

"The Pope is still awake," I motioned. She had a hand in mine and raised her head. Just then the windows darkened. "We are putting him to sleep." We watched the darkened windows for a moment, and then turned back, idly, through the square. I found one of the two round stones from which all the columns of Bernini are aligned, so that one could see through them in perfect symmetry. Above, on the portico over the columns, the cloaks and swords and books of great saints formed burly shadows against the sky. The moon was dazzling, in celebration, I thought, for the great things that had been accomplished in the basilica today.

Our feet were tired, and when an old man leaned forward from

his carriage to ask us if we wished to see Rome by night, I argued
with him for a while concerning the price. He knew I was an
American; I knew that it was very late. We compromised.

"Really?" Nadya expressed her pleasure as I told her. "That
sounds like fun."

The driver helped us adjust a blanket over our legs. She pressed
her knee against mine. I put my arm around her and she let her
head fall upon my shoulder in relaxation. *But she trusts me,* I
argued. The horse's hooves clattered over the stones and the
concrete. We headed toward the huge white monument to Vittorio
Immanuele, past the church of St. Philip Neri. The carriage came
out of the long canyon into the modern blue lights of the piazza
where Mussolini had once harangued shouting crowds, plodded
along around the silent circle, down past the Forum and the
Colosseum and the Arch of Constantine, took a turn, doubled
back, and began to ascend toward St. Mary Major. There it veered
left and circled the glorious, colored fountains at the head of the
Via Nazionale, then descended to seek out the fountain of Trevi
and the Via Veneto, mounted to the city wall, orange in the lights
of the evening, and descended again to the Piazza del Popolo and
the fountain at the base of the Spanish steps, and wound past the
shops en route to the Piazza Navona, and then across the river
to our *pensione.* It was an exhilarating, long trip. Behind the
clippety-clop and clatter of the horse, exulting in the scent of
oats and steaming manure, dizzy with alternate neon lights and
dark hulking cypress trees, Nadya and I brought our lips lightly
together again and again. What words did not open, a ride behind
a straining brown-black animal did, a ride in the silence and the
cold air and the lights and the ancient city.

Afterwards, I felt sorry for the driver and his horse—they had
given us more than an hour and there were few other sights they
could have shown us—so I paid him the higher price he had
asked before our compromise.

19

FROM THE POOLSIDE at our hotel on Capri the sky gleamed blindingly; it was like looking into lighted diamonds. Below, over the harbor, white sea gulls floated and dipped, suddenly plummeting toward the crystal blue water. We lay lazily in the sun, recovering from the trip the day before and weeks of accumulated weariness. We talked quietly. There was hardly anyone around the pool.

"What is it that you are afraid of?" I asked.

"I don't know. I don't even like to think about it." She lay on her stomach on a great blue towel. She wore a white bikini of some soft, fluffy material. There were light blue veins behind her knees, and creases under her rounded bottom. The lines of hairs down the inside of her thigh gradually turned silver and gleamed in the sun. On each heel rough, reddened cores of skin had been built up. Her toes were short, the cut nails innocent of polish. *My beautiful one,* I thought, *my lovely one!* And yet we had to talk our way through to liberty.

What I liked most about Nadya, in fact, was her difficulty in speaking about her emotions. She had a stubborn integrity. She knew just what she was feeling, one could count upon that; she was always fully present. She forced me to scrutinize my own feelings, so as not to give way to poses or to sentiments or to words I did not mean. On the other hand, her reticence made it difficult for me to speak. I was not sure how much I should probe. It was as though we were constantly exposed to one another, each of us talking from the pit of his stomach. It is rare to find persons who talk like that. I always came away from Nadya feeling scoured and clean, freer and more honest than before.

She began to ask more questions of me. Her eyes conveyed the movements of her own emotions. "One thing I don't understand about you," she rested her chin on her hands and looked away. "You are both innocent and—" she searched for a word. "Complicated."

I waited.

She looked at me quietly. "You aren't innocent."

I replied in a tone that accepted the charge. "Are you?"

"Maybe that is why I see it in you."

"What do you mean, 'not innocent'?"

"Oh—untrustworthy or something. As if your head is smart enough to work out a way for you to do anything. And still you would remain 'innocent.' "

A long pause. "Is that bad?"

"It is too much like me. It makes me uneasy."

"What you want is a man in whom there is no guile."

"Yes."

"A tall order."

"Don't you mind being told you're untrustworthy?"

"No."

"See? That same innocence." Her eyes shone with the pleasure of vindication; her confidence grew. "Don't you see? You *like* to accept criticism. But you really don't."

"A man of reason," I laughed.

"It's the sense of humor I think I like." She was looking out at the sea again, as if the words weren't spoken for me. Then she turned and her eyes were not judgmental.

"You don't care, then, if I'm not innocent?"

"A little."

"It makes you afraid?"

She nodded.

It seemed wrong to offer assurances. A long silence.

"What do you most want to be?" she asked, raising herself up on her elbows.

We were not looking at each other, but speaking quietly, at peace. I sat facing sideways, my outstretched foot almost touching her thigh, my other knee clasped between my hands. I was silent a long time without answering. The warm southern air stirred the trees of the courtyard.

"I don't exactly know," I said. "I want to be too many things. A writer, mostly. Sometimes I'm afraid it's only a dream. The world is full of people who want to write. It's another matter to find enough inside and to work. Sometimes I'm afraid of that. Of not being good enough."

"You should write. Your letters are beautiful."

"I think you like me better in letters than in the flesh." She set the invitation aside unanswered.

"You have to be a writer. That is very important to you." She was suddenly earnest. "No one should take that away from you."

"I like politics," I said. "I like to teach. I don't know what I want to do."

"That is the most amazing thing about America," she said. "In France, everybody knows. There are very few posts; you must work very hard to become accomplished. In America, a person has too many possibilities. Everybody wants to know what your 'major' is." She laughed, remembering, mimicking. "I was so afraid because I didn't have a major. But then I realized that everybody changes majors constantly. I used to make up a new major every week. It was so funny!"

"Mainly, I want to keep the future open. I think only a year ahead. After that, at the next turn, who knows?"

"Doesn't it make you nervous?"

"No," I laughed.

"Aren't you afraid of never becoming anything? That's what I fear most. That I'll only be a dilettante. I didn't like the Institute. I don't want to teach. And now . . . ?"

"Presiding over teas."

"Uuuh! Exactly. Like my mother. Uuuh!" She lay her head down in her arms, shook it violently, raised it again and laughed. "Do you believe in fate?" Her large eyes tested mine for a moment. The mole on her cheek shone in the sun.

"In a way."

"I do. I really do. People become just what they want to become. You think you are free, but something makes you do the very things you try to avoid."

"What something?"

"Impulses, the unconscious. I don't believe in stars, but sometimes I think that each life has a fate—a pattern ironic and painful and revengeful. Life is mostly pain."

"Who puts those ideas into your pretty head?"

"I'm a stoic underneath. I don't believe in optimism. I don't believe in change. Life is more like circles." Her brow contracted.

"I wish I knew why you were so afraid," I finally said.

"Why?" she asked. Her fingers picked at lint on the towel. "I don't want anyone to know me too well. I don't want to feel controlled."

"I wouldn't want to control you," I laughed. "I'm not trying to put you in analysis. I don't know how I stand with you. You make me afraid, a little." I watched triangles of sun flashing in the pool, diving, blinking, all the way to the bottom. The words were hard to force across my lips. I made an effort. "I love you, Nadya. You know that. But I don't know where I stand. I can't quite find you. I think you love me, a little; but I think you are afraid— afraid to let go. Or something."

She was trembling a little and sat up, facing the pool. "People really shouldn't talk like this," she said. "It's dangerous."

I waited.

She touched her stomach. "It hits too deep. Who knows . . . I can't say everything, because I don't know what I feel. I'm confused. I'm all tied up in knots. I don't know why."

"Is it—?" I bit my lip. I thought about the question a while and then decided to risk it. "Is there also someone else? Are you between two of us?"

She was disappointed. "No."

I was sorry I had asked and yet also was relieved. "What is it then?"

"If I knew, I could tell you, couldn't I? I really don't like too much analysis!" She stood suddenly, pulled at my arm, let go, and dived into the pool.

The sight of her lovely body moved me. Her long, lithe legs cut the water cleanly. She turned underwater and came back. Her half-exposed breasts seemed full of honey. She emerged, blond hair darkened and plastered to her face. She looked at me with a smirk of pleasure and challenge, then pushed away. My heart was restless for an insight into behavior I didn't understand, restless to find the key. I dove into the pool after her, clumsily. I tried to grab her ankles—pale fire in the light-rippling water—but she squealed and kicked away. She splashed my face when I came up for air and, though she was a better swimmer, she let me capture her when I gave chase. I put my arms around her chest, her breasts lying upon my arm, and pulled her backward. She was kicking and laughing. I pressed my mouth upon her cool lips and dunked her backward, both of us falling deep into the water, lungs bursting not only for air but with joy. We broke apart and stroked upward, broke the silken surface and laughed.

We did not sleep together at night. We had adjoining rooms, with a door between us. I respected her wishes. But it was difficult to sleep. She said as much herself. In fact, our lack of sleep became on the third day a source of many jokes. We sat around and walked the island. We played a short game of tennis, but Nadya, for all her energy, was a novice at the game and we tired. (The *pong!* of the balls in the sun made me think for a moment of Sarah, thousands of miles and many years away, and I was glad.)

"Say, if we don't get more sleep than this," I said as we walked from the clay courts, "it's not going to be much of a rest. I'm going to have to marry you to be able to sleep at night."

"Are you having trouble sleeping?" she asked archly.

"You aren't?"

She wrinkled her nose. "A little bit. I think I fell asleep just after the bells rang the Angelus."

"You got three hours. Stop complaining."

She ducked into her room and used the door as a shield. When I lunged for it, she closed it, snapped the lock, and laughed: "I'll call the house detectives!"

"You wouldn't dare."

The lock turned and the door opened. "No, I wouldn't." She held up her arms and we embraced. Shortly she said, "That's enough," and began to push away.

"Easy for you to say," I remonstrated. "It's really not quite fair."

Her lips opened, then hesitated. "I'm not trying to play with you."

"But you are."

Her eyes were confused and I could see the anger building. "If I do nothing, I'm too cold. A little, and you want more. What am I supposed to do?" The door slammed.

Still facing the white door, I rubbed the back of my head with my right hand and smiled. I sang in the shower, but not loud enough for her to hear.

That evening at dinner in the hotel restaurant we were just beginning our main course when I saw a man I recognized rising from another table with a girl. As they walked nearer, I studied his face. It didn't seem possible, but I was certain.

"Eddie!" I called. He looked at me for a moment and then brightened.

"Jonathan Svoboda! How are you, old man!"

I rose and we introduced the girls. His companion was black-haired and cute, an English girl. I explained to Nadya in a sentence that Eddie was an old school chum.

"What are you doing here?" I asked. "Won't you join us for a few moments? An after-dinner drink?"

He looked at his companion and agreed. It was the off-season, and not much was happening on the island.

"Working for the government," he said. "Really enjoying it. Did you see today's headlines?"

"The assassination?" I asked. "In Vietnam?"

He nodded, "I'm on my way out there."

"What on earth for? Who are you with?"

He hesitated only for a fraction of a second. "State. I suppose you're here for the Council. For *The Liberal Catholic?*" When I nodded—it was an astute guess—he continued. "I'll be in Rome for two or three weeks. I have some business there and a little free time. Then off for the Orient. I'm pretty excited."

"You should be. Pretty fast work."

"Connections. I'm really on a sort of training mission. Be very short. They want me out on the field, briefly, before the real training starts."

"Eddie Flanagan, diplomat!" He looked tough and strong in his new closely trimmed haircut and well-pressed gray suit. He looked as though he'd been taking out cute girls all his life.

"Not exactly," he laughed. "Say, don't let us interrupt your eating. Go right ahead. We'll do the talking. Washington is an exciting place, Jon. Maybe we can talk you into coming down.

Kennedy has the whole city popping. Lots of young people. Good morale."

"I thought he was having all sorts of trouble."

"Bound to. But things are just getting into gear. He'll do better with a large majority his second term."

The conversation continued on politics and Vietnam until we had finished eating. I was becoming uneasy because Nadya seemed a little bored. Our own conversations had been intimate and rewarding; we had begun to cherish them. But I could also see that Eddie wanted to talk. He invited us to join him and Evelyn for a night on the town, by which he really meant conversation. When I looked at Nadya, her eyes turned the decision back to me. I kept thinking that perhaps she and I had talked as much as we could alone, for now, and that it would be good to see how we could get through an evening on subjects that made me, if not her, come alive. Besides, I really wanted to talk to Eddie.

"Okay," I said. "Where to?"

We paid our bill and, just as I had guessed, our destination turned out to be a quiet lounge where soft music was being played. Eddie was a worse dancer than I was, but a bolder one. We danced. But mostly we talked. The conversation kept coming back to war. I could gather between the lines that Eddie was going to work out in the back country, on a pacification team of some sort. I was now guessing CIA. In any case, the subject of war seemed to fascinate him. Evelyn said she was too young to remember the Blitz, so Eddie asked Nadya about her memories of the war.

Silence. I could see that Nadya liked him. She held her forehead with one hand. "Mostly, I remember the bombing. If I hear a loud noise at night, even now, I break out into a sweat. . . . I was only three, not quite four. It was in the summer. We lived on a sort of estate and there were some German officers living next door, with guards."

She hesitated; she was not looking at any of us but at the table. "One day I went out into the garden without telling my mother, and I saw some soldiers stealing fruit. My little dog ran out the door with me and ran ahead and barked at the soldiers. One of them pulled out a large knife, a . . . a bayonet. He whacked Aldo and cut his front legs almost completely off."

She stopped and reached quietly for her glass. After a while, she went on. "The other two soldiers laughed. I carried Aldo back to the house trying to keep the legs from breaking off. I was sure it was my fault, because I was disobedient and let him out. Aldo kept bleeding and bleeding; my smock had to be thrown away. He died that night." Her voice was very soft.

Eddie sipped his Scotch.

"Then, just before the end of the war, they took my father and later . . . killed him. Somehow the two things came together in my mind. I felt I was responsible for that, too. And I am angry at him, I don't know why. I don't like war very much. Not very much."

Evelyn nervously sipped her bourbon. The conversation drifted to other things and later we parted. I wanted to keep the night coolness from Nadya. She was trembling. Some insight had frightened her and then released her.

When I had put on my pajamas, there was a knock at the door between us. I twisted the lock on my side; hers was already open.

"Are you lonely?" she asked. She was wearing a knee-length gown. "I need a hug."

"Should I come?" I asked, surprised.

"Please."

Quietly we walked over to her bed. I sat on the edge and she sat beside me. I put one arm around her. Her head fell slowly onto my shoulder. I reached the other arm in front of her, and she turned, looking upwards, for a kiss. The position was uncomfortable. We held the kiss for a long time, while a decision went back and forth in my mind like a tennis ball.

"Do you want me?" I said.

She nodded, and then leaned forward to kiss me so hard I thought she'd cut my lip. I started to tip backwards, then stood and let her swing around into the bed. As she knifed her legs under the sheet her skirt caught and a dark triangle of hair was visible. She held the sheet and smiled with a shy, childlike smile. I lay down beside her and we pressed our bodies together. The pounding of our hearts was audible—we paused in our kissing long enough to listen to them and to laugh.

"It feels as though your heart is inside of me," I said.

"It is," she said, licking my lips with her tongue and darting her tongue between my teeth. "It is." She sighed with pleasure and wriggled her body closer to mine. Side by side we pressed as close to each other as we could, as though we could merge, as though bodies should be tongues of flame instead of solid and tangible and strong and independent. Gradually our clothes became an impediment. I took her hand and guided it—it came hesitantly, timidly—to my penis. Her breath was short. I moved her fingers while she explored in silence. Then she hugged me again and brought her hands to each side of my head. My ears rang and I thrust myself against her. She felt the hardness jabbing into her belly, jabbing, and she pressed out against it. I pushed myself up on one arm and untied my pajama bottoms. She watched as I sat up into a faint pattern of moonlight and slid them off. She pulled her nightgown. I helped it over her head. Her breasts fell forward and I kissed them, squeezed them gently, playing my fingers back and forth across the hardened nipples. Then I lifted myself; my pants were tangled on one foot. I kicked—no results. She pulled them free. I lifted the striped top over my head, and pulled her down so that we could lie upon the pillow silently. Our hands were intertwined. Silently I pushed myself up and gently bit each nipple in turn, running my teeth around and around. I kissed every inch of her, and then lay back. She placed a hand upon my penis, and I walked my fingers slowly down her cool belly, pulled the hairs lightly, pressed into the warm folds. Her hand clasped mine. She was very wet and soft, waiting and eager. We lay silently for many moments, looking at the ceiling.

"Don't you wonder," my voice broke the silence, "why people ever do anything else?"

A specter in the darkness was troubling her; the unspoken tension was audible. "Have you done it often?" she barely whispered.

I was painfully sorry for every time. Instead of answering her, I kissed her lips, again and again.

"Have you?" she asked firmly, afraid, through the kisses. Her eyes, white in the pale light, were watching me.

"You don't want me to lie," I said. "And I know you won't understand. But it's not important—you have to understand that."

She pulled away. "Not important?"

"It means different things." Her body tensed again. "Please don't think of it. There were other girls. I was lonely. I was not in love with them. Not really, not in love."

"You just—do it?"

"You have to understand."

Silence. "I guess I do. I try to. It's just—" she turned her face away.

A long moment.

"Don't cry," I said. I had to shift my weight to relieve the pressure on my left elbow. I lifted my body from her and sat beside her, running my palm slowly over her side: her waist, her ribs, the side of her breast.

She turned her face back toward me.

I didn't want to say false words and so remained silent.

The low hum of machinery or electricity, some burden of civilization, moved the still air. Outside, the creatures of the night were singing.

"Say something," she whispered.

My voice was hardly audible. "I love you, Nadya. I really love you. I want you to marry me. I haven't proposed because I didn't want to rush you. I've known since the first week I met you that I would marry you, if you wanted to."

"I don't understand that."

"Understand?"

"How you can know so quickly. How can anyone decide so quickly?"

I shrugged. "I liked what I saw in you. What you said tonight— about your puppy, about your father—that didn't surprise me. I didn't know about it. But it didn't surprise me. The first time I saw you, I thought of you as a very sad person, someone who was very lonely. You were very beautiful and Mario said you were hard . . ."

"Mario!" she said with quiet contempt.

"Was there much between you?" I asked with calculation.

"Jonny!" she said with horror and even more contempt.

"You've had a lot of boyfriends, you know."

"Yes, but at a distance."

"Engagements."

"Yes, but it was never. . . . You're not being fair."

"The point is that I love you. I was afraid of you at first. My instincts told me to stay away from you."

"To stay away from me?"

"You are what is known as a man-killer. Beautiful, attractive, *quicksand*."

"Flattering!" she mocked. Then she laughed. "Afraid of me? Really? Afraid of me?"

I nodded in the moonlight. Then I lay back down upon the pillow and, side by side, we talked for a long time.

"Would you ever leave me? Do you believe in divorce?"

"I don't know what I think about divorce," I began. "I don't—"

"I believe in it," she said passionately. "Why should two people remain together if they don't love each other?" Her voice was amusing when she tried to imitate the tone of reasonable argument; she was best at passionate pronouncements, full of conviction. "The moment you don't love me, leave me—leave me alone, please." Then she rolled over and put a warm hand on my chest. "But don't go yet." She laughed.

"Don't worry," I said, taking her hand and stroking my thumb between each two fingers in turn. "Don't worry about that, ever. We're going to grow and grow together. . . ."

"Don't talk about the future, Jonny." She pulled the sheet over her head and turned to the wall. "It frightens me too much. Don't talk about marriage yet."

I pulled myself over against her and cupped my body to hers. Her bottom, soft and cool, was against my stomach. The skin of her back was silken, like ivory, smooth and cool. We lay in silence for a while.

"May we make love?" I whispered. "I love you."

She lay perfectly still for about a minute. I realized that it would have been better not to put the decision into words, but to let her decide little by little. Still, I wanted her to know what we were doing, and to share the responsibility. The gift is free or not a gift at all. But the effect of my words was to shatter her mood.

She nodded and began to turn. I held her in place and kissed the back of her neck. From behind I let myself approach and explore the wetness and the honey, pushing slowly back and forth near the surface.

"That feels so good!" she sighed, and twisted and pressed against me and kissed me hard.

We touched for a while, then proceeded slowly. We rested. We shifted to different positions. She was docile, yielding, and I tried to follow her lead. There was a kind of sacred silence. We worked toward the blinding swift moment. In the end, she did not quite reach a climax. She shuddered and I could hold no more and she was left stranded. But she came down slowly, clinging tightly to me. The air was cool; we had been sweating. She rose and padded to the bathroom. I watched the flesh of her soft bottom as it rose and fell with each step. The faucets ran. She leaned into the room—yellow light leaped instantly across the wall—and threw me a towel, half of which she had held under the warm water.

When she came back, her teeth were freshly brushed.

"I liked you better when you were you, not Pepsodent," I said.

"Oh, you did! Then you'll have to kiss it off."

She fell asleep in my arms. Pulling my arm out from under her, dead for loss of blood, I pulled away a little and looked at her. She was a child, and I felt like a child. *Father Juan*, I wanted to say, *Mount Carmel . . . !*

20

HARSH DAYLIGHT FLOODED the room. We awoke like strangers un-accustomed to each other. As Nadya brushed her teeth and dressed, she seemed uncomfortable. She said nothing about the preceding night. She was affectionate, in a reserved and hesitant way. Possibly she felt a contradiction between being married and not being married, a discomfort living under a partial fiction. She liked to keep the environment around her orderly. I kissed her before we descended to the hotel restaurant for breakfast; she seemed glad for the attentiveness.

After we had eaten, a front-page story in the morning paper caught my attention and made me set down my coffee cup. CZECH TRAVEL AGENT HELD IN PRAGUE. The subheading ran: *Soviet Jet Makes Unscheduled Stop*. I knew it was Karel Karazov before I read the account.

"What is it?" Nadya asked.

"Karazov has been arrested." I opened the paper so she could read it with me.

"Your friend?"

I nodded.

A United States citizen, the column said, was taken from a Soviet Ilyusha jet en route from Paris to Moscow, when the plane made an unscheduled stop in Prague. He was believed to be Karel Karazov, owner and manager of the University Travel Bureau in Morningside Heights, New York City. Unofficial reports said that Czech police and secret-service agents were waiting at the airport and forced Karazov to deplane. The Prague paper *Rude Pravo* accused Karazov yesterday of "espionage, treason and crimes against the State." Karazov, the dispatch continued, had been a prisoner of the Nazis in Dachau for three years, and then left Czechoslovakia in 1949 after having spent almost a year in a Communist prison outside Prague. He lived for a time in Italy, and emigrated to the United States in 1952, becoming a U.S. citizen in 1959. Friends and associates at the University Travel Bureau, which Karazov owned and operated, denied the charges. Karazov was making, they said, a routine inspection trip of accommodations recommended by the bureau to its customers.

A ball of cold lead grew larger in my stomach. "The trouble is last month he gave me a message to deliver in case anything happened to him." I was reflecting slowly. "He must have been expecting this. My thirty days aren't up yet."

"What do thirty days have to do with it?"

"Shh! Let me figure." As best I could recall, he had spoken to me on October ninth. It was now November third. "My responsibility lasts thirty days."

"Your responsibility? For what? Jonathan!" Her voice rose in warning.

"I promised Karazov."

"Promised *what*?"

"I can't say exactly. I have to try to remember his precise instructions. I didn't think anything would happen."

"Explain it to me. Explain everything to me."

"Don't be nervous. Everything will be all right. You're edgy this morning."

"That isn't fair."

"I didn't mean it that way, honey. I'm sorry."

"I wish you hadn't read the paper. I wanted you to talk to me."

I started to object.

"It's all right." She rose. "I'll see you in the room."

She was already gone. I tried to shrug, to dismiss the pain. My thoughts turned to Karazov. Was he in danger? I pictured him being shot. Where did that leave me? I felt like an instrument of forces I didn't understand. Nadya? Ridiculous. But in fact I knew very little about her, and everything I knew I knew from her. How paranoiac! I got up to go for a walk. Better to leave her alone. There would be nothing to say now, and we would only grate upon each other. I bought a pack of cigarettes and went outside on the terrace.

The briskness of November tinged the air. The skies were leaden and the port below was hidden in a bank of mist. Trees that yesterday were glorious and bright were today dark black lines in listless gray.

"Jon!" someone called from the lobby. Eddie Flanagan walked slowly across the terrace. When he came alongside me, he asked, "Leaving today?"

"About one."

"Think we'll leave, too." He squinted at the weather. "We were going to stay another day or two. Why so somber? Love life going badly?"

I shook my head. "Bad news about a friend of mine."

"Would I know him?"

"Sure you would. Karel Karazov, the travel agent."

"What about him?"

"He was taken off a Russian plane in Prague. They're holding him for espionage."

"Hmmm."

Our footsteps fell on the stones of the terrace.

"Tough break," he added. "Yes, I glanced over that this morning."

"Depressing," I said. I was deciding rapidly to say nothing more to Eddie. He was working for the government, and I had no idea what Karazov wanted hidden. If I kept a secret on the grounds of personal friendship, could I still be guilty of treason? I had no idea what I was involved in, or what the law required. To whom should I report it? And what if that resulted in trouble for Karazov? I decided not to say anything.

"Who's this Evelyn?" I asked.

"Oh, met her in Rome. Cute kid. Lots of fun. Nothing serious, you understand." He was grinning. His sport shirt was open; he wore the silver chain.

"I understand." I wanted to tell him about Cindy Lou but decided against that, too. The fog out over the black trees below was messy and discouraging.

"Your Nadya is pretty spectacular. I'd say she's got you by the balls."

"Think so?" I smiled and conceded: "I like her."

"Kinda shows, you know?" He punched me on the arm.

"Do you always wear a gun?" I said. I had seen the bulge when he pulled back his arm.

"Regulations," he smiled.

"State Department?"

"Well, you know," he shrugged and grinned.

"The pistol-packin' padre."

"You better believe it. Say, I'm pretty good with it, for a guy who never shot a gun. It's the New Frontier," he joked. "Limited warfare."

"At least now I know you're not with the Peace Corps."

"I flunked the entrance exam."

"You won't say then?"

"Can't."

"I don't mean to pry."

"We're old buddies." Another punch on the arm.

"You'll go back to the mainland with us?"

"If that's okay. We'll stay in Naples a day or so. See Pompei and all that jazz."

"I have to get back to work. You'll call when you get to Rome?"
"Intend to—you can count on it. We'll meet you here at one."

The next morning in Rome, Signorina Bianca gave me a fistful
of messages from Jack Prescott. He had called three times. While I
was beginning my breakfast, the phone jangled. He asked me to
meet him at a little coffee bar we both knew, not far from the
pensione. I hung up and returned to my lukewarm *caffè latte*. I
squeezed out the doughy center of a roll and wadded it into a
ball. I didn't feel like eating it this morning. I spread apricot
marmalade on the crisp crust and forced myself to chew it.
Everything had been going so well, and now I felt immensely
depressed.

Jack's story concerned the two Roman detectives he had hired
to follow Padre Georges. They waited a block from Jack's house
while Jack left for town. Twenty minutes later George arrived
in a gray Fiat. He and Marilou left together and the detectives
set out behind them. Apparently George suspected something and
lost the detectives in traffic, twisting and turning and doubling
back. The next day the same process was repeated. But this time
another car followed Jack's detectives. When the detectives lost
contact with George's car, they stopped to telephone Jack. While
they were in the booth, George's three detectives approached and
demanded to know who Jack's detectives were working for. Jack's
detectives didn't know what to say. George's detectives asked,
"Are you working for the Holy Office?" The suggestion offered
an escape. Jack's detectives slowly nodded, "*Si!*" They then
telephoned Jack to ask if that was okay.

"What did you say?" I laughed.

"I fired them. They were pretty hopeless. But I gave them a
bonus for that answer. Can you imagine George's face when his
men reported in?"

"It's comic opera," I said.

"But it's my wife." There were crow's-feet around his eyes but
he was still half smiling. "The bitch!"

"What next?"

"I'm going to fly to Paris next week. I've got to get to the
bottom of this. There are people there who know George.
Secondly"—he was painstakingly systematic and objective in his

speech—"I want to visit the Arab League office and discourage them from hiring her. She hasn't any future with George. He's going to drop her like a hot potato."

"What do you care?"

He looked miserably into his brown, milky coffee. "I can't get her out of my mind. I love her more than ever. I love her and I hate her. But I want her back. That filthy bastard isn't going to do a thing for her. She's just a little girl from a small town and he's doing a snow job. Adultery: it's so sophisticated. She's way over her head!"

"You better get some sleep. You're not going to make good decisions in the state you're in."

He raised his head and looked at me as if I was nuts. "That's pretty easy to say."

"Sorry. I'll keep quiet."

"I'm trying to be objective," he pleaded. "I'm trying not to act like a cuckolded husband. But, brother, it's tough."

My stomach felt like the uneaten wad of dough I had left on the table.

That afternoon I helped Nadya move her bags to the room next to mine. Our bodies longed for each other, yet we were combating some strange inward hostility. If we could only shut off our minds, perhaps everything would be all right. I analyzed and reanalyzed our relationship; I could not find the key. But even our despair somehow heightened the clamor of our bodies. The sight of her or the thought of her stirred coals in my loins until the ache became overpowering. Blindly, dumbly, almost like automatons we threw ourselves into each other's arms during the siesta hours, and then could hardly wait until evening. I do not know exactly what she was feeling: I am certain that she was as passionate, as insatiable, as desperate as I. Yet our love went badly. She could come to a plateau, but never through or over it—at least, I could not bring her. The harder I tried, the worse things went. In my intensity I would yield too quickly and instantly become limp and useless. Or else, after great exertions it would become apparent that, though responsive and willing, she could go no further. I ached from the activity; I felt drained and tired, and developed a light headache that seemed never quite to leave me. Something was terribly wrong: we could do so well by each other, and yet now we seemed to be destroying ourselves. I wished we had not gone ahead so fast. I wished I could see more intelligently what needed to be done. I wished we could both shut off our minds and be two gay, joyful animals. My wishes rose into the November skies in vain.

The Council, too, was going badly. Newcomers to Rome commented on how tired everyone looked. Rumors about the torpedoing of the Jewish document—in which the Council tried to take up a friendly and brotherly attitude, after so many centuries of neglect, abuse, and atrocity—filled the gray-clouded air. The pronounced theological anti-Semitism of the conservatives seemed to make Jewish–Catholic relations worse, not better. Moreover, other movements were afoot to block the affirmation of religious liberty, and still others to emasculate the document encouraging the ecumenical movement. The arguments on the floor of the Council were now pedestrian and predictable and mostly concerned with intramural affairs of the narrowest bureaucratic sort. I was beginning to regret having become involved in such churchy materials.

When I sat at my typewriter, I thought of Nadya. When I sat at a press conference, an image of her lovely body hung like a tapestry before my imagination. As we ate dinner together, gaily enough in front of friends, we secretly longed to be together. We were trying to kill something evil in each other. We had faith in each other, if only we could get past some unseen obstacle; we did not know what the enemy was or where to strike. Hence, there was a kind of dishonesty between us. We could scarcely talk about our problem together—our talking was done solely with our bodies. Perhaps for the uneducated such language is sufficient and, if so, there is no more terrible curse than education.

In any case, we doggedly pursed our lovemaking. We came to know every inch of each other's body, every hair, every irregular jutting bone, every softness, every pleasure spot. We tried to please each other; mute in words, we could at least do that for each other. We tried every position our whims or interest led us to. Gradually, Nadya, too, came to take the lead. We gave each other a course in sensuality. We used our tongues; it brought us to the highest pitch of surrender. It was the most intimate, boldest, most tender respect we could pay each other. The taste of musk, a coarse hair clinging to the roof of my mouth, the sweet-soft liquid on my chin and nose, the shudder and sudden turn, ended for a while in comfort and childlike resting in each other's arms.

Yet we were sometimes near tears in our despair. For soon the sense of oneness would dissipate, and we would become two, and we were no closer than we had been before: two bags of skin stretched over bone and two imprisoned egos unable to escape and find each other.

Yet it was not a mystique of unity we sought together, not some continuous ecstatic state. What we sought was an ability to see our lives together and to speak the truth. We had a month-long novitiate getting used to our bodies; it was crucial to put novelty and mere excitement behind us. We needed to be able to see each other as distinct human beings, Jon and Nadya, with separate life projects and interests and fears, and a common struggle for self-liberation up ahead. It might turn out to be a joint struggle, or a separate one for each of us.

We went once to an ecumenical service arranged privately by several priests we knew. Father Metzger was there, with ten others, together with ten or twelve English-speaking Protestant ministers, gathered around the side altar of a virtually empty parish church. The ministers read the prayers at the mass, including the epistle and the gospel. In the shadow of St. Peter's they read the prayers of the offertory and the canon aloud with all those present. The bread was raised and later broken; the wine was raised and later offered to all. At the moment for communion, Nadya joined me. As we chewed the bread and drank the wine, body and blood, I could not help thinking of our ancestors, who for centuries had celebrated this rite. I felt as though we stood in a very long procession. I felt proud of Nadya and myself. We were earning our emotional and personal freedom. There was no other way to do what we had to do, and we were willing to fight fears and guilts and hesitations.

Walking down the street afterwards, I asked Nadya if she had felt guilty going to the altar.

"No, not at all," she said.

"What would your mother say?"

"Ah, yes, in that sense. Yes, I had mixed feelings. But feelings are not guilt."

"What do you think of us?"

She smiled. "Disgusting."

"You don't mean that."

"No," she laughed. "Okay—" She paused. "Only that something is wrong."

"What is it?"

"I ask myself. I keep thinking it is my fault. In some way I am still afraid."

"You don't trust me."

"Oh no, I trust you. But perhaps you are right. There is something—"

"What is it?"

She shrugged. "I can't say it because I can't see it. I don't know what."

"I wish I could make you feel secure."

"And yourself. You are up, then down. You are not very settled either, Jonny."

"It is mainly the Council. And Karazov . . ."

"At least, you should talk about it. Do you realize how seldom we talk to each other? I feel perfectly useless to you. You tell me a few words about your work. But what do I really know? Am I supposed to be one-third of a human being because I am a woman? Good for bed but not for talk?"

"I think we talk a great deal. Compared to most couples."

"Hmmm. Maybe. But we are not most couples. And for me it is not enough."

"All right, then, let's talk. What do you want to talk about?" I tried not to allow the tone to be too childish.

"Not like that. That is the way not to talk."

"I'm serious. What do we talk about? Psychoanalyze each other? You're not being fair. I try hard to keep talking. After all, we've only known each other, essentially, a month."

"Oh, I know you try. It's just that—"

"That what?" I asked after a silence.

"It's hopeless, I guess."

"It isn't hopeless. We're making progress. Like right now. We just have to be honest with each other."

She flicked her eyebrows: "That's easy to say."

"How are we not being honest?"

"You're taking everything personally," she challenged me.

"Should I take it impersonally?"

"Jonny!" she whispered. We were walking in the Borghese gardens near the Piazza del Popolo. The leaves of the sycamores were yellow and brown with decay. The autumnal tang of death was in the air, sweet and sad.

My mood was defensive. I decided I had to change it and took a deep breath of air. The clouds above were leaden. Thousands of people lived underneath them; a busload of children and women and soldiers and old men disgorged at the corner. A child rolled a hoop on the sidewalk.

"You know you're very beautiful," I said.

She looked into my eyes. "That's nice."

"I love you."

She nodded as she walked.

"Is it too early to say that?"

"No, keep saying it."

"And you?"

She watched her red shoes step out in front of her for a moment. "I think it often, even when I don't say it."

"We have to talk more, remember?"

"I'll try."

Her eyes were bright again and we were happy for a time.

21

ONE WEDNESDAY in mid-November, just before the two o'clock press briefing, I noted a black Mercedes on the Via della Conciliazione. Several of us were sitting on the white stone benches enjoying the warm sun. When I glanced up, the two men in the car seemed to be studying me. I shrugged the impression off, but I retained the image of a man with closely cut blond hair.

The next evening, as I left a restaurant in Piazza Navona, I noticed a black Mercedes whose license plate bore the initials of the Diplomatic Corps. The same tall blond man was standing with his foot against the base of the foundation thirty feet away. My stomach reacted as if the man were in some way interested in me. That damn packet, I thought, is playing tricks with my mind.

I walked homeward alone. Nadya had complained of a headache and gone to bed; she was just getting over a twenty-four-hour flu. Signorina Bianca had made soup for her. The Council was boring her and she wanted me all to herself. It seemed unfair of her to suggest that I not work so hard; I took her almost everywhere I went.

The night air and the loneliness refreshed me. I longed to be alone; I needed it like air. I hoped that that did not disqualify me for marriage. For I loved being able to walk home to Nadya. "You just want me to be here." she had said. "You want me around. You take me for granted." I had quoted a writer who said marriage isn't based on passionate love but on affection as quiet as slipping into comfortable slippers. "And I hate being

a pair of old slippers!" she added. "I detest that idea. I'm not
just a shoe you can pick up when you like."

I smiled as I walked through the night. Poor little Nadya. I
neglected her. I really would have to change my life if I married.
The evening was crisp and beautiful. The brightest stars penetrated
the glare from the city, hundreds of them. Men in ancient Rome
and medieval Rome had seen those same stars, walking to their
loves. A nobleman was murdered by his lover's brothers, his body
thrown in the Tiber; he had jewels hidden on his person, but no
one ever found his body. That image led to another. I looked
back over my shoulder.

I had never believed in the demimonde of espionage. But I
couldn't stave off a feeling of fear. As I walked alone in the
streets, I longed for the days when I had been innocent and had
walked without anxiety. Which is the real world—the world of
every day or that of war? I kept shaking my head and recalling
childhood scenes so that my earlier sense of reality would come
back.

By the time I had reached the *pensione*, I was deeply wrapped
in strange emotions. I entered my room and, without turning on
the light, knocked quietly on Nadya's door. There was no answer. I
slowly turned the knob. I bent over her and kissed her forehead. I
adjusted the sheet over her bare shoulder and stood looking upon
her for several minutes. I retreated to my own room and lay
awake for a long time.

The next day, after the two o'clock briefing, the blond man
walked up to me on the sidewalk in full view of everybody.

"May I speak with you a moment?" He nodded toward the
Mercedes.

I froze. I was determined not to enter the car.

"My name is Jaroslav Palica," he said. "I am an aide at the
Czechoslovak consulate. I am told that you have testimony that
will help a friend of yours."

It was not difficult to play dumb. I said: "A friend?"

He studied my face with his gray eyes. "Karel Karazov."

"Karazov?" I was not very convincing.

"I am certain you know him."

I was embarrassed, and when he nodded again toward the car,

I felt obliged to go. His authority was vaguely threatening, as if there really were no choice.

I turned from him for a moment, thinking rapidly. "All right," I said, finding the courage to look him in the eye. "One moment." Before he could protest, I walked over to a friend of mine, who knew Nadya, and handed him my briefcase.

"Please tell Nadya that I was picked up to go to the Czech consulate. She'll understand. I'll telephone her as soon as I can. *It's important*," I said quietly.

Frisbe, from *The New York Times*, looked at me as if I was putting him on.

"Please call her right away," I said.

He looked at Palica and at the car and back to me. He still seemed puzzled, but I knew I could trust him. I rejoined Palica and he led me to the car. I was slightly dismayed when I looked through the back window and saw Frisbe still taking part in the animated discussion in front of the USO building. The driver sped us up toward St. Peter's, turned, and started out Via Gregorio Settimo for the countryside.

Palica turned in the front seat. I was alone in the back. "Karazov is well. He sends greetings."

I nodded.

He turned and said something to the driver in a Slavic tongue; I was not certain it was Czech. We drove for ten minutes, turned left, and headed down a narrow road along the hilltop that led, I knew, to the Russian embassy. Still not a word. To my relief, we passed under the aqueduct—the white dome of St. Peter's lay to the left across a field of grass—and drove past the armed guards at the gate of the embassy. Near the brow of the hill, at the city walls, the car slowed. We drove through Garibaldi's park overlooking the yellow tiled roofs of the city.

"Would you like to walk?" The blond man had already opened his door. I opened mine and got out. His face was lined and I realized that, despite his athletic frame, he was older than I had thought. He looked exactly like a man I knew in Conemaugh, the owner of a Texaco station—his name was Siftak—and I could imagine Palica in the green uniform, grease on his hands. The coincidence of images allowed me to forget my fears.

We walked up and down in the park along the stone railing,

in the midst of old people and children and a few tourists, a public and reassuring place. I began to understand that they would not threaten me.

"My business is very simple," Palica said. "You received a package from Karazov. He now requests it. I received a message from him to ask you for it."

I was frightened, very frightened. But I kept seeing Karazov's intense eyes. It seemed to me strange that the Czech had no note from Karazov, and had not met me under more sociable conditions—a drink, a lunch—as would befit mutual friends of a man in trouble. And of course he had not yet given the password. I was not going to play secret agent, and decided neither to admit receiving the package nor to deny it.

"You say that I have a package?" I asked quietly.

"Yes."

I bluffed: "Where *is* Karazov? The papers say he is a U.S. citizen. Hasn't Washington filed a protest?"

"He is well. Do you deny having the papers?"

He wasn't certain I had them. My voice faltered: "Karazov is an acquaintance, a friend."

"You knew him well." His tone was also uncertain. I noticed that Palica wore a silver ring with a blue stone where a wedding band would be. He had strong hairy fingers. We were standing at the rail, overlooking the cupolas and monuments and weather-worn roofs.

"He was my travel agent. He arranged my trip."

"You will not help him then?"

"I'd be glad to help him, as a friend. But Washington is doing all it can, isn't it?"

"What I am asking you is unofficial. I am Karazov's friend. Not a soul in the world will know. That is why we meet in a place like this. There is no threat involved. It is to help Karazov. He is in trouble."

"I would like to help him," I said.

Palica was exasperated. "Do you admit having the package?"

"You keep talking about a package."

"Do you deny having it?"

I looked him in the eye and forced myself to hold the gaze. His eyes were gray-green, willful, strong—but he did not know enough to be sure of his ground and he was trying not to threaten me.

"I wish Karazov well," I said. "Beyond that . . . ?"

He looked at me for a long time. I wondered what he was thinking and who he was. His blue shirt had been fresh this morning. I wondered if, like Eddie, he was wearing a shoulder holster. I thought of bumping against him accidentally, but warned myself against it.

Finally he said: "Mr. Svoboda, I suppose we must get back to town. Your sweetheart will be waiting for you. Karazov will be disappointed."

We left the railing and slid into the new-smelling car. The driver took me directly to my *pensione*, without directions from me. "Thank you for your trouble, Mr. Svoboda," Palica said. His face seemed lined, weary, and bored. I felt sorry for disappointing him.

"Thank you for the drive," I said. I looked at the driver and deliberately said good-bye to him, too. He nodded, without breaking his silence. I walked slowly inside. Then, when the car purred quietly away, I bounded upstairs.

Jack Prescott telephoned just after I had explained the whole situation to Nadya. We were sitting at the window. When Signorina Bianca knocked at the door, I arose, put on the raincoat I used as a bathrobe, and went out to the phone.

Jack explained that he had had the meeting with Metzger and the other priests. He told them about George and Marilou but, of course, they didn't believe a word of it. "They took it as proof I'm insane," he said.

"Did you tell them about the detectives?"

"Yes," he said glumly. "But George Georges beat me to it. He said Marilou saw them following her and became afraid. She called him to come help her. He said she was afraid I might kidnap the children or something. You see, I'm a monster."

I was silent a moment. "And naturally they believe him."

"Naturally!" His hostility cut through the poor connection. "What next?"

"I'm on to something in Paris. A friend of mine knows a gal who had an affair with some priest from Rome three years ago.

Broke up her marriage and then the priest skipped town. Sounds like George's work to me. And I want to check with the Arabs. Did you see the *Times* today?"

There had been another front-page story about the maneuvers of the Cardinal Secretary of State to scuttle the Jewish document. "Yes," I said.

"George-Georges is at it again."

"When are you leaving?"

"There's a plane at seven."

"You sound much better today. I'm glad."

"Well, I'm doing something." Silence. "Besides, I know I'm right. You know how I hate those bastards."

"That helps."

"You bet it does! See you in about a week." An afterthought: "Regards to Nadya."

My involvement with Jack and Marilou troubled Nadya. "I don't want to get married," she moaned. "I don't think I can take it."

I patted her hip. "You'll be all right."

"I mean it," she said.

"It'll take care of itself."

"Jon," her voice changed. "Don't see the Czech again. Go to the embassy. I know how these things go. They are very dangerous."

"I don't know who to call."

"Ask for the intelligence officer."

"I don't want to get messed up in something complicated. What if Karazov is working for the Russians?"

"If so, you should turn in the packet immediately."

An idea suddenly struck me. "I could call Eddie Flanagan."

"I'd call someone more official," she objected. "But that would be better than nothing."

"I'll call him today," I promised.

When I tried, he was out of town; a girl's voice told me he would be in Milan until Monday. I left my number and decided I could wait another couple of days.

Nadya and I had something to celebrate that night. In the afternoon mail I received a letter from a New York publisher accepting my thesis, *The Person Judges,* for publication. The house had a distinguished imprint, and they offered me a thousand dollar advance. I could see the book in print, with my name on it. I knew it would impress the department at Berkeley, where an offer would still be open next September. With the advance and a little more, Nadya and I would have money to stay until June. She had recently received a letter from the *Wall Street Journal,* inviting her to contribute three short articles on the fashion industry in Rome, Paris, and London. Her former boss had told her he was going to recommend her to the *Journal,* and with both of us at work we might have a comfortable spring. We toasted each other with champagne and had the best dinner we had had together, just the two of us. That night we walked both sides of the Via Veneto, and then through the darkened streets toward home.

My thoughts were full of hope and promise. More than anything else, I wanted to set to work on a two-volume study of human judgment as it operates in the arts and in action. What factors enter into a decision to do something, to let a line of prose stand or to revise it? I wanted to do a *Critique of Judgment* that might take me five or six years to begin to get on paper. Moreover, before settling down to the task, I wanted to fill up several notebooks with attempts to capture my own sensibility, with its own oddities and differences. How does one do that? How does one know that this incident and not that, these words and not those, will best reveal what one wishes to reveal? The most important things cannot be said directly: they are conveyed in ways of which we have only the dimmest knowledge. Precisely such factors, I wished to show, are the most influential ones in making judgments and decisions.

I now felt as though I had a goal again; I loved what would absorb me for a decade. Such a project fulfilled my secret yearnings. I had a dread of failing to throw up something solid against the sands of life; I longed to leave behind at least one work that would stand. The fact that so good a publishing house had accepted my first book, which seemed to me plainly inferior to what I hoped to do, eased a hidden insecurity. For seven or eight years, without having published anything more than a handful of articles, I had sustained myself on the image that I was a professional writer. My dreams seemed vindicated; I would not have to confess, as I secretly feared, that I had merely been pretentious.

It was good to be able to share my release with Nadya. I felt I was escaping from a kind of prison. I knew the rest would be good; the worst was over. Moreover, we were both gladdened by her decision to take on the assignment from the *Journal*. She knew more about business economics than almost anyone her age; she would try out her skills on the world of fashion. It was fun to look on her again as the professional woman. Seeing her from across the room, I could imagine myself being a little afraid of her—so sure of herself, so determined, so experienced. It made me very proud to be sitting at the table with her. We saw the world with new eyes that night. It was the best night we had together.

On Sunday, a special delivery letter came. The return address was yet another publishing house. The editors had been reading my reports on the Council and wanted to know if I would accept three thousand dollars as an advance, half on completion of the manuscript, half on publication, for a manuscript of sixty thousand words about the Council. I was sorely tempted by the money. It would guarantee our stay in Europe. But I didn't have an agent and wasn't sure what to do. The deadline was perilously close—March 15. They would speed up publication in order to have the book out by the end of June. The money was too attractive and I couldn't simply turn it down. The offer itself was flattering and the letter even more so. On the other hand a book on the Council would not help my career at all, might even hurt it; academic people would call it "journalistic," and I would be typed for years as a "religious" writer. Moreover, Nadya and I had more or less decided to travel together; she had to visit Paris and London, and I could keep my notebooks anywhere.

My emotions were confused. I had a great deal of factual information and anecdotal material I had not been able to use in my articles. It was a shame to waste it. I set my regular work aside and began making outlines of the book on the Council. If the original concept is correct, I told myself, the book will almost write itself and it will have an impact. Sheets with diagrams, cryptic sentences, and experimental titles gradually surrounded me.

When Nadya walked in with a small armful of parcels, I was in a world all my own, full of the joy and pleasure of creation. The unwritten book was gleaming and beautiful, its vision unmarred by the slow, painful, and clumsy steps of execution. I already saw enthusiastic reviews and large sales—I had no idea what an average sale is, how drab and unintelligent reviewers become when one's own book is at stake, how difficult it is in the flood of new books to be reviewed or even noticed, how difficult it is to place a new book on shelves where it may be seen for more than three or four weeks. I saw myself as a veteran author with two successful books almost overnight.

"But, Jon," Nadya said when she finished reading the letter. "What am I going to be doing, while you work on your book night and day?"

22

On Tuesday morning I was perplexed as I walked down the marble stairs of the *pensione*. I had decided to take a walk and "think about my book," although when it came down to it, I knew I would decline the second offer. In fact, the walk was going to be an effort to sort out my emotions and to decide what needed changing in my life. I desperately did not want to lose Nadya. Something had to be changed—I didn't know what. The sun was gleaming on the pavement as I stepped out the door. When I looked up, the black Mercedes was waiting in the shade on the other side.

Palica was already out of the car.

"May I see you again? I have a message."

I felt so low I didn't object. I climbed in the car and we set off. This time Palica sat in the back.

"Time is running out," he said. "Karazov must have the package. To be more exact, I must have it. We know that you have it."

"You have reasons to think I have it. You don't know," I said. I didn't feel like cooperating with anyone. I felt apathetic.

"You admit you have it, then?"

"No—"

He waved his hairy hand menacingly. "This is no time for games. You have it."

"Yes, I have it." What did I care? I was tired of pretending.

"Good." He smiled. "You will bring it to me this afternoon at four. Carry it in this." He unwrapped a thick book from brown wrapping paper. He placed a stubby thumb under one corner of the cover and lifted it. The book was hollow. "Is it big enough?"

I looked him in the eye, wondering whether to reply or not. "Yes."

"Good." He sat back and looked out the window as he talked. "We will come again in the car. Merely walk over and hand it through the window. Karazov will be eternally grateful."

"Is he dead?" I asked.

He smiled. "No, he is well. He will be grateful."

"I can't have it by four."

"Why not?"

"It will take until tomorrow." My tone was meant to convey a total stubbornness. I wanted time to talk to Eddie. Besides, there was a rough truth to what I said. I would have to go to the American Express office and the day was already crowded with interviews. I did not intend to give up the morning.

Palica pondered. "All right. Tomorrow. At eleven. We will find you."

"All right," I said. I was weary and I really didn't care. I didn't intend to give him the packet, and it was only a matter of how to avoid doing so. I had the impression that they were under orders not to create an incident—Karazov was an American citizen and there was international trouble enough. I hoped I was not being cowardly. I felt I should contact Eddie, but anything more than that might compromise Karazov. I hoped Eddie would know what to do.

That morning I received a letter from my brother. Dad's spirits, he said, had improved over the last few months. But he's still acting like a vegetable: eat, drink, watch television. "We try to get him outside, get him interested in things. But you know Dad. He's so goddam stubborn. He never did like cards or sports, and now even reading tires him. We bought him a tape recorder, hoping he'd recall some old memories and maybe dictate his memoirs. But he never uses it."

David added that he was definitely committed to running for Congress in 1964. He went to Washington and obtained a promise from the Kennedys that they would support him, and possibly visit the city for him. "The local committeemen sure got into line after that! It looks like I'll get the nomination for sure, and if we get a Kennedy landslide, I'll win the election easily. In fact, I'll win it anyway. The Democratic machine is collapsing and there are a lot of new faces supporting me. People are tired of Soldier—what has he done for this district in fourteen years? Don't bring any long-haired girls back to town and ruin it for me!!!"

About noon Jack Prescott returned from Paris. He met me outside the press office at the top of Via della Conciliazione and persuaded me to skip the initial briefing and go with him to lunch. His expression was a combination of grimness and excitement.

"I got the goods on George-Georges all right," he said. "You won't believe it. You won't believe it." He pulled me into a small trattoria around the corner. We stepped through the cool front room and out into a tiny courtyard where there were only two small tables. The eastward stucco wall was brilliant white. Supported by thin trellises, thick leaves flapped languidly in the air above us.

"George-Georges," he said triumphantly, "is a secret agent. He uses at least three aliases. And he has broken up not one marriage, but two." The dramatic effect was spoiled by the appearance of a meek waiter with straight black hair. Jack ordered hurriedly for both of us: "Tortellini soup and *saltimbocca*. Okay?" he asked me. I nodded.

"*Insalata?*" the waiter asked.

"*Verde,*" Jack replied impatiently.

"*Vino?*" the waiter meekly asked.

"*Vino di tavola. Bianco.*" Jack waved the waiter away. He turned eagerly to me.

I didn't like the obsession I saw in Jack's eyes. The worst thing

Marilou and George had done was that. "Where did you find out?"

"This friend of mine used to work for the embassy in Rome. He said George-Georges traveled in Russia for the Vatican, but also for the CIA. Did you know George speaks fluent Russian?"

"Of course!" I improvised. "The third Rome. The wave of the future."

"Anyway, my friend said George-Georges had two bank accounts in Rome, under other names."

"And the Dominicans didn't know?"

Jack shrugged. "One of the names he used is Farina."

"I've heard that name," I said.

"There's a story to it. He was running around with the wife of a navy lieutenant in the Middle East. After he threw her over, he kept her name."

"Gallant," I nodded.

"Emmy, the girl I told you about, the second one? She recognized his picture right away. She said she's practiced hating him for seven years. Except," Jack's voice went lame, "she got a divorce out of it." He was reanimated: "George-Georges used to tell her how much he loved Farina—talked about her incessantly. Emmy felt sorry for him. That's how it all started. Lonely priest falls in love and then, in sorrow, has to deny himself and leave the beautiful Farina. I wonder if Marilou's heard that one?"

When I didn't answer, he held up a thin box. "I can't wait to play this for you. I set a recorder under their bed. It was activated by voices and creaking springs. I have evidence enough to hang him."

"Good Lord, Jack!"

"It's self-defense, man. I'm not fighting for my wife anymore. I'm fighting for my sanity."

During the rest of the meal he elaborated the details he had learned, from whom, and the degree of evidence that he was able to accumulate. Emmy gave him a notarized affidavit identifying the photograph of Georges as the man who had betrayed her in 1956. The embassy official gave Jack the name of a man who knew the intelligence files in Rome. I asked Jack to let me have that number, in case I needed it. He was puzzled but let me copy it.

"I'm sorry," Jack said before we left. "I didn't mean what I said about Marilou. I love her. I'd take her back right away and forgive her everything. I don't want to lose the children." Tears filled his eyes. The wine had made him sentimental.

Eddie Flanagan had promised to come to the *pensione* early Wednesday morning. He drove up in a red Ferrari about nine. "Where did you get that?" I asked, thumping the smooth fender. "Borrowed from a friend. Where do you want to talk?" "Anywhere."

"This is Tom Andreotti," Eddie introduced the man in the seat beside him. "He's been on the case full-time." As Andreotti and I shook hands, Eddie grinned and turned in his seat, scrutinizing the buildings around the piazza. "By the way. Grapes grapes GRAPES grapes. Butter butter BUTTERfly!" He laughed at the expression on my face. "Get in."

I looked up and down the block while Andreotti climbed into the narrow back seat. "How did you—what is this?" I slid into the black leather bucket.

"No questions, please," he laughed. "Do you have the goods?" "Yes, keep driving."

"I really don't know much," Andreotti said over the roar of the motor and the wind. "When Eddie mentioned Karazov, he was put in touch with me. Our drop was being watched. Looks like Karazov sized it up and went to you. There was no way we could find out where to look. Apparently he didn't decide on you until the last moment. So we've had a frantic three weeks. Could have been anywhere in Europe, you know. He travels."

I nodded. "He told me I wouldn't be bothered unless something happened to him." We drove awhile and then I told Eddie about Palica and the Czechs. Andreotti wanted a detailed description of Palica.

Eddie grinned when he had heard the story; he slapped my knee. "You need help, call old Eddie."

"I wasn't going to give it to them," I said with bravado, which sounded a little false.

"I'll put both of us in for a medal," Eddie said, screeching around a corner. "The Grand Prix." He pronounced it pricks.

"You've got to tell me one thing," I said. "Who is Karazov working for? And Palica?"

"You'll have to figure out Karazov for yourself," Andreotti

said. "As for Palica, as far as I know he's on the other side."

"He didn't have the password." I mused.

"You did a pretty gutsy thing." Andreotti delivered it as praise only an amateur would get.

Eddie noticed and broke in: "Okay, where do we pick up the goodies?"

"American Express," I said.

"Why didn't you tell me?" A quick look over his shoulder. The car screeched in a U-turn and then spun down a right angle to the left.

I had the key in a comb case. We got the packet from the deposit box and Eddie slipped it under his shirt.

"We make another one just like it?" Eddie asked.

Andreotti nodded. He looked at me. "You don't have to go along with this. But it may give us an extra day. It might help Karazov."

I didn't have much choice.

We drove to a department store and bought a notebook. Andreotti stopped at a café and cut the binding of the notebook, so that the pages were loose. Then I wrote a series of numerals on each page, nine digits on each. We chose the digits at random. When each page was neatly numbered, we stacked them and slipped them back into their cover for stiffness.

"That should keep them busy for an hour or two."

"Longer if they send them away," Andreotti said. He wrapped the pages neatly in the brown paper, duplicating the original packet exactly.

We drove quietly back to the *pensione*.

"If they trouble you a second time, tell them you handed the packet to us. Anything happens to you, we know who to call." I couldn't tell if Andreotti was trying to frighten me.

Eddie spoke with a quiet laugh. "I'll let you off here. Be good."

"Thanks," I nodded. I didn't look forward to seeing Palica again.

"There won't be any more trouble," Andreotti repeated. "If you need help"—be leaned to one side, slipped out his wallet, gave me a card—"someone at this number can find me instantly."

"Thanks," I waved. The Ferrari sped off.

I walked home rapidly, breaking into a sweat. I hurried through the cool hallway, and up the stairs to my room.

"Jon?" Nadya called from the other room. She was combing out her hair. "What are you doing?"

"Hold that. Right there. The sunlight in your hair. Ah, if I were a photographer."

"What were you doing? Where were you?"

"I met Eddie, like I promised. He gave me the password."

"What password?"

"For Karazov's packet."

"Eddie?"

"Eddie Flanagan. You should have seen him laugh at the look on my face."

"I'm so glad you're rid of it."

"So am I, baby. So am I."

"But isn't that it there?"

I held it up. "A dummy."

"What are you doing with it?"

"Putting it in the book. Palica will be here this morning."

"Don't do it, Jon."

"They can't create an incident. Besides, there's nothing to gain by hurting me. I'm nobody. They know that by now."

"Don't you think they follow you? Don't you think they saw you with Eddie? You're always being watched."

I was hugging her and squeezing her bottom. "Not always I hope."

"Jon," she pushed away. "Promise me you won't."

"It means a few more hours of tension," I agreed. I didn't want to see Palica's face again.

"It's dangerous for people like you. It isn't your profession. You should stay out of it."

I was more ashamed of going back on my word to Andreotti and Eddie, however, than afraid of facing the Czechs.

"I'll be careful," I said and hugged her. She struggled at first. "You get yourself ready and we'll play all day! We can go to lunch—the whole day will be ours." I patted her bottom.

A few moments later I descended the stairs with the book. No car was in sight. I waited a full ninety seconds before the black Mercedes rounded the corner. My eyes scanned the buildings.

The Mercedes parked in the shade on the other side of the street. I walked across and handed the book over the thick plate glass of the half-lowered window. Palica tapped the cover and

looked inside. He smiled and said: "Thank you, sir. Karazov will
be very pleased." He reached a white envelope through the
window. "For your trouble."

I shook my head. "Karazov is my friend."

Palica smiled. "I'll tell him that. Good-bye." He waved and the
driver pressed the accelerator.

I looked up at the cobalt sky, and at the sun glistening on the
ancient pines around the Castello. I walked slowly across the
street. I didn't know then that Andreotti and Eddie were watching.

"*Buon giorno!*" The nine-year-old girl at the window greeted me.

"Good morning," I enunciated carefully, with a smile.

"Good morn-*ning*," she repeated with concentration, getting
the sound almost right.

"Good *mor*-ning!" I sang again, and smiled going up the stairs
to Nadya.

That was the first day Nadya was feeling really well, after a
week of convalescence. *The Liberal Catholic* had my last article
in hand, and I could await the events of the closing days for a
wrap-up. My obligations would then be concluded and Nadya
and I would be free to travel. We played and struggled, and lay
quietly and talked. We fell asleep and began to play again. I
marveled all the time how beautiful she was, and how lucky I
was to find her. It seemed too good. In that respect, Nadya and
I were similar: when things went well, we anticipated tragedy.

It was late afternoon when we went together into the shower
room across the hall. Her skin was less slippery than usual, and
cool. Her nipples were violet-pink and soft; water gathered on the
tips and dripped. Between her legs, when she turned, the hair
clung together in long dark lines. I kissed her upon lips that
smelled of silver water. She tweaked my shrunken, limp, and dismal
violet penis and began to laugh. I pressed her so close a vacuum
was created between our chests and a sound rang out between
us and we laughed under the running water.

"Let's go for a drive," I repeated under the final rinse.

"Okay," she brightened. "Where to?"

I shrugged. "Out into the country?"

"I'd like to get the air," she said, flicking a finger across the
dark beauty spot. "I haven't been out for weeks."

I called Jack and asked if I could borrow his car. He said sure—Marilou had it but wouldn't be using it—and we took a cab out to his apartment. Marilou met us at the door. We pretended and she pretended; the moments were awkward.

"Have fun," she said as we left.

"We'll have it back by seven," I promised.

"Keep it till late," she replied. "You might as well. Jack went out with friends of his. I won't be using it. Enjoy it while you can." She feigned a smile and withdrew behind the door.

We drove back into the city, and out along the boulevards leading past St. John Lateran's and the Baths of Caracalla.

"What did you think of Marilou?" I asked.

"I felt sorry for her."

"Why?"

"I liked her. I had expected someone—more beautiful, more sophisticated. It made me sadder. She seems confused."

"But you liked her?"

"A wife, a mother. Yes, I liked her. I didn't have the impression she is happy."

"She used to be quite happy. She was proud of the first baby. Even when I saw them last August, she was very happy. A very different person."

We didn't care to go down into the catacombs; we had each done that before. We walked around in the gardens. Thick brown leaves had fallen from the rows of shrubbery. We drove down to the monument to the hostages machine-gunned by the Germans after a platoon of soldiers had been bombed in the city. The immense violet stone covering the three hundred graves seemed disproportionate and pretentious. The statue of three chained victims was a caricature of proletarian figures. It was larger than life and meant to glorify, as if fascist art had won after all.

That evening we dined at a vine-covered trattoria in the countryside. The evening air was brisk; the accordion player was merry. Wide-eyed children looked at us dumbly, their parents, suspiciously. The lasagna was heavy. The paper napkins were tissue-thin, shiny, and hard; the wooden tables had suffered many rains.

The stars above were clean and precise. I held Nadya's waist tightly in my arm as we left, pulled her close and kissed her before climbing into the Fiat and again after sitting down. We drove in silence toward the city.

"Jon," she began. The little Fiat sped along the boulevards. "Yes?"

Fingers pulling a black kerchief through her other hand.

Gently: "I don't like being put on a pedestal. Don't you see how you think of me? It makes me feel way out there, ethereal. It doesn't feel like me."

"I don't understand."

Hurrying: "I feel as though you like me to be remote. You don't want me close. I don't like that." She shook her head rapidly. "The trouble is, I *do* like that. I was brought up to be a lady. Sweet. Gentle. I don't like it. I don't feel as if I'm living when I have to be like that. And that's exactly what you like. It scares me."

"I don't want you to be remote."

"Oh yes you do. You *keep* me that way."

"What do you mean?"

"Do we ever argue? Have we fought?"

"Why should we? I don't like to fight."

"With women."

"What's wrong with that?"

"Because you're putting me in a cage. I can't breathe."

The dim headlights made whitewashed trees leap out.

"I'm not putting you in any cage."

"Of course you are."

"You're putting yourself there."

"That's what I mean. That's where I am. I want *out*."

"Then *get* out." I affected control.

"You won't give me any help at all?"

My eyes were caught momentarily by hers. She was searching them for something. I grew uncomfortable.

"What are you trying to say?"

"You think of me as sweet and gentle, right?"

"Yes."

She rested her hand on my arm.

"You like to go to bed, right?"

"Yes."

"What else is there?"

"What do you mean, what else is there? I respect your work, your talents . . ."

"Yes, yes, yes. But I mean *me*. What I feel. I feel as if you keep missing me. I've been taught to keep people away. I feel more comfortable when I do that. But I was hoping you wouldn't let me."

"This is getting to be too much."

"Hold it a minute. It's my turn to talk. If you want to reach me, you better listen. Because you're missing."

"I don't understand. After everything we've been through . . ."

"But I'm not what I seem. Don't you understand?"

"You're deeper. You've suffered. I know . . ."

"You're missing the point."

"Well, help me."

"I'm trying to. . . . Don't you see, your impatience is what I mean. You don't like talking like this. You want me mystical and beautiful and undisturbing. Nothing petty, nothing complicated, nothing small. Well, I *am* small, see. You'll have to get used to it."

"C'mon, c'mon! This is fraudulent. It's sticky . . ."

"It's not fraudulent at all! You can't stand the truth about human relations. You'd rather have your pretty dreams. I just don't want to be one of your illusions." We stopped under blue-white lights. Her eyes were cruel and hard.

Suddenly I liked the stoniness. "Tell me more." I shifted into drive again.

"You don't have any sisters, right?"

I nodded.

"You don't have any idea how unpleasant women are to live with. You don't even care. You want a little romance, some service, and then: DO NOT DISTURB. I can see it hanging on your forehead. A little sign. The trouble is, I was brought up to be a wife for a man like you. And I won't do it. I can't stand the idea."

"I can't be that bad. I . . ."

"So it's exaggeration. The point is, let me in. Can't you hear me? Let me in."

"How am I stopping you from being what you want to be? You can't blame your lack of courage on me. If you want to be different, go ahead. I'm not stopping you."

She sat back in her seat. "Can't you hear yourself? 'Why should *I* give a damn?' You'll just sit there and watch me bounce like a puppet, while I go through my thing. You're so tolerant. So wise."

"Look, let's stop fighting."

"No, I won't! This is crucial." Her eyes spat iridescent fire through a film of tears. "You've got to let me be a woman, Jon, and stop this sweet lady business, or you'll only trap me."

"I'm not trying to lay down laws for you. For Chrissake, I'm only taking you as I see you."

"But you're not letting yourself *see*. You see me with only half your intelligence. You don't treat other people that way. You *want* to be blind—it's your version of love, or something. You're being childish."

She was swinging to hurt, and the blows were beginning to break through. Still, I couldn't abandon the line of defense I had already occupied.

"But I do see you straight. I can't help it if I love you."

"I'm not objecting to your love," she said quietly as I slowed the Fiat in front of the Prescott's apartment. "But I don't think you see me straight."

I pulled the key from the ignition lock. "So? What do I do now?"

"Look. Listen. Just try to see me as I am."

I felt defeated. "Well, I have years for that." We walked toward the Prescotts' door.

23

LESS THAN twenty-four hours later, Signorina Bianca met us at the door as we entered merrily from an early dinner. "President Kennedy has been shot," she whispered. She wiped her dark circled eyes with her apron. "They shot him, they shot him." She began to cry.

"Who? Where?" I asked as the news sank in.

"In Texas," she said. "They shot him in the head."

"Is he—only shot?" I asked. "Only shot? Is he dead yet?"

She shrugged. She pointed to the sitting room. "Imbeciles!" she cried openly.

I pushed by her; there was hope. Tears had escaped my eyes as I watched the inauguration on television; I had not realized, until they came, that the weight of being Catholic had been resting on my shoulders. Then I had grown excited by youth, intelligence, tough-mindedness.

The hushed, excited voice of the announcer read dispatches handed him. "*Il gióvane Presidente Americano è morto.* President Kennedy died at 12:17 at the Parkland Memorial Hospital in Dallas, Texas, felled by the bullet of an assassin or assassins unknown."

For three hours we listened. I was certain with enraged certitude that the killers were right-wing extremists, freedom-fighters, bigots. And then even that icy comfort was denied. Details were confused and contradictory. The radio and the television—we had them both on—were agonizingly slow, repetitive, constantly amending earlier reports. We went to bed cold, grief-stricken, and stunned. We clung to each other, and slowly began making a sorrowful and needy love.

In the morning bleakness began again. People walked silently and many cried; eyes were heavy. If to Kennedy, then who is safe? What nation or continent or planet can stand against the hopelessness?

It was not a day to be abroad. We needed familiar objects, sights, and noises. We could not explain to people that America is not like that, that the badlands no longer exist. (We did not then realize; we were still innocent.) Americans huddled together. The Italian and French papers editorialized and speculated; the hard, cold, iron facts were hard to obtain. Jack Prescott came to meet us before the mass for Americans at Santa Susanna. Eddie Flanagan called and met us at the church. A weak, shuffling little cardinal presided at a disgraceful service, his round shining face innocent of the pain we felt, mumbling the Latin, sliding through the routine gestures: not Christ, not Christ. We stumbled out through the crowds, revolted and enraged. Our dinner, poorly

eaten, sat ill upon our stomachs. Then came the sudden death of
Oswald: no comfort now in meaning or pattern or significance.

I wondered briefly in those hours what would happen to my
brother and his plans to run for Congress. The fabric of prediction
had burst apart.

When we got home that night, we found our rooms had been
searched. I telephoned Andreotti immediately. There was nothing
he could do. "They won't harm you," he promised me. He sounded
very sure.

Two days later the Mercedes slipped up beside me on a side
street near our *pensione*. Palica stepped out of a doorway behind me.

"I want the packet," he said. He walked me to the car, with
his hand in his right-hand pocket.

Inside the Mercedes, lethargic, uncaring, I told him: "Karazov
is my friend. You have no password."

"You will turn over the packet," he said.

"You're late. I gave it to a man who had the password."

"You lie."

"It was a priest."

He looked with steely eyes into my face. "His name?"

I shrugged. "I didn't ask. He gave me the password."

"It was the CIA," he said. He produced a small revolver and
held it in his lap.

The car had taken a turn and we were near the wall that ran
from the Vatican to the Castello. The street along the wall was
deserted. No one stirred in the buildings of weathered, aged stone.
Palica pushed my arm roughly and said, "Get out."

I kept my eyes on him. His fingers tensed and relaxed on the
small black pistol.

"Walk," he ordered, nodding toward the gate fifty yards away.

I studied the thin smile on his face, took my hand from the
door, turned away. My shadow fell ahead on the uneven paving
stones, which I could feel through my shoes. I expected at any
step to be pitched forward on my face. My ears strained to catch
every sound. I forced myself not to run, not to give them the
pleasure, not to lose any further dignity. I stayed near the heavy
wall—they could not run me down. I saw glints of maroon and

blue shimmering from the gray stones. My back prickled. Half the distance was covered. Now? My eyes blurred. I lost vivid impressions and began to weaken. I reached the corner and stepped around it. I ran several steps to mix myself into a crowd at the nearby market. I kept looking back, but no Mercedes followed.

My back was covered by a film of sweat. I drew deep breaths of air.

When I saw Nadya again, I held her tightly. She couldn't understand. I described the walk along the wall.

"The famous sense of humor!" she said bitterly.

"George-Georges skipped town Saturday," Jack told Nadya and me.

"Tell me everything from the beginning."

"I played Metzger one of the tapes. He didn't want to believe it, but apparently he went to the Dominicans. They gave George-Georges twenty-four hours to leave for Jerusalem."

"All the better for you and Marilou."

"No."

"Why not?" Nadya asked.

"George-Georges didn't go to Jerusalem. I checked at the steamship company." He looked at us with despair. "The bastard is hiding out in Rome somewhere. The Dominicans wanted him at sea, incommunicado, for a week. He'll take a plane and show up in Jerusalem on schedule. I know he will."

"My bet is he's gone," I said. "Too many people know him in Rome. The danger is too great."

Jack shrugged. "I won't be happy until he's chained down in Iceland somewhere." He brushed a hand through his thick touseled hair.

The next day Eddie Flanagan and I were having lunch at the American bar across from the USO. He confirmed an assertion of Jack's, that George-Georges was in the pay of Arab intelligence. There were strong indications that he was also employed by the Israeli secret service. "He has worked for us," Eddie said quietly. "And we think he was giving information to the Russians on his trips behind the curtain. He was working both sides then. No reason why he shouldn't now."

"He's for everybody," I nodded sourly.

Jack Prescott appeared at the doorway, scanned the tables, and then came over. "Nadya said you were here," he said. "Marilou has gone. Packed and gone. With the kids."

"When?"

"This morning. I left early to take Archbishop Stevens to the airport. When I came back, she was gone."

"No note?"

"Nothing."

"What do you make of it?" Eddie asked quietly, studying Jack. Their roles had been reversed since the Côte d'Azur.

"She couldn't have done it herself. The maid said a cab came and waited for her."

"She said nothing to the maid?" Eddie continued calmly.

"Not a word. At least Gabriella said she didn't. She told Gabriella to take the day off."

"What's your theory?"

"I don't have any theories. I'm out of theories." Jack held the thumb and forefinger of his right hand across his eyelids. "I still think George is in the city."

Eddie shook his head again. "What does it matter? He'll be in New York. London. Paris. And then he'll end up dead."

"Murdered?"

"Not necessarily. He'll drift, and always come out on top. He's probably studying Chinese."

Eddie slapped Jack softly on the back. "You'll get over it, boy."

A Southern fierceness crept into Jack's eyes. He said slowly: "I'll hate that woman as long as I live."

"It won't last that long," I said. Not hopefully.

The last week of the Council went badly. Opposition elements won their devious battle to separate the two documents on the Jews and religious liberty from the document on ecumenism, and to postpone the votes for a year. The texts were left in a fluid state, at the mercy of interim commissions dominated by conservatives. The majority seemed powerless to effect its will; the Pope seemed willing to temporize. "Let's face it," one red-faced Australian bishop said to me over coffee, "the Pope lacks guts." On the final, dismal Friday—black Friday as it came to be known because of

the failure of the majority to bring the key documents to a vote—
an American bishop told another reporter: "The cardinals thought
they were electing John XXIV; they got another Pius IX." The
Council lost another full day of discussion when the Pope sched-
uled a celebration for the fourth centenary of the Council of
Trent. The cardinal preacher—an Italian—linked Trent and Vatican II as twin pillars. As they parted for their homelands, the
gloom among reformers was thick.

Rome seemed empty after the bishops and their retinues de-
parted. The press corps shrank to almost nothing. I finished my
last report for *The Liberal Catholic* late that night and heaved a
sigh of relief.

Now, I thought the next morning, for the difficult decision. It
was the first day of freedom Nadya and I had had since she
arrived. I went for a walk, and sat in the gardens of the Castello.
Then I rose and crossed the river, walking through the narrow
streets of the medieval section, aimlessly and without purpose,
toward the shops of the Corso. Somewhere Nadya was buying a
winter coat, while I went to mail my article. She had been very
tired the last two weeks. The closing of the Council was a weight
off her mind; she had never been interested in it. She said she
looked forward to having me more to herself and getting away
from our accumulated bad memories of Rome. She seemed a little
nervous, as if the change of life required for traveling together
worried her.

Were we ready to marry? It was hard to imagine Nadya in a
kitchen. She wasn't going to like becoming a housewife in Berkeley.
As for me, I felt an imperious drive to concentrate upon my
work. From her perspective, I was a peculiarly selfish man—as if
no woman could ever rival my work in importance. She accused
me of never being vulnerable, of never needing anybody, of keeping my head in control at all times. "You don't let anyone inside
you," she told me quietly the day before. "Somewhere inside
you're like ice." I must have shown some vulnerability because she
came, then, and held me. "I didn't mean it the way it sounded.
You can be warm and affectionate. But somewhere . . ." The word
stuck. *Ice.* I suppose I am. You have to be, after a point. You
have to set goals and elect priorities and work very hard.

Who am I, really? I wondered. What ambitions do drive me? What am I really seeking? A tightly closed ego no one can penetrate?

I suddenly saw the possibility of turning some heat upon that iceberg. Maybe I could afford to yield up some of that mysterious drive within me. Wasn't Nadya worth it? I felt her cool buttocks pressing into my stomach. I loved her quiet honesty when she spoke to me, the courage of her penetrating criticisms. She made me feel more truthful. How could I live apart from her? No work in the world would be worth it. And maybe if I opened myself to her, I would discover secrets I would otherwise be incapable of learning.

The traffic on the Corso was moving swiftly and noisily. I walked halfway across and forced a large, lurching green bus to screech to a stop; the driver swore at me. The other lane cleared and I crossed. I hardly noticed anyone around me.

I needed more time to deal with myself. I thought back to the days in the seminary, the long, dry hours of prayer, the beginnings of the quest. To forfeit that is to forfeit everything.

I loved Nadya. There was no doubt of that. The thought of her drove sweetness through my veins. I longed for a truthful love, and I did not see how we would reconcile all we wished to do. But we would find a way.

I bounded up the steps of the *pensione* lightheartedly. I wanted to see her and to propose—if not marriage, then at least a pledge of marriage until she was ready to say the word.

Signorina Bianca was somber and fearful. Nadya didn't answer my calls. I found a white envelope on the bed. I looked around and absorbed the feeling of the room. I didn't have to read it but my fingers tore it open.

My dearest Jon:
I want to marry you. I love you. There is no uncertainty reflected in what I want to say. It is truthful, and thus I know you will respect it.

We are not ready for marriage yet. In another year, perhaps. For my part, I have not straightened out the professional side of my life. I don't think I could stand the strains of making a home, having babies, etc. Given the lessons of the last few weeks—which have finally caught up to me, overwhelmed me—I'm not sure I could stand the emotional strains, either.

(Is marriage doomed to disappear, now that women have the right to a professional life? I can't be alone in the fears that sweep through me. Am I? . . . *I don't want to marry.* Half of me doesn't.)

Dearest, I know I hurt you when I accused you of being cold. You have been gentle and loving, and I have talked more with you than with anyone in my entire life. I doubt that anyone will ever be more open to me, or closer to me. I am not an easy person to approach. I have my own iceberg.

But you, too, hesitate. I know you do. You will be generous and say you do not. That is why I leave you this way. I could not bear to face you again; I would weaken; I would never go away.

And yet we are not ready. Maybe in a year. I know the separation will do us good. You told me once you spent four years (out of eight?) preparing for the priesthood. Did you ever dream it would take longer to prepare for marriage? . . . I will do some writing for the *Journal,* and sit in on some seminars in London, and get some things out of my system. Don't worry about me.

Darling, please forgive me for stealing away. I love you too much to risk seeing you just now. It has taken me weeks to find the courage to do this much.

Separate, we will be free. I dread the risk of losing you.

Please do not follow me. It would take the truth out of everything. You would win, but I would be only a shell of myself.

Shall we plan to celebrate the publication of your book in Paris? With champagne?

And most certainly with love,
Nadya

I held the thin blue paper in my hand.

"I'm very sorry!" Signorina Bianca was already crying.

"It's nothing," I told her gently. I picked up my jacket.

She nodded.

I walked without seeing anything. I grew sweaty and tired. For the best? All I could hear in my ears was farewell, another farewell. I didn't think I could take very many more. I found myself at the foot of the Spanish steps, looking up past the twin towers of the church of the Trinità and into the cool sky. I walked across the piazza and slowly climbed the medieval steps.

After I had been at the balustrade a long time, a taxi driver, with his hands in the pockets of his knee-length coat, nodded his head toward his cab. I climbed into the narrow interior, full of dread. He turned lazily in his seat and looked at me.

end of the beginning